DIGGING UP TROUBLE

THE LEAFY HOLLOW MYSTERIES, BOOK 2

RICKIE BLAIR

BARKLEY
BOOKS

DIGGING UP TROUBLE
Copyright © 2017 by Rickie Blair.
Published in Canada in 2017 by Barkley Books.

ISBN-13: 978-0-9950981-6-9

To receive information about new releases and occasional special offers (and a
free story), please sign up for my mailing list at www.rickieblair.com.

Cover art by: http://www.coverkicks.com

DIGGING UP TROUBLE

CHAPTER ONE

I SHIFTED on my camp stool, rubbing my bleary eyes with both hands. When I looked up again, the scene in front of me hadn't changed. Storage shelves, stocked with cases of beer and maple syrup, spanned one wall of my aunt's Victorian-era basement. The deception was flawless—until you tilted your head at just the right angle.

I heaved a sigh, and called out, "I can keep this up forever, you know."

No reply.

Perseverance was Number 2 in *Top Ten Tips for Success in Life*, one of my most comforting self-help books, so I was confident my persistence would be rewarded. My new friends Emy and Lorne had long since given up. Four weeks earlier, my outstretched hand had disappeared into one of these beer cases—followed by the ten most terrifying seconds of my life. But Gideon, my aunt's next-door neighbor, convinced Emy and Lorne that it was merely an elaborate burglar alarm.

Which was quite a stretch, since most Leafy Hollow residents didn't even lock their doors.

Maybe I would have believed Gideon, too, if I didn't know of my aunt's astonishing number of sprains, torn ligaments, and broken bones over the years. I couldn't ask Aunt Adeline, though, since she was missing. Her car had plunged through a railing and into the river, and my sixty-five-year-old aunt was "presumed dead."

I didn't believe it.

Which was why I spent hours in her damp and musty basement every day, staring at boxes of Molson Canadian, hoping for answers.

A synthetic voice boomed overhead, jolting me out of my reverie. "Verity Hawkes?"

I jerked upright on the stool, my heart in my throat. "Yes?" I croaked.

The holographic shelves of beer wavered and disappeared. Metal walls parted to reveal the electronic console and blinking monitors I'd seen only once—and then only for minutes. As soon as Control realized I wasn't Adeline Hawkes, the panels had slammed shut.

Identical gray faces with sharply defined features—like colorless ventriloquist's dummies—appeared on each of the monitors.

"I'm not Adeline, but I want to help," I blurted. I had to talk fast before Control shut me out again. "Tell me—why is the fate of our nation at risk?"

"You're not cleared for that intelligence."

"But... you already told me about it."

"Only because you impersonated Adeline Hawkes. Fortunately, we recognized your deception in time."

My mouth gaped as I absorbed this insult. "Deception?" I asked, my voice squeaking. "I'm not the one engaged in dirty tricks. In fact—"

"You must prove yourself," the voice boomed. "With a test."

I scrunched my forehead. "What kind of test?"

"We can't tell you that."

"Then how will I—"

"A suitable candidate will recognize the danger and mitigate it."

"What?" I hadn't even seen the test and already I was confused. "What if I fail?"

Control's multiple faces looked bored. "There would be... consequences." The images swirled into concentric ribbons as if disappearing down multiple drains. "Don't try to contact us," the voice called as the screens went black.

"Wait," I said, leaping to my feet and jabbing at the keyboard. "What do you mean? What—"

The metal walls rumbled. I took a hasty step back. Air gusted across my face as the panels clanged shut inches from my nose.

"—consequences?" My voice trailed off.

The beer cases re-appeared, glimmering in the basement's dim light. I stared at them with a hand pressed to the pulsing vein in my neck.

A faint *beep, beep, beep* sounded in my ears. With a start, I realized I'd been hearing that noise for the past ten minutes.

3

It was coming from my cell phone. Wincing, I glanced at the screen.

I was late for the biggest event to hit Leafy Hollow village in years. Emy was going to kill me.

With a final scowl at the silent hologram, I dashed out the door.

———

If I hadn't been in such a hurry, I wouldn't have catapulted down the village hall stairs. But then I wouldn't have met tear-stained Isabelle Yates and complicated my life—again.

I was racing up the broad marble steps when we collided. I twisted in the air, reaching for the banister, but just missed it. Lurching and flailing, I bounded off every other step on my toes until I reached the bottom. I grabbed the newel post with both hands and swung around, clasping it to my chest, pleasantly surprised to be vertical.

"Oh, my gosh. I'm so sorry," said a lanky woman trotting down the stairs in her leather ballet flats. "Are you all right?"

I released the post and straightened up.

"That was my fault," she said, reaching out an arm. "Are you hurt?"

"Not at all," I gasped. "I'm fine."

Untrue, but Mom raised me to be polite. Sometimes, I even managed it.

"Verity Hawkes," I said, flexing a wrenched elbow and holding out my hand.

"Isabelle Yates." She gave my fingers a quick pump. Her brown eyes were rimmed in red and her lids were puffy.

When she adjusted the fringed leather purse slung over her shoulder, I noticed a plain gold wedding band.

"There you are," a voice called from the landing above us with a petulant tone.

Isabelle stiffened. She twisted her head to look up, one hand at her throat.

I glanced up as well. My bestie, Emy Dionne, was holding a tall stack of white cardboard boxes tied with string, with her chin stretched up to anchor the top one. "Where have you been?"

"Emy, you'll never guess what..."

My voice trailed off as I noticed the pudgy man with rumpled hair, wearing khakis and a pink cotton shirt, who stood a few steps behind Emy. He was glowering at Isabelle.

Beside me, I heard Isabelle's quick intake of breath.

When the man noticed I was looking at him, he drew back, then stepped away, into the auditorium. I glanced at Isabelle, who smiled feebly at me and lowered her hand.

"Sorry I'm late," I called to Emy, gesturing at the steps. "I had a little tumble down the—"

"Well, get up here," she said, struggling to rearrange the cartons, "I could use some help."

Isabelle leaned in to touch my arm. "I'll be back with my suitcase," she whispered. She cast a last glance up at the landing before turning to dart through the lines of people streaming in the front door.

I stared after her. "Did you say suit—"

"Are you coming?" Emy called.

Clearly, the village's big event took precedence over a crippled friend. Muttering, I trudged up the steps—shamelessly massaging my elbow. My attempt to elicit sympathy was wasted. Emy was so frantic she wouldn't have noticed if my arm had been lying on the ground.

At the top, I rescued three boxes stamped with 5X *Bakery* from the stack that dwarfed her tiny figure. "Sorry. I meant to get here sooner. When I was in the basement just now, Control finally—"

But Emy didn't hear me. She was looking in the direction Isabelle had disappeared, frowning.

Before I could ask why, she turned and strode toward a fold-out banquet table along one wall. I followed. Emy had a lot on her mind today. There would be time later to bring her up to date. After dropping off my load of boxes, I glanced around. Containers swamped the table. "How many cupcakes did you make?"

"Ten dozen. Plus five dozen scones, five dozen cheese puffs, and five dozen pigs in a blanket," she said, tying her long black curls behind her neck with a ribbon. "Wait," she said, frowning. "Where's the clotted cream for the scones?" She bent over to rummage through the plastic milk crates under the table. "Got it," she said, hauling out a stainless steel bowl with a snap-on lid.

I assumed the pigs in a blanket didn't come from Emy's other business, the vegan takeout that shared a door with the bacon-loving 5X Bakery. It seemed an odd joint tenancy. But as Emy told me when we first met, the southern Ontario village of Leafy Hollow was a small place and shop owners "have to double up."

"How many people are they expecting?" I asked, helping

her move the boxes and whisk a white linen cloth over the table.

"Two hundred. I hope I made enough."

Raising my eyebrows, I studied the mounds of boxes. "I think you're covered."

Lorne Lewins—my helper at Coming Up Roses Landscaping—hustled up, carrying a massive aluminum coffeemaker. "First one," he said, drawing out the "s" with his soft lisp and placing the urn on the table. He turned his head to conceal the gap between his two front teeth—a habit he adopted only when speaking to Emy. Lorne's strapping, five-foot-ten frame was usually garbed in jeans and a T-shirt, but he'd traded up to a long-sleeved denim shirt, open at the throat, and khakis for today's event. "I'll get the other one," he said, running a hand through his rumpled brown hair and turning to the entrance.

"Is the Leafy Hollow Historical Society paying for this?" I asked Emy.

She nodded. "Zander and Terry are thrilled about their first big event. Getting that historian from Britain was a huge coup, apparently."

"So Terry's not wearing his hiking boots today? Or his spandex unitard?"

Emy giggled and punched my arm. "I saw Terry this morning. He had on a sports jacket and a silk bow tie. Very handsome—debonair, even. They're both nervous, though."

"Why? After one of your cherry-custard chocolate cupcakes, nobody will care what that historian has to say about Prudence Bannon."

Emy crossed her fingers in a "don't jinx it" gesture.

Prudence Bannon was Leafy Hollow's favorite heroine, a plucky girl who slogged miles through the bush to warn British troops of a planned attack on a supply convoy during the War of 1812. That hike was usually attributed to Laura Secord—or "that woman" as Leafy Hollow residents call her —but according to local lore, Prudence did it first. Without chocolate.

Until now, no respected academic had been willing to validate this local legend. But Edgar Nesbitt-Cavanagh had made it his life's work to study a war that most Europeans considered merely a skirmish. The Oxford-educated historian found Prudence Bannon fascinating.

Many Leafy Hollow residents were history buffs, proud of the village's role in the early nineteenth-century conflict that forever separated Canada from the U.S. But most simply expected the Society's initiative would spark a boom in business. As a former bookkeeper who knew how easily businesses could fail, I hoped they wouldn't be disappointed.

So far, though, there was no sign of the featured speaker, even though the hall was filling up. I cast a wary glance at the people pushing in through the front door. When I agreed to help Emy, I hadn't stopped to think what it would feel like to be in a room with hundreds of people. I pressed my hand against the vein in my neck, willing it to stop throbbing.

I craned my neck to look up at the ceiling, a deliberate attempt at distraction. I'd lived in Leafy Hollow six weeks, but today was my first visit inside the honey-colored stone walls of the village hall. I gazed at the auditorium's soaring windows, thick crown molding, and multi-tiered chandeliers.

An easel by the stage held a six-foot-tall rectangle covered with a blue cloth.

I wandered over to take a peek. "Is this the new portrait of Prudence Bannon?"

Emy, snipping strings with a box cutter and flipping open cardboard lids, glanced up with a frown of concentration. "I think so. Can you—" She waved anxiously at the empty serving platters.

I hurried back to the table. While we worked, I told her about my encounter with Control.

Her eyes widened. "It's not a burglar alarm?"

I narrowed my eyes at her. "You didn't really believe that, did you?"

She shrugged before returning her attention to the platters. "You should move out of Rose Cottage."

"Move out? Why?"

"Who knows what that thing will do next? It's not safe."

"If I move out, Control will think I'm not interested in helping. And then I'll never find Aunt Adeline." I kept the cryptic warning about *consequences* to myself. Emy gestured at a china platter bedecked with violets. I handed it over and watched her arrange cupcakes on it. "Besides," I added, "it might be fun."

"Fun?" Emy gave me a worried glance before gathering up the empty cardboard boxes and stowing them in a milk crate. She swept her gaze across the laden table. "I think we're ready," she said.

Lorne walked up with the second coffee urn and set it next to the platters.

Emy glanced at the coffeemakers. "Should I turn those on now? They take an hour to brew."

I reached for a cheese puff. "Have you tested these?"

She slapped my hand away with a smile. "Stop that. Can you find Zander or Terry? Ask them if they want the coffee ready before the talk ends."

I suspected the audience for this "historic lecture" would need caffeine as soon as possible. But maybe that was just me. I glanced around. Over two hundred people had crowded into the hall. As they walked past us on their way to a seat, they eyed the overflowing platters. If this event didn't get underway soon, we might need an armed guard.

"There's Zander by the door," I said. "I'll ask him about the coffee."

Zander Skalding—his semi-mohawk at odds with his conservative blue suit and pale, round face—was talking to a tall man in an Ontario Provincial Police uniform. The officer's back was to me, but I recognized those broad shoulders and the straight black hair that stopped just short of his collar. Detective Constable Jeffrey Katsuro turned around, and I also recognized his dark eyes—and their effect on me. Jeff had been out of town for weeks on a training course. During a previous conversation, he'd promised to give me a bowling lesson. I hoped he hadn't forgotten.

Jeff smiled at me. *Later*, he mouthed. With a last remark to Zander, he walked out the door and down the marble steps that led to the street. As usual, I admired his... uniform.

I had no time to ponder what *later* meant before a blast of static from the microphone behind me caused me to jump. I turned to see Terry Oliver on the stage.

"Hello, everyone," he said, grinning.

Emy was right—Terry's periwinkle-blue sports jacket, yellow shirt, and navy bow tie set off his mahogany skin, shorn head, and athletic build to perfection.

"Welcome to the Leafy Hollow Historical Society's 'Celebration of Prudence Bannon,'" he said into the mic. "Our honored guest will be here soon." Terry tapped the microphone, creating another blast of static. The audience winced. Terry leaned in closer to the mic. "Thank you for your patience." With a grin and a wave, he clattered down the three steps at the side of the stage.

I exchanged glances with Emy from across the room. She bent to turn on the coffee urns.

Walking back to the table, I was surprised by how many faces I recognized. Not bad for someone who hadn't left her Vancouver apartment for two years. My therapist would have been proud. Still, I acutely felt the growing crush of the crowd, especially when someone bumped into me from behind. I took a deep breath to calm myself and started forward again.

A loud whisper made me pause.

"What do you mean, you need more time?" a man asked. "You said the same thing a month ago. Why so long?"

"Please, Nick, not here," a woman whispered.

"Then where? Why won't you talk to me?"

"I told you."

"Tell me again."

"Let go of me," she said, louder than before.

I recognized that voice. I twisted my head to look behind me.

Isabelle Yates yanked her arm away from the grip of the florid-faced man beside her. It was the same man who'd glared at her from the landing. Isabelle pivoted on her heel and hurried toward the exit. She was wheeling a small suitcase.

I stepped between the pink-shirted man and the exit, blocking his way.

His watery blue eyes met my gaze. "Mind your own business."

I didn't move, silently counting while ignoring my throbbing vein.

"What are you gawking at?" he asked, scowling.

"I'm sorry. I thought I saw someone I knew." *Nine. Ten.* That should be long enough. With a shudder, I ducked around him and walked over to the table. All the way there, I felt his eyes grazing my back.

CHAPTER TWO

THE PERCOLATORS HAD BEEN BUBBLING and spitting for forty minutes by the time Terry took the stage for the third time. He tapped the microphone, and the audience members cringed again at the burst of static. "We're running a little behind schedule, folks, but Mr. Nesbitt-Cavanagh should be—"

A commotion at the entrance drowned out Terry's words.

"Plenty of fridge magnets for everyone," called a man's voice, punctuated with a hearty guffaw. "No need to push."

At the back of the auditorium, late arrivals crowded around someone I couldn't see, even after standing on tiptoes and craning my neck. Since I'm five-foot-ten, that meant the new arrival was extremely short. So this must be—

"There's Wilf," exclaimed a woman with long blonde hair seated opposite our baked goods table. She twisted in her chair, waving her manicured hands over her head. "Wilf," she called. "Over here."

I recognized the sparkly rings and impeccable grooming of Nellie Quintero, the real estate agent who told me my aunt's home, Rose Cottage, was unsalable in its present condition. I owed her for that. A less ethical realtor would have taken the commission and run.

The men and women surrounding the new arrival stepped back. As the throng parted, I recognized the beaming face of Leafy Hollow councilor and lawyer Wilfred Mullins at its center. Wilf was under four feet tall, but his buoyant personality ensured he never got lost in a crowd.

He waved at Nellie, then high-fived his way through the auditorium toward his reserved front-row seat, handing out business cards and magnets.

"Verity!" he said as he approached our table. "How's my favorite client?" Without stopping to hear my answer, he slapped a magnet onto my palm and gripped it in a hearty shake. "Looking good."

Then he was gone, trailed by his gray-haired assistant Harriet, who clasped a royal-blue upholstered cushion to her chest as she battled the crowd. It looked like one of those orthopedic seat supports, but on steroids.

As they swept past us, I bent my head to examine the rubber fridge magnet in my hand. The headline, printed in an antique font, read:

The Prudence Bannon Memorial Waterpark

And in smaller type:

Opening Soon in Leafy Hollow, Near the Old Rendering Plant. Bring the Kids!

In the top left corner was an oval, daguerreotype portrait of a young girl who could have been Prudence—except that photography hadn't been invented at the time. A tiny map with a red star in the middle took up the opposite corner. Wilf's head was superimposed over a curling blue wave at the bottom, his hand raised in a thumbs-up.

Harriet dropped the pillow on a front-row chair. Another commotion ensued when three people reached out at the same time to help Wilf onto the blue booster cushion. He waved them away.

With a practiced hop, Wilf landed on the cushion and scooted up against the chair's back. Grinning broadly, he rubbed his hands together. "Let's get this show on the road."

Terry—still waiting on stage—tapped the microphone again. This time, the audience members groaned. A few stuck their fingers in their ears in protest.

"Ladies and gentlemen," Terry said, "Mr. Nesbitt-Cavanagh isn't here yet—"

Dozens of people rose to their feet and thundered toward the baked goods table.

I backed away to clear a space in front of the nearest coffee spigot while Emy handed out paper plates. When she wasn't looking, I sneaked a cheese puff. I bit into the flaky, cheddar-packed pastry with a sigh of pleasure.

"While we're waiting," Terry continued, "Reverend Daniel McAllister of Leafy Hollow Community Church has agreed to unveil our wonderful new portrait of Prudence Bannon."

A tall, thin man in a black suit, white clerical collar over a lavender shirt, and broad wire-rimmed glasses bounded onto the stage. His straight dark hair was parted on one side. The longer side dipped over his forehead, an unsuccessful attempt to hide a hairline that started well back of his ears, although he couldn't be much older than forty-five. The minister's chin melted into his neck as his lips spread in a big smile, but his eyes twinkled when he regarded the audience. Not much of a looker, Reverend Daniel, but the essence of affability.

"Thank you, Terry," he said into the mic. "And thank you, Emy Dionne, for the wonderful treats. Now if we can just get you away from the Catholics, those cupcakes would be terrific for growing our Sunday school class."

Emy mock-rolled her eyes before smiling back.

"But seriously, save a cherry-chocolate one for me," McAllister said. He smiled at the audience for a beat before adding, "I'm only kidding about the Catholics, you know. Wonderful people. It's not their fault that Adam was a Protestant."

Several spectators chuckled. I suspected they'd heard this joke before.

"You didn't know that?" McAllister asked, nodding sagely. "Only a Protestant could stand next to a naked woman and be tempted by a piece of fruit."

Like Wilf, McAllister knew how to play to a crowd. As the minister launched into another joke, I scanned the seated audience until my gaze reached the back of the hall. The red-faced man who had grabbed Isabelle stood by the entrance, arms crossed, scowling at McAllister.

"Emy," I whispered, "don't look right at him, but who's that man by the back door? The one in the long-sleeved pink shirt?"

She glanced sideways at him. "Nick Yates," she whispered back. "Isabelle's husband."

"Is he mad at Reverend Daniel?"

She puffed air through her lips. "He's mad at the world."

On the stage, McAllister embarked on the official part of his task.

"Prudence Bannon," he said, "was only eight years old when she overheard Yankee sympathizers outside her father's inn in Leafy Hollow planning a strike on a British supply run. Those wagons were packed with fresh beef, salted pork, and barrels of rum. Since we all know an army marches on its stomach, this was a serious threat. Our plucky Prudence hiked ten miles through the bush to warn the British troops. The provisions train was rerouted, the attack averted, and the rum delivered as promised."

A few people in the audience applauded.

"Sadly, this brave child's contribution to the war effort was never officially recognized," McAllister said. "But now, the newly funded and re-organized Leafy Hollow Historical Society has taken up her cause." The minister nodded at Zander and Terry, who stood by the side of the stage.

Terry graced the crowd with a jaunty two-finger wave and a wink, but Zander's moon-shaped face was drained of emotion. Like me, he was uneasy in a crowd.

I took a step back to lean against the wall, wondering if McAllister would mention that the Society's new funding came from a murder victim. Zander's mom, Yvonne Skalding, had left her entire estate to the historical society in a move that shocked everyone—especially her son.

"Let's take a moment to recognize Zander and Terry's contribution," the minister said, leading a round of applause.

Nope, no mention of Yvonne—possibly because she'd

been a sharp-tongued shrew. And no mention of her daughter-in-law Kate, Zander's ex-wife. Kate left Zander after he declared his love for Terry—and Yvonne's will had been read. No one in Leafy Hollow missed her, either.

I liberated another cheese puff. I considered a cupcake as well, but Emy was guarding them like a mother hawk.

"And now, our artist, Madeline Stuart—could you stand up, please, Madeline?" McAllister asked, nodding at a woman in the front row.

The artist rose to her feet. Sweeping unruly crimson curls off her forehead, she twisted to face the audience and made a shy bow.

Beside Madeline sat a handsome, slightly built man with light brown skin, dark eyes, and medium stubble. Xavier Roy, a local filmmaker, wore rimless glasses under a black ball cap, and a gray hoodie. He balanced a video camera on his lap.

"And now—" McAllister said, extending his hand toward the easel as if he were on *Wheel of Fortune.* Zander, his lips pressed together, plucked up a corner of the cloth with a trembling hand. "Prudence Bannon," the minister boomed.

Zander whisked the cloth away, bundling it up in his hands, and then stepped back.

There was a long moment of silence while the crowd examined the portrait.

Prudence's enormous left eye stared out at us from under a frilly lace cap. There was no sign of her other eye. It could have been a profile view, except that both ears were visible. Beneath her chin, a tiny triangular body was draped in gray, with a Union Jack trailing from one hand.

A child's whiny voice broke the silence. "Why is her head so big?"

"Shhhh," his mother hissed.

I crammed the rest of the cheese puff into my mouth so I could clap with both hands. Others joined in. Soon, Madeline was blushing. She waved and sat down.

"Thank you, Madeline," McAllister said into the mic, "for that... riveting portrayal of our heroine."

Another smattering of applause.

"I see that Mr. Nesbitt-Cavanagh has joined us, so I'll turn this event over to him."

Finally. Heads swiveled to face the entrance as a short, stout man wearing a tweed jacket, pin-striped shirt, and paisley tie shuffled down the aisle toward the stage. The bags under his eyes, furrowed lines beside his nose, and sagging jowls suggested an elderly hound dog. An untidy stack of papers stuck out from under one arm. A pipe clamped between his lips jerked up and down as he walked.

Zander trailed him up the aisle, looking anxious. "Sir? No smoking, please. Mr. Nesbitt-Cavanagh? There's no smoking in the hall." Zander picked up his pace, flapping a hand at the historian. "*Edgar,*" he pleaded in a loud whisper.

The historian ignored him and mounted the three steps to the stage. Once there, he yanked the still-smoldering pipe from his lips and balanced it on the edge of the lectern. A faint aroma of tobacco wafted throughout the room.

Nesbitt-Cavanagh cleared his throat, wiped his face with a linen handkerchief, which he then tucked into a pocket, and picked up the mic.

"As you know, it has been my life's work to study the Anglo-

American War of 1812," he said in a gravelly voice. "While most European historians consider this conflict to be a mere adjunct to the Napoleonic Wars, I believe it warrants rigorous scrutiny in its own right. For instance, the Treaty of Ghent..."

There was a renewed assault on the cupcakes and pigs in a blanket.

"We might need more coffee," I whispered to Emy as the historian droned on.

"No kidding," she whispered back, "and possibly CPR."

Eventually, Nesbitt-Cavanagh got to the point. "I have been asked to confirm the tale of Leafy Hollow's Prudence Bannon. After an exhaustive academic study"—he surveyed the room, prolonging the moment—"I find that I cannot."

"What?" came a startled exclamation from Terry. His smile had vanished. "You what?" He stepped toward the stage.

Nesbitt-Cavanagh held out an imperious hand to stop him. "Furthermore, I have determined that the entire Prudence Bannon history is nothing more than a fanciful ruse."

When no one broke the stunned silence, he raised his voice and added, "It's a fake."

Cupcakes paused, halfway to mouths. Several people rose to their feet, muttering.

Wilf Mullins, his face red and contorted, pointed at the historian from his front-row perch. "How dare you, sir? You're an invited guest. How dare you mock our community?"

Mutters of agreement came from the crowd.

"I serve the truth," Nesbitt-Cavanagh said. He picked up his pipe, took a quick draw, and exhaled a stream of smoke. "No one was more saddened than I to discover that such an entertaining story was entirely fictitious."

"Liar!" Wilf roared. He jumped to his feet, scattering fridge magnets onto the floor. "Liar!"

The muttering rose in volume. More people stood up. The crowd was getting ugly.

McAllister, who had been standing off to one side while the historian addressed the group, hurried up to grasp the mic. "Please, folks," he said, "let's give Mr. Nesbitt-Cavanagh a chance to explain. Sir, can you tell us your reasons for this... startling hypothesis?" He passed the microphone back to the historian.

"It's not hypothesis, it's fact," Nesbitt-Cavanagh said, holding the pipe in his hand. "Prudence Bannon never existed."

Even McAllister was speechless for a moment.

The historian pressed his advantage. "My upcoming book will document the entire investigation. I call it *The Legend of Leafy Hollow*."

The minister's jaw—such as it was—dropped almost to his chest.

Nesbitt-Cavanagh continued. "My book will be available this autumn, followed by a documentary currently in production with a major filmmaker."

In the front row, Xavier rose to his feet with his camera in one hand, turned to the crowd, and waved. "Hello, I'm Xavier Roy. You'll see a lot of me in the next few weeks—"

"Sit down, Roy," the historian broke in with a wave of dismissal. "I said a major filmmaker."

Roy gave him a startled look before dropping back into his chair with a frown. He shook his head, mumbling to Madeline, who patted his arm.

That was the last straw for Wilf Mullins. He strode to the stage and grabbed the front edge with both hands, glaring up at Nesbitt-Cavanagh. "Are you trying to make this village a laughingstock?" he demanded.

The professor ignored him.

McAllister held up a hand, looking uneasy. "Permit me, Wilf," he said. He pressed his lips together as he collected himself, and then turned to the historian. "Mr. Nesbitt-Cavanagh," he said, carefully enunciating each word. "Prudence Bannon is buried in the Bannon family vault behind the Leafy Hollow Community Church. She died in 1815 at the age of eleven. How can you say she never existed?"

"I assume you're referring to the inscription on the crypt that reads, 'Sweet Prudence, taken too soon?'"

"Of course."

The historian took another draw on his pipe and exhaled before replying. "That was the Bannon family dog. An English pointer bitch, if I'm not mistaken."

The mutters turned into shouts, the first five rows emptied, and the crowd surged for the stage.

"Wait!" Nesbitt-Cavanagh thundered, waving a document above his head. "I can prove it." He handed the paper to McAllister, who took it with a frown.

The audience stared, open-mouthed, as the minister read it.

"You can't do this," McAllister spluttered, slapping the back of his other hand against the paper he held in his fingers. "It's not right."

"It's absolutely right," Nesbitt-Cavanagh replied. He stuck his chin out at the audience. "Tomorrow morning, we will open the Bannon family vault and exhume the supposed remains of Prudence Bannon. That document"—he pointed to the paper in McAllister's hand—"contains authorization from the attorney general himself."

With a black look, McAllister tore the paper into shreds. The pieces fluttered to the floor.

The historian flicked a hand. "That's only a copy. The original is perfectly safe."

"You can't do this," McAllister said. "Under law, the owner of a burial ground must agree before a body can be exhumed. And the owner in this case is the church. And we don't agree." He crossed his arms and glared at Nesbitt-Cavanagh.

"No one can own a corpse," the historian countered, "since a human body is not considered property. It's called the 'No Property' rule."

The crowd was following this exchange as if it were a Wimbledon throw down. Their heads swiveled back to the minister.

He narrowed his eyes. "Maybe not, but it's an indignity to a dead human body, and that's definitely against the law."

The historian smiled. "A law enforced by the attorney general." He paused. "Who shared a room with me at Oxford."

Game, set, and match to Nesbitt-Cavanagh.

A single hand, holding a chocolate cupcake, poked up through the throng. The hand swung back and then heaved its missile at the historian.

Nesbitt-Cavanagh ducked, and the cupcake struck McAllister full in the face. His eyes widened as he wiped cherry custard off his cheek. "Please, let's—"

No one heard the rest of the minister's plea.

"Liar!" someone shouted. More baked goods shot through the air, landing on the stage, the backdrop, and the lectern. Emy slapped a lid on the container of clotted cream and pushed it out of sight behind a coffee urn.

Several audience members leaped to their feet, trying to stop the carnage. Their soothing words went unheeded by the battalion of pastry tossers. Everyone else retreated to the exits, heads down.

Xavier Roy stayed behind to film the melee. He paused only once, to eat a cheese puff that landed on his camera lens.

On the stage, Nesbitt-Cavanagh cowered under a stack of cherry-custard-stained papers held over his head. When a pastry-covered sausage smacked him in the side of the face, he made a break for it down the center aisle.

His way was blocked by Nick Yates, who marched toward him with a chocolate cupcake in one hand and a maniacal gleam in his eye. Nick let fly with a wicked swing, and the pastry arched through the air.

A split-second before impact, Nesbitt-Cavanagh jerked to one side.

The cupcake smacked into Prudence Bannon's eye, breaking into two. Cherry custard dripped down the painting.

Madeline Stuart shrieked and clapped both hands to her mouth. Nesbitt-Cavanagh yelped and ran wild-eyed from the auditorium. Xavier Roy followed, still filming.

As the auditorium emptied after them, I surveyed the mess with a sigh. I should have eaten one of those cupcakes while I had the chance.

CHAPTER THREE

EMY, Lorne, and I stared at the deserted auditorium with our mouths hanging open. Fridge magnets littered the floor, and a few chairs were toppled. I bent to pick up a half-empty cup. A coffee-soaked sausage jutted up over the rim. Cringing, I put the cup down on the table.

Heaving a sigh, Emy rested her hands on her hips. "I'm not dealing with this," she said, shaking her head.

Over by the stage, the chocolate cupcake on Prudence Bannon's face slid down the canvas and dropped to the floor with a *splat*.

"Let's pack up your stuff and leave," I said.

"What about the coffee urns?" Lorne asked.

Emy frowned. "Take them back to the kitchen. It's not our job to clean them, anyway."

After that, we only took a few minutes to flatten the empty cardboard boxes and cram them into the milk crates. A few lonely pastries remained on the platters. Lorne and I put them out of their misery.

Emy cast a last glance around the auditorium. "That's it. Lorne, can you start loading the truck?"

"On it," he said, picking up two crates and hurrying through the front door. Emy and I followed with more.

"Watch your step," I said on the stairs, although I was the only one likely to trip. Unlike my giraffe-ish five-foot-ten, former gymnast Emy barely hit five-two. Her diminutive shape and tousled black hair were adorable, but eclipsed by her enormous smile, which lit up whatever room she was in. I'd seen grown men dissolve into putty under its power. She also made the best lemon meringue pie I'd ever tasted. It was a mystery why she was still unmarried in her late twenties. I assumed her first flame —a wealthy older man who bought her a bakery on Main Street before moving on—was a tough act to follow. Certainly, no one ever bought me a building. Or anything bigger than a china mug printed with *Souvenir of Yukon*, come to think of it.

"So, who's Isabelle Yates?" I asked as we stood on the sidewalk by my aunt's aging pickup, waiting for Lorne to unlatch the tailgate. *Coming Up Roses Landscaping* had been freshly re-stenciled on the driver's door.

"My cousin. She's two years older than me."

"She looks a lot older."

"I know. Izzy works in the library, and Mom's been dying to give her a makeover."

"But why the suitcase?"

"Izzy is moving in with me for a while. Until... well, I don't know actually." Emy sighed. "Years ago, she used to

27

babysit my brother and me. She was a lot livelier then. But that was before—" Emy stopped talking as Lorne leaned over the edge of the truck bed to take our crates.

We handed them up and headed back inside for more.

"Before what?" I asked.

"Her boyfriend dumped her the year they graduated from high school. They were high-school sweethearts and everyone expected them to marry."

"What happened?"

"I don't know all the details, but Mom says Charlie—that was his name, Charlie Inglis—wanted to skip university and move to Alberta to work in the oil patch. He and Isabelle had a huge fight over it."

We gathered up the rest of the crates and headed outside. Lorne stacked them in the back. "That's the last of it," he said, jumping down from the truck bed and latching the tail-gate. "I can walk home from here, unless you need more help."

"We're fine," I said. "See you tomorrow."

Emy and I climbed into the truck for the three-block trip to her bakery.

"What happened to Charlie?" I asked, starting the engine and turning out of the parking lot.

"Nobody knows. He left Isabelle a note to say he was leaving for Alberta without her. That was the last she heard from him. It was a mean note, according to Mom."

After pulling up outside the 5X Bakery, I hopped out of the cab—ignoring the parking meter—and propped open the bakery's bright red door. I unpacked the milk crates while Emy carried them in.

The "5X" in the shop's name was a reference to the Dionne quintuplets, Depression-era celebrities. They were a passion of Emy's mother, Leafy Hollow's chief librarian Thérèse Dionne. I winced at the thought of Thérèse. I had only two more weeks to finish *Anna Karenina* for her book club. *Anna* was a literary classic. It was also a doorstopper—eight hundred and sixty-four pages. I wondered if I had time to take a speed-reading course.

I followed Emy inside, pausing to inhale the intoxicating aromas of cinnamon, lemon, and cocoa that wafted through the open kitchen door. The glass-fronted counter that spanned the side wall ended at a café table at the back. I'd spent at least two of my six weeks in Leafy Hollow sitting at that table, wolfing down walnut-caramel scones and Darjeeling tea.

When I first arrived in Leafy Hollow, battling anxiety attacks, Emy befriended me. We were both in our late twenties, both on our own. I liked to think she recognized a kindred spirit. But whatever sparked our friendship, I might have resumed my shut-in ways if it hadn't been for her. She joked that I only liked her for her mouthwatering cupcakes, scones, and pies. I assured her that was true.

Today, though, I'd had enough of people in general and Leafy Hollow residents in particular. Not to mention mysterious holograms with hidden agendas. "Are you okay to do the rest by yourself?" I asked.

Emy smiled and flicked her hand. "Nothing to do. Go home."

I drove slowly through the village, prepared to brake while passing the restaurants and stores on Main Street. You never knew when a pedestrian would amble out in front of you.

Leafy Hollow straddled the edge of the Niagara Escarpment, a rugged rock face that runs for hundreds of miles through the province of Ontario. Most of the village was in the valley, including Main Street's quaint shops. My aunt's home was on the plateau above, surrounded by forested conservation areas whose rivers cascaded over the escarpment in a series of waterfalls.

The tallest spot, Pine Hill Peak, loomed as I headed up the two-lane road. I grinned at the tiny figures waving from the lookout, three hundred feet above my head.

At the top, I drove another mile and then into Rose Cottage's driveway. I maneuvered around Aunt Adeline's ruined Ford Escort and the pop-up trailer parked alongside. Carson Breuer, the carpenter who lived in the trailer, must be sleeping one off. He had an almost encyclopedic knowledge of nineteenth-century structures, but I was paying him a lot less than the going rate to repair my aunt's neglected home. Our arrangement worked fine for Carson since his laid-back approach to life did not currently include a fixed address.

The agreement also served me well. I'd spent some of the happiest summers of my childhood in my aunt's home, and I intended to restore Rose Cottage to the shipshape place I remembered.

Not today though.

For the rest of the afternoon, I planned to curl up on the battered sofa with a beer and my well-worn copy of *Ten Paths to Clarity through Tidying Up.*

My dream of a peaceful end to a hectic day evaporated the moment I stepped out of the truck. My aunt's next-door neighbor, Gideon Picard, was waiting for me on the porch. I halted, closing my eyes with a sigh, before slamming the door. The last thing I wanted was an encounter with an aging would-be action star.

"Why are you here?" I asked as I mounted the steps and glared at the gray-haired man in a wicker chair leaning precariously against the wall. His shirt sleeves were folded to the elbows, displaying sinewy forearms, and his worn leather belt cinched a trim waist. Gideon's hair, which matched the gray mustache that trailed from each end of his upper lip, was caught up in a samurai top knot at the back of his head. I suspected his hairstyle predated the current trend by at least four decades. "Have you finally decided to explain about that thing in my basement?"

Gideon's top knot bounced as he dropped the chair's front legs onto the floor and rose to his feet. "I told you, I can't. You're being unreasonable, Verity."

"I think I'm doing pretty well for a woman with a murderous hologram in the cellar."

Normally, Gideon was as talkative as the statue of Leafy Hollow's founder in the village square. Whether his silence masked hidden depths was impossible to determine. I had often tried to stare him down, but his blue-tinted octagonal glasses always threw me off. It was like talking to Ozzie Osbourne—before the reality-TV years.

It had been six weeks since the police dragged my aunt's empty car from the river. They insisted she was dead. I was equally adamant that Aunt Adeline was nowhere near the last of her nine lives when her Ford Escort plunged through that railing. And I intended to find her. Which was why I was living in a mid-nineteenth-century stone cottage in an idyllic southern Ontario village, instead of holed up in my high-rise Vancouver apartment on the other side of the country.

Correction—strike "idyllic."

Leafy Hollow officially lost its peaceful status for me within days of my arrival. I was implicated in two murders and almost became a murder victim myself. Then, once I'd unmasked the killer and things were settling down, the mysterious talking entity known as "Control" threatened to blow the whole place up.

And the man who knew what it all meant wasn't talking.

I repeated my question. "So? Why are you here?"

Gideon shrugged—his signature move. "Ran out of tea."

Shaking my head, I unlocked the front door and stepped over the threshold. Unasked, he followed me in.

We walked through to the kitchen. I opened a cupboard and pulled out my aunt's painted tin canister with the faded Scottie dogs. I handed it to Gideon.

After extracting two tea bags and dropping them into mugs, he took the kettle to the sink. He filled it and placed it on the stove. "Sorry I didn't bring donuts," he said, flicking on the burner.

With a pang, I recalled the sugary topping and soft, doughy interior of Tim Horton's maple-glazed, my favorite. Although retired, Gideon worked at Tim's two days a week. I narrowed my eyes at him. Given the number of cheese puffs

I'd eaten at the village hall, he was out of luck with that strategy.

"Stop trying to change the subject," I said.

"Or what? You'll pop me again?"

His reference to the *one time* I landed an uppercut on his jaw was unmerited. I'd followed it with a knee strike and spinning-heel kick because, well, in for a penny, but he'd deserved it. Besides, there was no point in taking years of Krav Maga lessons only to let them lapse. "Are you going to keep bringing that up forever?"

With another shrug, he gestured at the fridge. "Milk, please."

I took out the milk-bag pitcher and filled the moose-head creamer on the kitchen table.

"Anyway," he said. "The hologram—as you call it—isn't talking."

"Says you." With a smirk, I recounted my early-morning conversation with Control. I leaned back on my heels, expecting a reaction.

"Hunh," was all I got.

I gave a puff of exasperation. "Is that all you have to say?"

Gideon added a raised eyebrow.

I sagged against the counter, temporarily defeated. "At least tell me how it knows I'm not Adeline."

"Because you're too young."

"How does it know that? Unless..." I leaned my head back to look at the ceiling, remembering the clicks and whirrs in the attic I heard on my first day at Rose Cottage.

Gideon poured boiling water into the mugs and handed me one before stirring milk into his. "No idea." He headed for the back door, raising the mug in his hand. "I'll return this later."

I followed him onto the back steps, watching as he turned right, ambled across the yard, and plunged into the hedge that separated my aunt's property from his. Because using the driveway would be so... normal. The cedar branches shook like Fangorn forest as he disappeared.

"This isn't over," I muttered before returning to the kitchen.

CHAPTER FOUR

LORNE WAS YAWNING in the passenger seat as we pulled up outside the Leafy Hollow Community Church the next morning. Reverend Daniel, shaken by the day's events, had called me the previous evening to ask if we could come by early to spruce up the cemetery before the media circus hit. The church was one of Aunt Adeline's landscaping customers, and I'd inherited it along with the rest of Coming Up Roses' clients. Normally, we only cut the lawn and did a little pro-bono weeding, since the parish purse didn't stretch far, but this was an emergency.

"I'm not happy about this development," McAllister said over the phone, "but we must try to look respectable for the cameras. We owe it to the village."

"You couldn't stop the exhumation?" I asked.

"No," he said with a heavy sigh. "It's going ahead. Tomorrow morning at eleven." He had muttered something under his breath that sounded suspiciously like a swear word before hanging up.

The fieldstone church had multi-paned stained glass windows and a square bell tower that rose over the double front doors. Carson had told me the church, built in 1840, was a perfect example of the era, a monument to the early settlers' determination.

The minister's home stood on one side, about fifty feet back from the road. On the other side of the church, willows and elms shaded a hilly cemetery. A split-rail fence separated the graveyard from a cornfield behind, where a footpath ran through the field to the river two hundred feet away.

I got out of the truck and stood a moment to survey the gravestones. When I first arrived in Leafy Hollow, some residents had been reluctant to let me cut their lawns. I was a little hurt by that. Yes, I was a murder suspect at the time, but it's not like I was chasing them through the streets with hedge clippers.

No one here had complained though.

The cemetery reminded me of a miniature subdivision, with winding pathways that twisted and turned among the gravestones and doubled back upon themselves. A hand-written map that identified each resident hung from a hook in the vestry. But one grave was easy to locate. The Bannon family vault dominated the site from its position atop a hillock in the middle of the cemetery. Parishioners arriving for Sunday services couldn't help but see its carved marble angels, their wings streaked with age. It must have been even more impressive when the Bannon patriarch, Joseph, was reburied in the tomb after the new church was built. Carson told me the family's marble vault had replaced a more modest crypt outside the original wooden structure.

It was the only burial chamber here. Most of the Leafy Hollow congregation members preferred the simpler graves that populated the rest of the cemetery.

Today, the Bannon family crypt would be the center of attention once again. Which meant we had to tidy up the long-neglected shrubs and perennials that surrounded the vault. Even its metal door was choked with weeds.

I'd also promised Daniel to trim the perennial beds that ran the length of the cemetery's front fence, in case the news crews decided to take a "panoramic shot." While Lorne unloaded the lawnmower from the pickup, I gathered up a rake, an edger, and some hand tools and headed for the plots, grinning. Six weeks ago, I would have thought an "edger" was part of a jigsaw puzzle.

I plunged the sharp, long-handled tool into the first of the weed-infested gardens and dug out a shallow strip of lawn, then repeated the motion along the entire border until it was smooth and symmetrical. After raking up the clumps of soil and grass I'd removed with the edger, I pulled a pair of clippers from the leather holster on my belt to dead-head the dried blooms. The perennial beds that fronted the cemetery had been a personal project of the previous minister's wife, but Daniel McAllister was unmarried, which meant there was no one to take on the many unpaid tasks of a minister's spouse.

I set about trimming the neglected day lilies, roses, and

irises. When Lorne finished the lawns, he came over to help. I handed him a weeder, and he plunged in. Fifteen minutes later, I looked up to see him ripping out a clump of common ragweed.

"Good grief," I said. "This garden is a disgrace."

Lorne grinned at me—remembering, no doubt, that when I first arrived in Leafy Hollow, I couldn't tell ragweed from radishes. But that was before I discovered my aunt's *Journal* and her collection of gardening books. I'd always been a quick study, and the Latin I learned as a child—my mother had been a professor of ancient languages—helped me memorize Aunt Adeline's notes.

Lorne reached for another weed. This one was three-feet high with fuzzy, serrated leaves.

"Stop," I blurted. "Don't touch that."

He froze and shot me a questioning look.

"*Urtica dioica,*" I said. "Stinging nettle. You'll be scratching for days if it touches your bare arms."

I recalled the handwritten notation in the margin of my aunt's *Encyclopedia of Garden Plants.* "'Grasp the nettle' might be practical advice for Spartan soldiers, but the rest of us should take care," she wrote. "*U. dioica*'s needle-sharp hairs inject nasty chemicals into your skin, including formic acid. Be happy you're not in Australia—their version of stinging nettle is the world's most-painful plant."

Lorne went back to the truck for a long-sleeved shirt and heavier gardening gloves, while I scanned the cemetery for more nettle. I found some trampled and broken among weeds at the base of the Bannon monument. Maybe someone else tried to clear the site and quit when they realized what they were up against. Lorne brought over the shovel to help take the nettles up by the roots, and I re-edged the perennial beds around the vault, clearing away everything that blocked the door.

Once it was tidy, I stepped back and leaned on the edger to assess our progress. I caught a movement in the corner of my eye and jerked my head around.

An elderly man, his white hair brushed straight back off a furrowed forehead, stood under an elm tree by the far edge of the cemetery. His bushy eyebrows, mustache, and beard matched his hair. He had one hand cupped against the chest of his drab olive jacket as if he was holding something.

Since he hadn't passed us, I assumed he'd come up the path from the river. Maybe he didn't know about the nettles. I dropped my edger and walked toward him, intending to warn him. "Hi, there," I waved. "I'm Verity."

His face showed no sign he'd heard me. As I stepped nearer, I saw that his quilted nylon jacket was dirty and worn. His pants puddled so far over his running shoes that the back edges were torn and hung in strips about his heels. He clutched his hand tighter to his chest.

I stopped about four feet away. "Can I help you?"

Lorne came up beside me. "Hey there, Ford," he said. "How ya doing?"

He ducked his head. "Okay."

"Ford comes here often, don't you?" Lorne said in a louder voice.

Ford ducked his head again. "Yes." Still clutching his chest, he scanned the cemetery. "I'm here last night." He took a quick step forward and grabbed Lorne's sleeve with his free hand. His eyes were wide, the pupils black and dilated. "I can't help him."

"Help who?" Lorne asked, gently prying Ford's fingers off his shirt.

Ford muttered something under his breath, and pointed to the Bannon family vault. "Him."

"We can't help him, either," Lorne said with a chuckle. "He's past our help."

But Ford had lost interest in the monument. "Is Isabelle here? Want to show her something."

I frowned. *Isabelle Yates?* "I don't think so," I said. "Why would—?"

"She's a Sunday School teacher here," Lorne offered. "And I think she helps out in the office."

Ford swiveled his head to the fence behind him. "Goin' back."

"Wait, there could be nettles along the path," I said. "Let me come with you. I'll cut them down." Scanning the ground for my pruners, I realized they were gone. I looked at Ford, noting again the suspicious bulge under his jacket. "What have you got under there?" I asked. "Can we see?"

He took a step back in alarm. "Not yours."

"I'm sure it's not, but—"

Lorne placed a hand on my arm. "It's okay, Ford. We won't take it, I promise."

Ford's hands shook as he looked from Lorne to me.

Even if he did have my pruners, I could recover them later. "I promise, too," I said.

The mischievous grin that transformed his expression was a delight. He took a step nearer, reaching up to unzip his jacket while still holding on to the suspicious bulge with his other hand.

I took a startled step back when the bulge started to squirm.

A tiny furry face with enormous blue eyes popped out of the opening.

"*Meorrrw*," it chirped.

"It's a kitten," I said, my voice almost a squeak. I reached out a finger to stroke its head. "Does it have a name?"

"Not this one."

"There are others?"

"By the river."

"I'd love to see them."

With a nod, Ford zipped up his jacket and turned to go, still holding on to the kitten. I made to follow him.

"Verity, shouldn't we finish up here before the exhumation?" Lorne asked.

"What am I thinking?" I slapped my forehead and called after him, "Ford, can I come by later?"

But he had already disappeared through the gap in the fence. I saw his bushy white head through the slats, headed for the river. Which was good. Considering I'd only recently adopted a stray cat of my own—not to mention a rooster—I didn't need another pet. Besides, I suspected that General Chang wouldn't enjoy sharing his tins of *Feline Fritters*.

"Where does Ford live?" I asked Lorne as we resumed our work.

"He has a camp down by the river, with an old pup tent he found somewhere. At night, he builds a campfire. The village moves him into a shelter in the winter, but in the summer, he insists on staying out here."

At my shocked look, Lorne shook his head. "People drop off food for him, and the public health nurse visits him. Reverend Daniel looks out for him, too. No one's been able to keep Ford indoors for long. As soon as the snow melts, he's back at that camp."

"Does he have a last name?"

"Not that I've ever heard. Maybe the nurse knows. They must need a last name to get benefits for him, but, for all I know, they could have made one up."

"Where did the kittens come from, then?"

"Ford looks after a feral-cat colony by the river. It's really something. You should take a look. He even builds sleeping crates for them."

"Isn't that hard on the wildlife?"

"The birders think so. It's an ongoing dispute in the village. Some people want the feral cats rounded up and put down, while others claim they keep the rats under control and should be encouraged." He chuckled. "Then there are people like Ford who just like cats."

"How does it keep going?"

"Volunteers from the local shelter trap the new arrivals. The vet neuters them, and they take them back."

"Who pays for it?"

"Nobody. The vet does it for free."

I made a mental note to pick up extra tins of *Feline Fritters* next time I was in the store. We picked up our tools and headed to the truck, intending to park it out of sight before the onslaught.

"Which side in the feral-cat debate do you come down on?" I asked.

"I stay out of it." Lorne blew air out his cheeks while he latched the tailgate. He ducked his head at the road. "Well, look who's here." He dropped his voice to a whisper. "And not to see me." Lorne flashed his eyebrows, then climbed into the passenger seat and closed the door. Traitor.

I turned to face the shiny black pickup pulling up on the shoulder. The green-and-gold letters of *Fields Landscaping* gleamed on its doors. A tall, rugged blond stepped out of the cab and strode up to us with a grin. His snug green T-shirt displayed impressive pecs.

"Hi, there," said Ryker Fields. "Need a hand?"

"We're fine," I said. "Finished, in fact."

Ryker shaded his eyes with one hand and swept his gaze over the perennial beds. "And you did a great job. But you should have called. I would have been happy to help. It's for a good cause, after all." He lowered his hand, turned his cool blue eyes on me, and flashed his trademark sexy smile.

I tried not to notice the effect it had on me.

"Yes, well, it's all done," I said. "But I appreciate the offer. Gotta go. Reverend wants us to clear this area for parking." I waved briefly and turned to the truck.

"Don't forget my other offer. It still stands," he called.

That was a reference to our much-postponed dinner date. I nodded weakly. "I'll get back to you." I climbed into the truck, revved the engine, and pulled out.

Ryker watched us drive away, leaning against the side of his truck with his arms crossed. A pose calculated to show off his washboard abs.

"Why don't you go to dinner with him already?" Lorne asked.

I leaned over to whack his arm. "None of your business." To be honest, I didn't know the answer. My husband Matthew had been dead for two years. His illness and passing had been the most wrenching event of my life, and I'd hidden from the world ever since. Most people would consider it time to move on—or at least share a plate of nachos with somebody other than Netflix. And there was no doubt that when it came to Ryker Fields, few unattached women in Leafy Hollow would say no. I cast a wry glance at the rearview mirror. That was exactly the problem.

After parking the truck up the road, I splashed bottled water on my face and ran a comb through my hair. Dressed for church or not, I didn't intend to miss my first exhumation —regardless of who, or what, was in that coffin.

By the time we walked back to the church and ducked through the side entrance of the cemetery, cars packed the shoulders of the road. A camera van from the television station in the nearby city of Strathcona held down a coveted spot in the church driveway, closest to the graveyard. A beefy man in jeans and a striped shirt with rolled cuffs emerged, hoisting a camera onto his shoulder. He followed a short woman with a pert blonde bob across the grass toward the Bannon family vault.

McAllister came out of the manse and strode down the sidewalk and around the church, coming out behind the monument. He looked awful. Even from forty feet away, I could see bags under his eyes that testified to a sleepless night. I edged closer. I knew the exhumation upset Reverend

Daniel, but I hadn't realized how much until this moment. He didn't really expect to find a dog in Prudence Bannon's coffin, did he?

McAllister rubbed his hands together, looking lost, as a crowd gathered in front of the crypt.

CHAPTER FIVE

THE MINISTER STOOD by himself until Isabelle Yates walked over and placed a hand on his arm. He patted it without looking at her. Isabelle murmured something I couldn't hear.

McAllister nodded at her words, still without looking. He appeared to be searching for someone in the crowd. With hundreds of people in attendance, it would be hard to spot any one individual. This audience was easily double the one at the village hall. I suspected today's crowd had been lured by the delicious possibility of scandal rather than a desire for historical accuracy. I noticed a few dogs in the crowd, straining at their leashes. So either way, Prudence would be represented.

McAllister brushed away Isabelle's hand and trudged up to the entrance of the Bannon family vault. He couldn't have moved any slower if he was the body being interred.

The television cameraman set up on the other side, opposite McAllister, while the blonde woman waited. "Testing," she said, raising the mic to her lips and giving the camera a bored look. "Testing."

I scanned the gathered villagers and then the road, looking for Nesbitt-Cavanagh. The historian hadn't arrived yet—no surprise there—although Xavier Roy was in the front row, camera at the ready. He wore the same black baseball cap he'd worn at the village hall the day before, but he'd abandoned his gray hoodie in favor of a black T-shirt that read, "Director of Photography."

Given Nesbitt-Cavanagh's dismissive comment about a "major" filmmaker, Xavier and the historian must have patched up their differences. There were no other videographers in evidence.

Nick Yates stood against the back wall, wearing the same long-sleeved pink shirt despite the heat. His face was even redder than usual, and sweat glistened on his forehead. He tracked Isabelle with his eyes, but he made no move to approach her.

Someone poked my arm. I jerked around to find Emy at my elbow.

"What are you doing way back here?" she asked. "You can't see anything."

I didn't want to admit that the crowd made me nervous so I simply said, "I'm not dressed for a religious ceremony." I spread my hands to show my muddy feet, grass-stained T-shirt, and wrinkled khakis.

"Who cares? We're not in church, not technically. And frankly, your outfit makes more sense in this heat than this long-sleeved dress I'm wearing." Emy pushed a damp lock of hair off her forehead and heaved a sigh as she glanced around. "Could it be any hotter?"

"I thought you'd be used to it after all those hours toiling over a hot oven."

She made a wry face. "You'd be wrong. Come on. Let's move up to the front. I don't want to miss anything. This will be good."

Emy pushed her way through the crowd, beaming at everyone we passed while towing me behind her like a tug boat pulling a freighter. People always assumed petite women were delicate. *Hah.* If they'd ever watched Emy wrestle a heavy, full-sized sheet pan of organic whole-wheat bread loaves from a shoulder-high oven while muttering curses under her breath, they might reconsider.

"Sorry," I said as we barreled through the crowd. "Oops, sorry."

We had almost reached the front row when a uniformed arm thrust out to stop me. I glanced up, straight into the dark eyes of our local detective constable. I immediately regretted my wardrobe choices.

"Wow, you're here too," I said with my usual impeccable poise. I tried to brush away the grass stains on the front of my shirt, smudging them even more.

"Apparently," Jeff replied, his eyebrows rising.

"I only meant..." My voice trailed off. What *had* I meant? Why did I get so tongue-tied around Jeff? After all, we'd once bonded in my kitchen over a pair of red lace D-cups. Not mine, I hasten to add. "Are you... interested in history?" I asked.

"The village council requested a police presence at this

event, and I was available." The corners of his lips twitched. "Now that I see you're here, I understand why they thought it would be a good idea."

I took the high road, ignoring his feeble jibe. After the Skalding murder case, even Jeff admitted that I'd been a big help. I was proud of that. Up to then, the only mystery I'd ever solved involved dubious accounts receivable. "Why, are you expecting trouble?"

"Let's check. Emy, did you bring any cupcakes?" Jeff asked without taking his gaze from my face. His eyes crinkled at the edges.

"Nope," she said.

"Then I think we're probably safe."

"What do you mean he's not here?" came a loud voice from behind Jeff.

It was Wilf Mullins, and he sounded annoyed. "Why are we waiting, if that blasted historian can't be bothered to get out of bed?" The front row parted to reveal the tiny councilor tugging at Jeff's sleeve. "Katsuro. Good. You're here. You should disperse this crowd. No point in everyone hanging around if nothing's happening."

Without waiting for a reply, Wilf released his hold on Jeff's shirt and marched over to McAllister. "Reverend, let's call a halt to this circus," Wilf said.

Xavier swung his camera onto his shoulder and peered through the viewfinder to film their exchange.

"Nesbitt-Cavanagh isn't here, just as I predicted," Wilf continued. "Didn't I say he was a lying blowhard? He's probably on a plane headed back home by now with his tail between his legs."

Xavier moved in closer.

Wilf whirled to stare at him with his mouth open. "What are you filming?" he asked, advancing on Xavier.

McAllister stepped between them. "I think it's the documentary," he offered.

Wilf ducked around McAllister and pointed a finger at Xavier, who tilted his lens down to focus on Wilf's face. "Document this," he said, scowling. "Edgar Nesbitt-Cavanagh doesn't know what he's talking about. It's an absolute disgrace that he's come here to desecrate the grave of such a brave young girl. The village of Leafy Hollow will not stand for it. *I* will not stand for it."

The television cameraman also swung his lens in Wilf's direction, after tapping the reporter on her shoulder and pointing at the pair.

Wilf twisted his head so that he faced both cameras, and then raised his voice. "Nesbitt-Cavanagh hopes to profit from this outrage by publishing an extremely dubious volume. But we must not let commerce override decency. We must honor Prudence Bannon's sacrifices, not besmirch her memory."

Wilf was really getting wound up. I wondered what sacrifices of Prudence's he was referring to. Blisters, maybe? And now, *commerce* was bad? What about the Prudence Bannon Memorial Waterpark? I took a few steps back to ensure my smirk wasn't within camera range.

The blonde television reporter thrust her mic in front of Wilf. "Mr. Mullins, would you call this exhumation a travesty?"

Wilf pressed his lips together as he regarded her, and then he nodded. "Yes, that's correct. A travesty." He raised his chin as murmurs grew in the crowd. "We should call it off."

"Yeah, call it off," a voice shouted from the crowd.

Others joined in. "Call it off."

A worried-looking Terry worked his way through the crowd, followed by Zander. Terry had exchanged his dapper outfit of the previous day for a more laid-back hooded polo shirt and khakis. Wilf pointed at them. "These two fellows know the truth."

"And you are?" the reporter asked, holding the mic up to Terry's face.

"I'm Terry Oliver, and this is Zander Skalding. We jointly run the Leafy Hollow Historical Society. Mr. Nesbitt-Cavanagh is here at our invitation."

"Were you surprised by his contention that Prudence Bannon never existed?"

"Surprised? Definitely. That's not at all what he's been telling us."

"So this is a recent development?"

Terry nodded. "Very recent."

"I understand there was an altercation at yesterday's dedication ceremony?"

Terry shifted uncomfortably. "There was an academic difference of opinion."

"Is it true that Mr. Nesbitt-Cavanagh was assaulted with a pastry?"

Terry reeled back with a look of astonishment. "Of course not."

Good answer, I thought. Pork sausage was definitely not a pastry.

"Where is Mr. Nesbitt-Cavanagh today?" the reporter asked.

"We don't know. He promised to be here an hour ago."

Wilf shuffled up. The reporter turned the mic to him.

"Our alleged historian"—Wilf spit out the word—"kept over two hundred people waiting for forty-five minutes at the village hall yesterday. He's probably planning another grand entrance."

Muttering erupted in the crowd.

"But we won't let him," Wilf continued. Turning to face the onlookers, he raised his voice. "Let's end this travesty right now."

The mutters turned to chants. "Shut it down. Shut it down."

Wilf must have brought along his own cheering section. People didn't usually get this worked up over something that happened two centuries ago.

McAllister tried to speak, but his comment was drowned out by the chanting. The reporter swiveled to face him. The crowd hushed.

"Could you repeat that, Reverend?" she asked.

"I'm afraid"—McAllister cleared his throat—"we have to go ahead." He lifted the document in his hand above his head and raised his voice. "The attorney general's instructions are clear, and our local church assembly assures me that we have no grounds on which to refuse Mr. Nesbitt-Cavanagh's request." He lowered the paper. "Unless Mr. Nesbitt-Cavanagh withdraws his application, we must open Prudence Bannon's coffin and send her body for analysis."

Two black-capped attendants from the local funeral

parlor stepped forward and nodded at McAllister. The minister glanced sideways at Isabelle, who gave an encouraging nod. He pulled up the key chain that hung by his side and selected an antique skeleton key, then turned it in the lock. With a creak of aged iron, McAllister hauled the door open.

Xavier and the television cameraman jostled for the best vantage point, and the funeral attendants walked over to the entrance. The minister stepped into the vault.

For long seconds, we held our breath, waiting for him to emerge from the crypt.

The murmurs grew louder as people pressed closer. Jeff moved from the side of the vault to stand in front of the crowd with a hand resting on the nightstick hanging from his belt. Everyone knew he had no intention of using it, but they halted their advance anyway.

When I craned my neck, I could see through the crypt door, but the minister's back blocked my view of anything beyond.

Starlings rustled in the trees surrounding the cemetery while we waited.

Inside the crypt, McAllister said something. It was inaudible to the crowd, but Isabelle, standing right outside, jerked her head around with a startled expression. She pushed past the funeral attendants and into the tomb.

A second later, a scream echoed off the vault walls and into the churchyard. An alarmed flock of starlings burst from the trees, the birds' wings beating furiously as they rose into the air.

Jeff ran to the crypt. "Stay back," he shouted over his

shoulder as he disappeared inside. The crowd pressed in, holding its collective breath.

The birds swirled overhead, chattering and shrieking. Gradually, they returned to the branches.

McAllister emerged, his expression stricken, holding up Isabelle who was leaning on his arm. Her face was as pale and gray as the streaked marble walls of the crypt. "Horrible," she whispered. "Horrible."

As both cameramen swooped in for close-ups, I darted to the entrance of the vault.

Jeff was inside, crouched beside something. He leaned over to peer at an object, giving me a clear view of what lay beyond. I clapped a hand to my mouth to stifle my own scream.

Edgar Nesbitt-Cavanagh lay on the floor of the crypt, his limbs twisted and contorted. He had on the shabby tweed jacket he'd worn at the village hall a day earlier, but there was no pipe between his lips. His eyes were cloudy and his gaze fixed. I knew he was dead. His face was the same dull blue I'd seen before on a lifeless body.

At least no one could suspect me of having anything to do with this corpse.

As my shadow fell across the body, Jeff looked up.

"Don't touch anything," he said, getting to his feet and shooing me out the door.

CHAPTER SIX

THE POLICE RADIO crackled as Jeff spoke the same code for a homicide I'd heard once outside Rose Cottage. "...ten-forty-five, Leafy Hollow Community Church..." He held up a hand as the two cameramen crowded in. "Stand back, please."

"No, we have to—" they objected.

"Stand back, please," Jeff repeated, more forcefully.

It only took seconds for the news about Nesbitt-Cavanagh's body to travel through the crowd milling about the cemetery. Even though Prudence Bannon's exhumation had clearly been upstaged, no one seemed interested in leaving. They gathered in small groups, murmuring to each other and craning their necks to peer into the vault.

Madeline rushed up, crimson curls bobbing, only to be stopped by the outstretched arms of the constable on guard duty. "Edgar?" she called, ducking her head around the cop who was holding her arm. "What's happening? Edgar?" She tussled briefly with the constable as he tried to move her back.

Edgar? Nesbitt-Cavanagh hardly spoke to Madeline at the village hall. How could they be on a first-name basis?

The cameramen jostled as they moved in for close-ups of Madeline's horrified expression. Xavier elbowed the other videographer in the ribs and stepped in front of him. For a small guy, Xavier had gumption. No wonder he was a "Director of Photography." I smirked for a second, and then gasped as a hearty slap from the television cameraman sent Xavier stumbling out of the way. At the rate these two were going, Jeff would soon have another murder on his hands.

The television reporter stood beside Wilf Mullins and raised the mic to her lips, facing the camera. Xavier grabbed the cameraman's shirt and tried to wrestle him to the ground. The cameraman shoved him out of the way.

"The dead body of British historian Edgar Nesbitt-Cavanagh has been found in the Bannon family vault, here at Leafy Hollow Community Church," the reporter said. "Were you surprised by today's events, Mr. Mullins?" She lowered the mic to Wilf's face as the television cameraman zoomed in.

Wilf stared at her, openmouthed. It was the first time I'd seen the garrulous councilor speechless. With a look of horror, he shoved past her and marched over to the minister. "McAllister," he demanded. "What the fudge is going on?"

The minister only shook his head, looking stricken. Beside him, Isabelle rubbed her hands together, muttering.

With a burst of sirens, two police cars pulled up outside the church, light bars flashing. Doors opened and slammed, and four constables strode across the lawn to the vault.

"Guard the door," Jeff said to one before turning to confer in low tones with the other three.

Wilf was complaining to anyone who would listen. "Why didn't someone tell us he was suicidal?" he insisted.

Reverend Daniel stood still as stone, his horrified gaze fixed on the Bannon family crypt, almost as if he couldn't see the four-foot-tall man tugging at his sleeve.

"McAllister, you're a minister, for heaven's sake. Why didn't you do something?" Wilf released his grip and pivoted to glare at the tomb and the police. "Didn't I say that man wasn't right in the head? This is your church. You're supposed to be in charge. This is a disgrace."

The television reporter, still trying to get a quote from the councilor, placed a hand on Wilf's arm. "Mr. Mullins—"

"No comment," he said, shrugging off her hand and holding up his own. "No comment." He stalked off, still muttering.

Wilf marched right past Emy, who was hurrying to Isabelle's side. Emy squeezed her cousin's shoulder, handed her a tissue and murmured something in her ear. Lorne darted through the crowd to help. Emy and Lorne set off in the direction of the manse, propping up Isabelle, one on either side.

Isabelle appeared to be in shock. So was I. Leaning an arm against the crypt, I lowered my head, trying to catch my breath as knots of people swirled around me, everyone talking at once. My tongue felt thick and my chest had tightened.

I looked up as Nick brushed past me, hurrying after Isabelle, Emy, and Lorne. He placed a hand on his wife's shoulder from behind. "Isabelle?"

Emy flicked Nick's hand away. "You can talk to her later," she said.

He scowled, eyes flaring. "Why shouldn't I talk to her now? She's my wife. She's upset. She should come home with me."

Emy shook her head. "Not now, Nick. Please."

Nick grabbed his wife's shirt. "Isabelle?"

Lorne turned. With a determined air and a strong arm, he parted Nick from the two women.

Nick had at least forty pounds on the much leaner Lorne. For a second, I held my breath, fearing a confrontation. But Nick took a step back, lips pressed together. Scowling, he turned on his heel to return to the road.

His route would take him past Madeline, who stood by the vault entrance with her hands clapped over her mouth. She hadn't moved since being brushed aside by the police.

Poor Madeline. She was having a tough week. First, her portrait was ruined, and now her champion was dead. At least, I assumed Nesbitt-Cavanagh had championed her work. At least, the outspoken historian hadn't been among her critics.

The bubbly, red-haired artist was also a client—albeit unpaid—of Coming Up Roses Landscaping and a friend of my missing aunt. I wanted to tear myself away from the sidelines to see if she was okay. But I couldn't. I didn't know if it was the heat or the shock, but the air around me was shimmering and I was having trouble catching my breath. The past few weeks had been so peaceful that I'd forgotten how quickly an anxiety attack could flare up. I watched dully as Nick approached Madeline.

To my surprise, Nick paused when he reached her. "Are you okay?" he asked.

"I'm fine." She bit her lip, looking as if she might break into tears.

"Why don't I take you home?" He offered his arm.

She leaned on him with a grateful look. "Thank you, Nick. This has been a blow."

"You'll feel better when you get away from here," he said in a soothing tone.

I watched with my mouth open as they trudged past me. Maybe Nick Yates wasn't so bad after all.

A movement near the vault caught my eye.

Xavier emerged from the crypt with his camera in his hand. He must have ducked inside before the officer on guard took up his position. Jeff looked up, his eye caught by the same movement, and frowned. The constable, looking sheepish, moved nearer the crypt's entrance.

Meanwhile, Xavier was grinning broadly, an unusual expression for someone who'd just seen a dead—and probably murdered—body. Perhaps that was old hat for a "Director of Photography," but I couldn't understand how he remained so calm. Even my brief glimpse of Nesbitt-Cavanagh had left me shaken. But Xavier had been up close and personal with the corpse. Judging from their dispute of the previous day, there was no love lost between the two men, but it seemed cold-blooded.

Before I could give it any more thought, a second, much-bigger television van screamed up in front of the church and shuddered to a halt, the antenna dish on its roof wobbling.

Strathcona Live—an affiliate of a national network—blazed in multicolor print on the sides.

Good thing Wilf hadn't witnessed this latest arrival. The Legend of Leafy Hollow was about to go viral. I pictured the headline: *British Prof Slain in Crypt Shocker*.

The man who emerged from the unit had coiffed brown hair, a ready smile, and gleaming teeth. His face matched the larger-than-life portrait painted on the van. A woman followed—whom I took to be the producer—and then a video-grapher wearing sunglasses and a safari jacket. Xavier eyed his camera, which was the biggest so far. I could smell the testosterone in the air.

The female producer exchanged a few words with the reporter and cameraman already on the scene. Then she marched over to Xavier. I held my breath, expecting a prickly encounter. But their brief conversation ended in smiles. The producer handed Xavier her business card. I suspected Xavier's exclusive footage of the vault's interior was about to hit the airwaves—and make him a healthy profit.

Xavier pocketed the card with a sly smile and shouldered his camera to resume filming.

One of the constables unspooled yellow caution tape and stretched it across the vault. Another cordoned off the church's carved wooden doors and the concrete walkway leading up to them.

With a wince, I recalled that Lorne and I had cleared the area around the crypt that morning. It was possible we'd destroyed evidence.

"Verity?" came a voice from behind me.

I whirled, expecting to find Jeff waiting to question me.

But Zander and Terry stood behind me, looking woeful. Zander's moon-shaped face was paler than usual, and his semi-mohawk less jaunty. "Does this mean they won't open Prudence's coffin after all?" Zander asked.

I looked from one to the other, baffled. "I guess so, but why are you asking me?"

"We thought... with your experience, you would know how these things are done."

My experience? My stomach churned as I recalled my last dead body. "Guys, I've only been at one other murder scene, and I was too upset to take notes. Sorry."

Terry leaned over Zander's shoulder. "So it is murder, then?"

"It must be. The minister had to unlock the vault to get in."

"Ohhh, right," Terry said, narrowing his eyes and nodding. "See, you are experienced."

I stared at him. Maybe I was, because it occurred to me that we only had the minister's word that he unlocked the crypt. No one else tried the door. He could have inserted the key and only pretended to unlock it. *And why would he do that, Verity?* my inner voice asked.

I hated my inner voice. It was so rational.

A hand squeezed my shoulder, and I turned. When I realized it was Jeff, my knees went a little weak. "Hi," I blurted, much too loud for such a tragic scene.

His expression was solemn under the peaked cap that shaded his eyes. "Can you take Reverend Daniel back to the manse? We have to clear the area."

"What should I tell him?"

"Tell him to stay there and we'll talk to him later," Jeff said over his shoulder, walking toward the church

"He's not a suspect, is he?" I asked, remembering the ring of keys clattering by the minister's side and wondering if I should mention my theory about the lock.

"Just tell him," Jeff snapped without looking at me. He swiveled on one foot and walked back, looking contrite. "I'm sorry." He was about to add something when the television cameraman gave Xavier a mighty shove.

Xavier stumbled back and toppled onto the grass. He scrambled to his feet, adjusting his rimless glasses. "Hey, dumbass," he yelled. "Try that again."

Jeff sighed, and then stepped between the two men with his arms spread to hold them apart. "You'll both be barred from the scene if you can't behave." Jeff nodded at the constable guarding the crypt, who walked over with a questioning look. "Escort these gentlemen outside the fence, please."

The videographers, still arguing, were marched back to the road. No sooner had the constables retreated than the two men hoisted their cameras to their shoulders to interview bystanders. There were more than enough witnesses to go around, but the men followed each other and filmed the same people, determined not to miss any matching sound bites.

I turned to McAllister. His gaze was riveted on the open vault door and he seemed unable, or unwilling, to move. "It might be important," he muttered, looking at the crypt.

I knew what it felt like to stumble across your first murder victim. Zander and Terry called it "experience," but my discovery had been one of the worst days of my life. In fact, this whole event was giving me flashbacks—not only of that dead body, but also of the deaths of my mother and Matthew. I struggled to push it all out of my mind. "Reverend Daniel," I called, trying to get his attention. "Daniel. Let's go to the manse. The police can talk to you there."

He ducked his head at the vault. "Poor man. I should have listened to him."

I assumed he meant at the village hall meeting. "You did. And now, you should go home."

McAllister nodded, and we set off for the minister's house together, walking through the cemetery and around the church. Jeff and the other officers were clearing the scene, one gaggle of onlookers at a time, moving the spectators behind the fence.

Lorne and Emy, with Isabelle between them, were almost out of sight. As we followed them to the manse, I glanced over my shoulder. Jeff was crouching outside the entrance to the vault, pointing out items in the grass to a white-suited technician. Should I go back and tell him that Lorne and I had cleaned up the site?

I decided against it. There would be plenty of time to bring that up later. McAllister looked pale and miserable. He needed to go home and regroup. Anyway, Nesbitt-Cavanagh's body was inside the vault, not outside. And Lorne and I had never been in there.

That wasn't the only reason. I was desperate to sit down, lower my head between my knees, and close my eyes until my heartbeat returned to normal. After that, I intended to return to Rose Cottage, lock the door behind me, and draw a hot bath. Then I would try to erase from my mind the image of

Nesbitt-Cavanagh's milky pupils and unfocused gaze. How could I have been so close to another dead body? Was I jinxed? I pictured my tranquil Vancouver apartment, with its view of a sliver of Burrard Inlet, and wished I was back in my tiny living room, reading my favorite self-help book, *Organize Your Way to a Better Life*. At the moment, I couldn't even organize my thoughts.

We walked past Zander and Terry, who were conferring in low tones by the vault.

Terry held out a hand as we passed. "Verity, can we talk?"

"Later," I said. "Or come along."

They fell into step behind us.

As we trudged, I saw Ford standing by the back fence, head bowed, and remembered his words. *I'm here last night. I can't help him.*

Ford looked up and saw me. He shook his head, muttered something inaudible, and disappeared through the fence and down the path. I knew how he felt. I wanted to disappear, too. A chill ran down my spine and I paused for a moment while Daniel shuffled on. If Ford was in the cemetery the previous night, he might have seen Nesbitt-Cavanagh's killer. I narrowed my eyes to watch his gray-haired head vanish down the path.

If Ford saw the killer, did the killer also see Ford?

CHAPTER SEVEN

WE SAT around the wooden harvest table in the manse's light-filled kitchen, listening to sparrows rustle though the honeysuckle vine that twined over the open window. The blue-painted cupboards that lined the walls were faded and worn. Nicks and scratches in the polished tabletop attested to decades of wear. The church kitchen was fully modernized, but I supposed the members didn't want to pamper their minister's home with the same attention.

As we sat numbly, lost in thought, Emy bustled about brewing tea. She poured it over ice, added lemon and sugar, and served us in mismatched glasses from the cupboard. Lorne got up to help her. Isabelle sat beside the minister, watching his face intently and patting his arm. He seemed not to notice.

I sipped my iced tea and wondered who bought the fresh lemons. Judging from the TV-dinner boxes in the bin next to the sink, McAllister didn't fuss much over his bachelor meals.

Normally, whenever Lorne and I arrived to cut the church lawn we'd find him in his den, hunched in front of the computer or engrossed in one of the books that lined the walls, oblivious to the dishes stacked in the kitchen sink. Even today, the glass of iced tea sat untouched by his elbow.

With a heavy sigh, McAllister picked up the remote control that lay on the kitchen table. A television sputtered on—one of those boxy ones of ten years ago, not a flat screen —from its perch on a shelf over the microwave. The *Strathcona Live* anchor—recognizable from his giant profile on the news van—sat before a huge projected picture of the church.

McAllister turned up the sound.

"Police have not yet identified the body found this morning in a crypt at the Leafy Hollow Community Church, but local sources confirm that it's British historian Edgar Nesbitt-Cavanagh." The anchor swiveled his head to face the second camera.

Judging by the fancy set and huge video-screen backdrop, this was not the local affiliate, which had only one studio camera and an overhead mic that occasionally slid into the frame, followed by a hand snatching it back. No, this was the national broadcast—McAllister's worst fear.

"Mr. Nesbitt-Cavanagh was in the village to speak at a gathering to commemorate Prudence Bannon," the anchor continued, "a young girl who delivered beer to the troops in 1812, according to the villagers." His lips twitched into a slight smile, making me think the word "pitchforks" would soon follow.

Zander lowered his head into his hands with an audible groan, rumpling his faux-mohawk. "That's not what we told them," he muttered. McAllister didn't reply. Our normally sharp-witted minister seemed to have been struck dumb.

"We spoke to Mr. Nesbitt-Cavanagh before yesterday's gathering," the anchor said. "Here's a clip of that interview." The image behind him grew until the historian's face filled the screen.

At the mention of an interview, Zander jerked his head up out of his hands to stare at the television. "Terry, did you know about this?"

Terry shook his head. He stood up and moved closer to the set.

"Sir, can you tell us what you intend to say at today's gathering?" asked the interviewer.

Nesbitt-Cavanagh took the pipe from his mouth and looked directly at the camera. "I'll be presenting an explosive allegation about what I've come to characterize as The Legend of Leafy Hollow." He emphasized *Legend* with gusto.

"So you do not endorse the local myth?"

Terry's eyes widened. *Myth?* He mouthed the word with disgust and slapped the side of the television.

"Certainly not," Nesbitt-Cavanagh said. "It's time the truth was told."

His image dissolved into that morning's scene at the cemetery, dominated by the looming angels of the Bannon family vault. The camera panned over the crowd waiting outside the crypt.

McAllister nodded at the television. "The grass looks good," he said. "Thanks, Verity."

It was impressive that he could find something positive to

say about the day's events. Our minister was always a glass-half-full kind of guy, but this was above and beyond.

His optimism didn't last.

"Although... I never dreamed we would be on the news for something like this." He dropped the remote on the table and slumped in his chair to watch the rest of the clip.

We all watched it. Even though we knew what was coming next, it was impossible to look away.

The anchor talked in the background, over video footage that featured close-ups of Isabelle's shocked expression, Madeline's tears, and the minister's stunned silence.

"A warning to our more sensitive viewers," the anchor said, "this next clip contains graphic images."

The screen darkened. It took a second or two before we realized this must be Xavier's film of the vault's gloomy interior. The camera swung wildly from one side of the vault to the other, its light picking out stone coffins in the gloom. Then the viewpoint lowered to the ground and focused on a stark white hand.

Isabelle gasped and turned her face away as the camera swept over the historian's body. I peered at the screen, focusing on a shiny foil square that protruded from Nesbitt-Cavanagh's jacket pocket. My eyes widened. *Was that a giant chocolate bar?*

Odd, the things you noticed when you were in shock.

Emy picked up the remote and muted the sound.

McAllister pulled a handkerchief from his pocket with a trembling hand, removed his glasses, and wiped their lenses.

No one spoke.

I'd seen similar clips often enough on the news, but never

had I felt such a sense of indignation—outrage, even. It angered me that a village that had been so kind to me was being treated so unjustly.

Although, to be fair, the residents had accused me of attempted murder after my arrival in Leafy Hollow, and some of them boycotted my aunt's landscaping business, but that was a misunderstanding. At its core, the village was a kind place. A gentle place. A place where even feral cats received a second chance at happiness. A place where—

I mentally slapped myself. It had been a long and depressing day, so perhaps that was why my inner Pollyanna was emerging. I needed to return to Rose Cottage and reacquaint myself with reality.

Rising to my feet, I rinsed out my iced tea glass and left it in the kitchen sink. "Daniel, do you want me to drop off the key to the vault on my way through the cemetery?"

McAllister didn't look up. He was examining his glass as if the iced tea had transformed into wine.

"Daniel?" I asked, trying to get his attention. "The police will want to lock the tomb for the night."

"What?" He looked startled.

"The key to the Bannon family crypt. Do you have it?"

McAllister shifted in his chair and pulled the rattling key chain from his pocket. He laid the ring on the table with a clink, thumbing through it until he reached a heavy iron skeleton key. He extracted it from the ring and held it up. "This one?"

"We should give it to the police, don't you think?"

"I can do that," he said dully, but he made no move to rise.

I felt a rush of irritation. McAllister didn't seem to realize this was a crime scene, even though the flashing lights of the squad cars outside were a dead giveaway. The day's events had shocked everyone, but the man was a minister. He should be accustomed to dead bodies—they were a standard feature at funerals. His behavior was odd, to say the least.

I raised my eyebrows at Terry, who looked perplexed for a moment and then nodded. He walked over to the minister and held out his hand.

"Zander and I will drop it off for you."

With a silent nod of thanks, McAllister handed over the key. The men walked out the kitchen door. I watched as McAllister picked up the key ring and slid it back into his pocket.

"Are those the only keys to the crypt?" I asked.

"What do you mean?" Isabelle asked, her brow furrowed.

"I only wondered... that's such an old key. Are there duplicates? Or is that it?"

McAllister took a sip of iced tea and replaced the glass on the table. "There's another set. But not here."

I must have looked confused, because Isabelle stepped in to answer.

"I have it," she said, reaching for her purse. She pulled out a duplicate key chain and clinked it onto the table. "I... help out from time to time. In the church and the manse. On a volunteer basis."

The fresh lemons in the fridge suddenly made sense.

"That's great, then," I said. "We can tell the police you don't need the other key back."

Isabelle and the minister exchanged glances.

McAllister cleared his throat. "Is that necessary?"

"What do you mean?"

"It might... complicate things. If the police know about Isabelle's keys, that is."

I glanced at Emy to see if she'd caught his meaning. She was staring at the tabletop, her lips pursed. I recognized that look. Emy was pretending not to listen. I should do the same, before someone accused me of withholding evidence.

Time to change the subject.

"Daniel, when we were cutting the lawn, there was an older man—Ford—hanging about. Do you know him?"

"He's been here for years," Isabelle replied, still speaking for the minister. "We take him food every week, and he sometimes comes up for Sunday services. He's harmless, poor man."

"Is Ford his only name?"

"I don't think anybody knows. When he first arrived in the village, he used to wander the aisles at Canadian Tire. He was especially fond of the automotive section, so that's why everyone calls him Ford." She shrugged.

"Is he allowed to ramble about the churchyard?"

"Of course. He does odd jobs for us. Cleaning gravestones, that sort of thing. I'm afraid Ford's not quite—" She shrugged.

I nodded. "That explains it, then."

McAllister looked up sharply. "Explains what?"

"Why he was here last night, in the cemetery."

"Ford was in the cemetery last night?" The minister leaned forward to hear my answer, his lips parted. It was the most animated he'd been since the discovery of Nesbitt-Cavanagh's body.

"Yes. In fact, he said the oddest thing. He said he'd seen—"

A hammering on the front door made me jump.

"That'll be the police," I said, pushing back my chair.

Isabelle jumped up and scurried to the door.

"What did Ford see?" the minister asked, tapping his fingers on the table. "Verity?"

Before I could answer, Jeff walked into the kitchen and rational thought fled my brain. Gosh, that man looked good in a uniform.

I mentally slapped myself again. Which of my inner Veritys conjured up that ridiculous notion? I hoped the flush I felt didn't mean I was blushing.

Jeff flashed me a quick smile before turning to McAllister. "I have a few questions for you, Reverend." He slid out his notebook, flipped it open, and gestured to a chair. "May I?"

At McAllister's nod, Jeff pulled out the chair and sat at the table. He raised an eyebrow at Lorne, Emy, and me.

"We should go," Emy said, jogging my elbow.

"What?" I asked. "Oh, right. We're leaving, Jeff."

"Thank you," he said, pulling a small pen from the notepad's coil.

"You don't need Izzy, do you?" Emy asked, taking her cousin's arm and leading her to the door. They turned to look at Jeff.

He placed his notebook on the table while studying

Isabelle's face. "No. I'll talk to you later, Isabelle. You should go home."

"She's staying at my place if you need her," Emy said over her shoulder as we walked out the kitchen door.

Jeff nodded and turned to McAllister.

At the roadside, Emy opened the passenger door of her neon yellow Fiat 500 and nodded for Isabelle to get in.

Isabelle took a step back. "I think I'll stay. There's paperwork to do in the church office, and Daniel won't be in any mood for it." She glanced uneasily over her shoulder. "He might not even have time, what with the police investigation and all."

Considering the size of the boxy little Fiat, I felt that was a wise choice.

Isabelle walked off, and I turned to go.

"Wait." Emy moved closer and dropped her voice. "Can you come by the bakery in half an hour? I need your advice on Izzy."

"Why?" I asked.

"Shhh," Emy said. She glanced in the direction of the church, but Isabelle had her back to us and showed no sign that she'd heard. "I don't want her to know I'm worried."

"I can't, Emy. I'm exhausted. We still have two lawns to cut today. After that, I intend to go home." *And never leave*, I silently added.

"I can cut those lawns without you," Lorne said.

"Yes, but—" I began.

"It's no problem," he broke in. "They're right down the street, and the truck is already parked there. You can pick it up later." He stuck out his chin. "I'll write up the invoices, too."

I stared at him with my mouth open. "Really?"

"Yep." He ducked his head at Emy, who looked puzzled. She had no idea that her mother Thérèse and I shared a secret about Lorne—Thérèse, a literacy tutor, was helping him perfect his reading. He must be making rapid progress—which I had expected. Whatever difficulty had prevented Lorne from learning to read in school, it wasn't lack of brainpower.

"Okay," I said, a grin spreading across my face. "That takes care of my excuse." For some reason, my desire to hole up in Rose Cottage had vanished. Maybe it was the thought of Emy's delectable cupcakes. "But I'm going home to change my clothes first." I held up a hand as Emy indicated the Fiat's open passenger door. "Thanks, but I think I'll walk."

It was a beautiful summer day and a stroll might clear my head. Or at least help me forget about the body in the crypt.

Emy drove away, and I set off in the opposite direction. I had taken only three steps before someone called my name. I turned to see Zander and Terry trotting after me.

"Verity, please help us," Terry said with a frown. "If we don't get this thing under control, the Society will have to shut down."

Zander was puffing from the exertion of racing to catch me, but the athletic Terry wasn't even breathing heavily. "Where are your bikes?" I asked.

"At home," Terry said. "We're not dressed for cycling."

"I'm sorry about the Society. I'd like to help, but there's nothing I can do."

"You can ask Jeff Katsuro about the suspects."

"What? No, I can't. And anyway, what difference does it make to the Society who the suspects are?" I asked.

"It's obvious, isn't it?" Zander asked in a shaky voice. "Nesbitt-Cavanagh accused us of fraud yesterday. And now he's dead."

Shaking my head, I resumed my walk to Rose Cottage. Zander and Terry fell in step beside me.

"How does that make you a suspect?" I asked. "Wouldn't you be better off if Nesbitt-Cavanagh was still alive? Even if he cast doubt on Prudence Bannon's achievement, at least people would be talking about it. No bad publicity and all that."

The two men exchanged glances and grim looks.

"If the Society is closed due to fraud allegations, then it won't exist anymore," Zander said.

I sighed in exasperation. "I can see that, but—"

"If it doesn't exist, we can't carry out my mother's bequest. She left her estate to the Society. Which means—"

"The money would revert to you," I broke in.

"Exactly. And that makes us suspects in Nesbitt-Cavanagh's murder."

They looked at me expectantly while I mulled over the implications.

"We don't expect you to find the killer right away," Terry prompted.

"That's good, because I won't," I said. "Honestly, I think you're worried about nothing. If you were after your mother's money, it would make more sense to keep Nesbitt-Cavanagh alive. And either way, I couldn't do anything to help you."

"Not true," Terry said with an emphatic wave of his hand. "You solved the mystery of a five-year-old accident that killed two people—long after the police gave up."

I paused at this reference to the tragic death of Jeff Katsuro's wife in a hit-and-run. Wendy Katsuro had been blonde, petite, and only twenty-six when she died. I liked to think the truth helped Jeff to heal, but it wasn't an experience I wanted to revisit.

"And almost got myself killed in the bargain. No thanks, guys. I promised Jeff I wouldn't investigate anything else, and I'm not going back on my word."

"Still," Terry insisted. "You did solve it. And this time, there's only one victim and the body's still fresh. At least you could try to find out what the police are thinking."

"No," I said. "No, no, and no."

Terry opened his mouth, but before he could add anything I crossed my hands in the air in an emphatic gesture. "No."

He frowned. "Sorry, Verity. It's just that it's depressing—to think we had drinks with the guy only two days ago and now he's dead."

"Was that the night before the village hall meeting?" I asked, intrigued despite my better judgment.

"Yeah, we picked him up at the B&B and took him to Madeline's to view the portrait. Then we all went to Kirby's for dinner and a drink."

So Nesbitt-Cavanagh and Madeline had met before the village hall debacle. I couldn't resist asking the obvious question. "Did he and Madeline get on well?"

"I think you could say that," Terry replied, goosing Zander. "Wouldn't you say so, Zee?"

"Well, let's put it this way, Tee. When we left Kirby's, they were in a booth, both starting on their third strawberry margarita."

I couldn't picture Nesbitt-Cavanagh drinking any cocktail that included an umbrella—I would have bet on Scotch with a splash of water—but perhaps he was letting his hair down.

"What happened after that?"

"No idea, but Madeline was hanging on his every word, wasn't she, Tee?"

"I'll say, Zee," Terry replied, giving Zander a playful nudge.

These nicknames were getting old fast.

But Zander and Terry's disclosure raised another question—for me, at least. How did the boring Nesbitt-Cavanagh manage to enchant the bohemian Madeline? I pondered this during the last hundred feet of our journey. At the driveway, I thanked them for accompanying me.

"Did Madeline talk to Nesbitt-Cavanagh yesterday after the village hall meeting?" I asked.

"Didn't you see them?" Zander asked. "They got into her car outside the hall and drove off. Everyone was milling about in the auditorium, on the stairs, and even out on the sidewalk. So Madeline took Edgar out the back door and they gave everyone the slip."

"Well, except Xavier," Terry added. "He caught up to them."

"Oh, you're right, Tee. I'd forgotten about that. He was ticked off, too."

"Xavier was mad at Nesbitt-Cavanagh?"

"I'll say. You must have noticed the way Edgar dismissed him at the meeting." Zander imitated the historian's pinched expression as he repeated, "'Not *you*, Roy. I said a *major* film-maker.' After the meeting, in the back hall, Xavier was screaming at him."

"What did he say?"

"Called him a bastard. Said they had an agreement. '*You promised me*.'" Zander shrugged. "Stuff like that."

"I think," Terry said, looking thoughtful, "that Edgar hired Xavier to do the documentary, and then, at the last minute, hired somebody else."

"And didn't tell him before the meeting?"

"Obviously not."

"Did you see Nesbitt-Cavanagh after that?"

"Nope. We called the B&B that night to see if he needed anything and to check a few details about the exhumation the next day—"

"We were hoping we could persuade him to call it off," Zander broke in.

"But he wasn't there," Terry said.

"So Madeline was the last person to see Nesbitt-Cavanagh alive," I said.

They both nodded thoughtfully.

Except for the killer, my inner voice added.

CHAPTER EIGHT

AFTER SEEING Zander and Terry off, I trudged up the driveway of Rose Cottage, ducking around the ladder leaning against the eaves. I gazed up at the pair of saggy-assed jeans perched on the upper rungs. My handyman was on the job.

"Hello, Carson," I said. "How's it going?"

Carson twisted his head to look down. "You're back." He climbed down the ladder and turned to face me. With a grin, he pulled a hand-rolled cigarette from behind his ear and a faded book of matches from his wrinkled shirt pocket. "It's going good." He placed the cigarette in his mouth and cupped his hand to strike the match.

Reuben fluttered off the roof and landed at his feet.

"That rooster's taken a shine to you," I said.

Carson took a puff and exhaled before replying. "Been giving him sunflower seeds. He seems to like 'em."

Reuben had been my pet since I liberated him from Zander's ex-wife, Kate—who intended the scrawny bird for the pot as a grim send-off for her dead mother-in-law—but I planned to give him to Carson when the handyman stopped living in my driveway. If he ever did. Carson's pop-up trailer had been a fixture for weeks. It sat next to my aunt's rusting Ford Escort. Ruined by its plunge into the river, the car had become Reuben's nighttime coop.

Which renewed my worries about my other tenant. "Have you seen the General today? He didn't come back this morning."

Carson shook his head. "Tomcatting around, probably."

"I guess."

"He'll be back."

I nodded. Referring to General Chang as a tenant was wishful thinking on my part. The one-eyed, rumpled gray feline had insinuated himself into Rose Cottage two days after I arrived. But if he could talk, he'd insist that I was the tenant and he the landlord—make that *overlord*. I patted the pocket of my khakis, where I'd stowed the package of liver treats I'd bought that morning.

"I think I'll go out back and call him."

"Good idea. Before you go, what do you want me to do about the box gutters?" Carson dropped his cigarette on the flagstone walk and ground it out under his foot.

In the weeks that Carson had been restoring Rose Cottage to its original state, I'd learned not to question his mystifying knowledge of nineteenth-century architecture. Not that the knowledge was mystifying—more like edifying. But Carson didn't seem like the type to pore over books on history or architecture. Most nights, he sat on a camp cot outside his tent trailer, worrying his pocket flask.

On our first meeting, he had explained that my aunt's four-room bungalow was an excellent example of a "worker's cottage" from the mid-nineteenth century. Carson walked me around the outside, pointing out defining features like the fieldstone walls, mullioned windows, and built-in gutters lined with coated steel. But my aunt had let Rose Cottage lapse into disrepair. With almost no cash in her bank account —or mine—I assumed my only recourse was to sell.

Nellie Quintero, the realtor, talked me out of it. *Fix it up first*, she'd said, *and you might change your mind.* Excellent advice, especially since I believed Aunt Adeline wasn't dead and would return.

It was Nellie who suggested Carson. And we'd come to an arrangement. The local lumber yard opened a tab for my cedar shingles and supplies, and Carson accepted partial payment until I could afford the rest. It was why I let him camp in the driveway.

He'd already replaced the shingles on the roof, so I no longer needed aluminum pails indoors to catch drips when it rained. The built-in gutters were the next item on Rose Cottage's to-do list.

"The gutters?" Carson asked, raising an eyebrow.

With a hand shading my eyes, I studied the wooden cornices that ran along the roof edges, trying to look knowl-edgeable. "What do you advise?"

"Keep 'em. If you look after 'em, they'll last for decades. The linings should be repainted every ten years or so."

"Are they due for that?"

"Not yet."

"How will I know?"

Carson scrunched up his eyes and pointed at the cornices. "If you see water stains on the overhang, or sagging, that means water's getting through." He lowered his hand. "But don't wait for that. Repaint in the next couple of years to be safe. Once the metal rusts, it doesn't take long before you've got a mess on your hands."

"What has to be done now?"

"Not much. With some metal cleaning and joint solder-ing, those gutters'll be good as new." He leaned his head back, examining the roof. "And they look a darn sight better than those new aluminum jobs."

I considered mentioning that aluminum eavestroughs hadn't been "new" for at least fifty years, but I thought better of it.

"How much would that cost?"

"Not bad. Mostly labor."

I gave an authoritative nod, hoping Carson couldn't tell I had no idea what "joint soldering" was. "Let's do that, then."

"Right-o." Carson pulled his flask from his pocket and sauntered over to sit in the camp chair outside his pop-up trailer. We'd long since stopped pretending the flask contained coffee.

Reuben followed, halting every few steps to tilt his head and study the ground, hoping to spot a caterpillar.

With a sigh, I turned and clumped up the worn steps to the porch, avoiding the rotted spots in the planks. Leaving the door open to catch a breeze, I walked through the living room and into the kitchen at the back of the house—which I knew, thanks to Carson, had been added in the early twentieth century so that the homeowners no longer had to cook in the backyard. I leaned on the counter and looked out at my aunt's expansive garden.

A loud "*meeoooww*" drifted in through the open window.

General Chang jumped onto the railing of the back porch, tail swishing, and regarded me through the window with his slightly unnerving one-eyed glare. "*Mrack.*"

I leaned over and reached out to open the back door. "Hey there, buddy. Where've you been?"

The cat sashayed past me to check his bowl. At the sight of the dry kibble within, he batted the dish with his paw and looked up at me. "*Mrack?*" He batted it again, in case I'd missed the message.

I bent down to ruffle the fur under his chin. The General's bedraggled ears attested to years of backyard battles, as did his missing eye. Neither prevented him from roaming the neighborhood though. "I'm not leaving out fresh food for animals who can't be bothered to come home for dinner," I grumbled. Straightening up, I opened the drawer that held the can opener.

The General rubbed against my leg. Probably just a coincidence that he picked the side with the liver treats. I pulled the package from my pocket, tore it open, and tossed him one.

He pounced on it and chewed it thoroughly, then sat up, waving his paw in the air.

I tossed him another, and he chased it across the floor. I chuckled while spooning *Feline Fritters* into a saucer. "You better hope your next owner knows where to buy those treats." It was a running gag with us that the General would have to charm a new guardian when I returned to Vancouver. I was confident he was up to the task. A good thing, because once my aunt returned, I intended to resume my reclusive ways.

So why wasn't I looking forward to it?

I gazed through the window at Aunt Adeline's tattered garden, rolling my shoulders to ease out the kinks acquired during my attempts to revive the spectacular flower beds I remembered from my childhood. Digging, pruning, and planting were tough work, especially added to the hours I was putting in to stave off bankruptcy at my aunt's landscaping business.

A few corners were looking better, but I'd barely made a dent. The garden stretched almost four hundred feet before melding into the black ash, sugar maple, and spruce trees of Pine Hill Valley. A few yellowing leaves hinted at the fall colors to come. I should stay long enough to enjoy those at least. I frowned, remembering Control's "test." What had I let myself in for?

"Anybody home?" called a voice from the front door.

I put the saucer on the floor and walked into the living room. A black-and-white OPP cruiser was parked on the street outside Rose Cottage. The impossibly handsome Jeff Katsuro stood in the doorway in his immaculately pressed uniform.

And I was still wearing a grass-stained T-shirt and cutoffs. *Darn.* Although, Matthew had always said I had great legs. With a twinge, I glanced at his photo on the mantelpiece before moving to the open door with a smile.

"Have you come to question me?"

"Not at all." Jeff chuckled wryly. "Unless you want to confess."

I tilted my head as if considering my answer. "Nope, not today. Lemonade? Beer?"

He stepped across the threshold. "Thanks, but no. I came by to check up on you."

"That was kind of you. I'm fine, though."

Jeff took a step nearer and looked into my eyes.

My stomach slid south.

"Are you sure?" he asked. "That must have been a rough morning for you. Sorry you had to see the body."

If Emy had been present, she might have counseled me to burst into tears, lean my head against Jeff's chest, and play the vulnerable damsel in distress. But I couldn't do it. Maybe because I really was prone to anxiety attacks and didn't want to cry wolf.

Or maybe because, two years after Matthew's death, I still found it hard to flirt. Even with someone as appealing as Jeff.

Besides, Emy also thought I should try it on with my main landscaping competitor, the blond and ripped Ryker Fields. Despite her own lack of interest in romance, Emy had no problem doling out advice to others.

"It's not my first dead body," I said.

Jeff nodded. "As long as you're fine, I'll get going. Lots to do."

I wanted to let him leave, but my conscience got the better of me. "There's something I have to tell you."

He leaned in, looking curious.

"About the... investigation."

Jeff said nothing while I told him what Lorne and I did around the crypt that morning.

"Where is the material you removed?"

"It wasn't material, exactly. Grass, some soil, a few weeds. That's all. There weren't any clues in it."

"Where is it now?"

"Lorne's probably dumped it. I'm sorry. Is it important?"

Jeff ran a hand through his hair. "Why didn't you mention this at the cemetery?"

"I didn't think of it until later."

He pulled out his notebook and pen. "You said the weeds outside the vault had been disturbed?"

"Yes. It looked as though someone tried to pull them out and didn't do a very good job. At least, that's what I thought at first, but I later realized they might have been trampled by someone walking over them." I made a face. "Or dragging something through them."

"Where was the trampled portion?"

"Right in front of the entrance to the crypt. Sorry."

Jeff made a few notes and returned the notebook to his pocket. "Is there anything else you forgot to tell me?"

"Nothing. I'm really sorry about the weed removal. I should have told Terry to tell you about it when he returned the key."

Jeff flashed me a sharp look. "That was your idea?"

At least I'd done something right. I smiled at him. "Yes. I knew you'd need it to lock up the crypt."

He didn't smile back. "That key was evidence. It should have been left on the minister's key ring until we established chain of custody. Not to mention that handling it could have corrupted the forensic exam."

"Forensic exam? Of what? Are you suggesting the killer

stole the key, then returned it to the minister's key chain, but forgot to wipe off his fingerprints? That's ridiculous." I scrunched my eyes shut for a second, hastily adding, "I meant to say, that's *unlikely*."

"Assuming it was a he."

"It must have been. Nesbitt-Cavanagh was a big guy. A woman wouldn't have been strong enough to drag his body into the vault."

"A woman could have led him there. Killed him inside the crypt. And then locked the door from the outside."

I put a hand on his arm and leaned in. "Is that what happened?"

"Stop fishing."

I lifted my hand. "Sorry. Force of habit."

"It's a habit you should lose—"

I bristled, preparing a snappy comeback, but he finished the sentence before I could speak.

"—for your own protection. I don't want anything to happen to you." The corners of his mouth twitched up, and he gave me one of his soulful stares.

Well, in my imagination it was soulful.

"Thanks. I'll keep that in mind."

"Make sure your doors are locked," he added with a tap on the frame as he walked out onto the porch. "Oh..." He turned around. "I haven't forgotten about our bowling lesson. Just waiting for things to settle down."

I tried not to focus on Jeff's butt as he strolled to his cruiser.

He drove off with a brief wave and I went back inside, locking the door as instructed. While running water to warm up the shower—my aunt's ancient hot water heater needed advance notice before attempting anything hotter than tepid —I remembered something I'd forgotten to tell him. Ford's garbled account of his nighttime visit to the cemetery.

How did he put it? *I'm here last night. I can't help him.*

But Isabelle said Ford wasn't quite... right. An assessment I had no problem accepting after my own encounter with him. Ford could have been talking about last night, or something that happened a decade ago.

I should talk to him again. Lorne said the feral-cat camp was worth a visit, and I wanted to see the kittens. I'd go tomorrow. And while I was there, I could ask Ford what he saw at the cemetery.

I dropped my T-shirt and cutoffs into the laundry hamper and stepped into the shower.

Fifteen minutes later, I'd changed into yoga pants and a silk shirt and towel-dried my hair. I tossed the General another liver snack before heading for the door. I planned to walk down the road, meet Lorne if he was still around, and drive the truck down the hill to Emy's bakery.

As I opened the door, I stepped back, startled.

Gideon stood on the porch with his hand raised to knock. He lowered his hand. "I have an idea," he said.

I suppressed a sigh. Why did this man never call ahead?

"About Aunt Adeline?" I asked.

He nodded.

I ushered him in and closed the door. We'd exhausted the documents on my aunt's laptop without finding a single clue that might lead us to Aunt Adeline.

"Shoot," I said.

"Remember me telling you about those thefts in Quebec?"

"The Maple Syrup Caper? I thought that was a joke."

"Not all of it." He looked sheepish.

"But you said my aunt wasn't involved." I put my hands on my hips to reinforce my glare. Before my own encounter with Control, Gideon had told me my aunt once worked for a shadowy sub-government entity. He didn't tell me what she did for them. It could have been typing. As a child, I'd been told my aunt ran an office-services company. But I found that hard to reconcile with the injuries she sustained over the years. *Car accidents*, Mom always said. Yet, my aunt's old Volvo never had a scratch on it.

Gideon ignored my comment. "After that incident, we cultivated friends in the candy world."

"Candy? You mean drugs?"

He tilted his head at me and narrowed one eye. "Jelly beans, gummy bears, chocolate bars?"

"Are you making fun of me again?"

"Candy is a multibillion-dollar global industry."

"I don't see the connection."

"The dead guy in the crypt had a chocolate bar in his pocket."

"Yes, but—wait, how did you know that?"

"Irrelevant."

Prying information out of Gideon was exasperating. I'd realized early on that I needed to pick my battles. I let his knowledge of the murder scene—and how he got it—pass.

"So, he died with a chocolate bar at the ready," I said. "They're popular snacks."

"It's a message."

"Who from?"

"Someone who doesn't want Nesbitt-Cavanagh's book published."

With a sigh, I walked to the sofa and slumped onto its worn cushions. The General jumped onto my lap, and I absently stroked his back. It *was* possible the ill-tempered Nesbitt-Cavanagh was murdered because someone objected to his version of Leafy Hollow history. Several people would be affected if the Prudence Bannon tale was fake. Wilf Mullins would have to abandon his ambitious waterpark plan, Xavier Roy couldn't make his documentary, and Zander would be suspected of trying to liberate his mom's estate— and Terry for helping him. And if a dog was buried in the crypt, Reverend McAllister and his church would be publicly shamed. Quite a list.

But try as I might, I saw no connection between the murder of an irritating, smug historian and a chocolate bar. "That's ridiculous. And it has nothing to do with my aunt."

Gideon slapped the wall in frustration. "Listen to me, darn it."

I clutched the General's fur so tight that he twisted out of my grasp with a hiss and jumped to the floor. "I *am* listening. Talk faster."

"Do you have something more important to do?"

I glared at him. "As it happens, yes." We had talked endlessly about my aunt's disappearance, and I was fed up. "You've shared no real information with me about Control, or what my aunt did for them, or what that... thing in the basement really is. This is just more idle speculation."

With a scowl, Gideon leaned over to pick up a well-thumbed copy of *Organize Your Way to a Better Life* from the coffee table and pointed to the stack underneath it. Next in line was *Best Foot Forward: Your Illustrated Guide to Sock Drawers*.

He waved the volume at me. "Is this your idea of reality?"

I stood up and snatched it from his hand. "That's none of your business." I replaced *Organize* on top of the stack and lined up the edges of the books. For some reason, tears sprang to my eyes. I bit my lip to fight them back. General Chang rubbed against my leg, purring. I bent to pat him, not trusting my composure enough to face Gideon.

"I miss her, too," he said.

I glanced up at him. Gideon turned his head away. His lips were set in a tight line, but there was a quiver in his cheek.

Swallowing hard, I rubbed the back of my hand across my face. I dropped onto the sofa and gestured to the armchair. "Okay, tell me about the chocolate."

Gideon sat down. "Cocoa, not chocolate."

"What's the difference?"

"Global trade in chocolate is worth nearly one hundred billion a year. But it all starts with cocoa. You can make millions by affecting that trade even marginally."

"That doesn't sound like something a Leafy Hollow resident would do—or even could do."

"No, but the Syndicate can."

"You mean the criminal group that Adeline mentioned? How would they do that?"

"Nearly three-quarters of the world's cocoa is grown in

West Africa, mostly on family farms in The Ivory Coast. Someone's buying up those farms. Consolidating. Control production—control the price."

"How do you know about these purchases?"

"Our new friends told us."

"What do agricultural deals in West Africa have to do with my aunt? Or Nesbitt-Cavanagh?"

"I think he stumbled across those land deals and put them in his book."

"Good grief, Gideon. *The Legend of Leafy Hollow* is about events that occurred two centuries ago. On this continent."

"Have you seen a copy?"

"No, but—"

"Then how do you know?" he fired back.

Even for Gideon, this was a tenuous connection. I clasped both hands in my hair, lifting it up in a gesture of frustration. "How is my aunt involved?"

"Don't know yet. We have to search her laptop, see if they knew each other."

"Nesbitt-Cavanagh and Aunt Adeline?"

He nodded.

"I have a better idea. Why don't you go down to the basement and ask Control?"

"When we find Adeline, she'll talk to Control. Until then—"

"No." I sprang to my feet and jabbed a finger at his chest. "You know more about this than you're telling me. I demand to—"

"Stop," Gideon thundered, his eyes flashing behind his

blue lenses. A second later, he regained control and lowered his voice. "You're ignoring a significant lead."

"A chocolate bar? How can I take that seriously?"

"What would you take seriously?" He waved a dismissive hand at my stack of self-help books. *"Ten Easy Steps to Finding Lost Relatives?"*

I stared at him, my gut churning. "You should leave," I whispered.

He stalked across the room and out the door, shaking his head.

I dropped back onto the sofa. I was no closer to finding my aunt than when I'd arrived in Leafy Hollow. And now I'd alienated the one person who believed—as I did—that she wasn't dead. I was repairing Rose Cottage so my aunt would have something to come back to. Ditto my attempted revival of Coming Up Roses, her landscaping business. But I was kidding myself. If Aunt Adeline was alive, why hadn't she come home? Or, if she couldn't return, why didn't she send a message more meaningful than the cryptic Latin puzzle that was her only real communication to date? *"Ave,"* she wrote and hid it in her car. It turned out to be a reference to the Latin philosopher Cicero. I'd interpreted that note, thanks to my childhood love of puzzles gleaned from my mother. But it was a sorry substitute for the real thing.

If fixing up Rose Cottage was only a make-work project, wouldn't I be better off at home? In my high-rise Vancouver apartment, with my glimpse of a sliver of Burrard Inlet, my well-meaning neighbor Patty's incredible inedible brownies, and—yes—my self-help books? I glanced at Matthew's portrait on the mantel. He had always been so sensible. His feet had been firmly rooted in reality. Which lent me the courage to soar. I thought of the plans we made together. None of that would happen now. For two years, I'd refused to face up to that, too. Without Matthew, I was untethered. I was free to go where the wind took me, and it brought me to a tiny village in southern Ontario and a cottage hewn of stones wrested from streams and fields nearly two hundred years ago. The people who built Rose Cottage refused to give up, despite the odds. They wouldn't have been cowed by a holographic entity that refused to explain itself.

I rose to my feet and headed for the door.

CHAPTER NINE

"WHY DID you say that about my keys?" Isabelle asked.

McAllister looked up from the table. Jeff Katsuro had left, and he and Isabelle were alone in the manse kitchen. She was fussing about, brushing non-existent crumbs from the worn wooden surface. Her lips pressed together in that way she had whenever she was puzzling out a Sunday school lesson. Or the latest Kardashian story in those supermarket tabloids she kept under the boot tray in the vestry.

"What do you mean?" he asked.

Isabelle straightened up, a crumpled dishcloth in one hand. "You said it would complicate things if the police knew I had a set of keys to the church. What difference would it make?"

"Well..." He trailed his fingers across the back of his neck, wondering how much to tell her. "Wouldn't it draw attention to the crypt?"

She made a face. "More than the dead body in it, you mean?"

He tried to chuckle, but the tightness in his throat prevented him. It wasn't the crypt that worried him. He should have been honest with Jeff. He placed his hands against the table's edge and pushed back, stretching out his arms as if trying to push the truth away.

"Jeff wasn't here long," Isabelle said. "I just walked to the road and back and he was already leaving."

"There wasn't much to say."

"So you didn't tell him about my keys?"

He said nothing.

Isabelle filled the sink with soapy water and plunged in the empty glasses.

"You don't have to do that."

"I don't mind." She shoved the dishcloth into the first of the glasses and swished it around, then rinsed the glass under the tap and placed it on the drain pad.

He reached for his own glass, but Isabelle had already dumped it in the sink. Craving water for his parched throat, he leaned forward and set his palms on the table.

"Don't get up," she said, drying her hands on the tea towel that lay beside her on the counter. "What do you want?"

He sank back into the chair. "Water?"

She opened the fridge door and pulled out the filtered water jug—Daniel had never heard of such a thing until Isabelle insisted on buying one for the manse—and a lemon, which she placed on the cutting board. As she reached for a paring knife, he objected.

"For heaven's sake," he blurted. "I don't need a lemon slice in it. Just water."

She stared at him, the knife poised above the lemon.

"Sorry," he said.

Isabelle returned the lemon to the fridge and opened the freezer door. "Ice?" He shook his head, forcing a smile. Her lips pursed again as she filled the glass and placed it in front of him.

He drained the glass in a few gulps and wiped his mouth with the back of his hand. "Thanks."

Isabelle crossed her arms and smiled feebly. "So, the keys?"

The woman was like a dog with a bone.

He slammed the empty glass on the table. "Forget about the keys."

She took a step back with a hand at her throat, a hurt look in her eyes.

"I'm sorry," he said. "It's been a trying day. I think..." He looked around the kitchen. The cupboard doors and kitchen appliances he saw every day seemed unfamiliar—their contours, their colors. It was as if he'd never been here before. "I have work to do in the church." He rose to his feet, suddenly resolute, and dropped a kiss on her head. "Can you let yourself out?"

Looking pathetically pleased with the kiss, she nodded shyly and gestured at the sink. "I'll just take a minute to tidy up here first."

When he turned at the door to look back, Isabelle was scrubbing the tabletop again. She flashed a friendly wave.

He went out the back door, hoping to avoid the parishioners and reporters who were milling about in front. A few had eased under the yellow police tape to congregate outside the church's front doors. McAllister darted through the perennial bed between the manse and the church—his size eleven Hush Puppies scattering the mulch and bruising the plants—to the side door in the church vestry. He had almost reached it when a voice yelled from the direction of the road.

"Reverend! Do you have a moment?"

McAllister threw himself at the vestry door and twisted the handle. With a sidelong glance, he recognized the reporter and cameraman from the local TV affiliate bearing down on him. He waved while shoving open the door. "Thanks for coming out," he called, slamming the door just as the reporter reached it, a microphone in her outstretched hand.

"But, but—"

McAllister twisted the lock into place. Ignoring the reporter's frenzied knocks, he stood for a moment with his forehead against the door, inhaling the room's mingled aromas of wood rot, damp stone, and dry-cleaning fluid. Isabelle insisted on having his vestments cleaned on a rotating basis. When he'd forgotten to air out his gown before the last quarterly communion, old Mrs. Terrace had looked at him as if she suspected him of drinking the sacramental wine.

The knocks ceased. He straightened up and turned to the door in the opposite wall.

Then, "Reverend Dan! A word?"

Startled, he glanced over at the vestry's mullioned window, six feet above the ground. The reporter's head appeared, disappeared, and then appeared again. He realized with a start that she was jumping up and down like a jack-in-the-box. He would have to apologize to Verity for the damage done to the perennial beds today. And after they looked so nice on television, too.

"Reverend Dan!"

Shaking his head, he darted across the tiny room and into the church. Once in the main building, he slowed to a more reverent pace as he walked through the nave on his way to the basement stairs that led down from the lobby inside the double front doors. While he'd normally take a moment to appreciate the sun glowing through the rows of stained glass windows onto the polished arms of the curved wooden pews, today there was no time for reflection.

He avoided looking at the communion table, which lacked one of its heavy pewter candlesticks, as he walked past.

McAllister trotted down the wide stairs that led down from the nave on his way to the lower floor. Here, the stone foundation walls—laid in 1840 by the same Scottish masons who'd built much of the village—were plastered over, and then painted so many times that the storm windows in their three-foot-deep wells hadn't been unlatched in decades. The latest color, a pale blue, was called "robin's egg," according to Isabelle. It looked the same as the previous blue to him.

Down here, the temperature dropped at least ten degrees from the church overhead, where a few feeble air conditioning units were unable to keep the summer heat at bay. The cooler temperature in the basement meant that its thick stone walls were damp with humidity on hot days. In the worst heat waves, they wept. In his more reflective moods,

McAllister wondered if that was the explanation for the "weeping" statues of angels and saints that intrigued more demonstrative religious orders—a simple case of condensation as water changed from gas into liquid. He should write a paper.

No time for that today, either. He hurried through the basement—past the tables and chairs arranged in circles for Sunday school classes, the neat stacks of old hymn books, and the colored pictures taped to whiteboards. Jesus riding a donkey was a favorite subject of the under-fives. He glanced over at a board and slowed down. One of the crayoned drawings on display featured a bearded Jesus—his arm flung around the shoulders of a donkey—aboard a rocket ship, its tail glowing red. The ship was headed for a red orb crudely labeled *MaRs*. He paused to consider the picture and then moved on with a shrug. At least the church's outreach mission was alive and well.

At the basement's far end, he wrenched open a thick wooden door, flicked on a light switch, and entered the only unfinished part of the structure. A decade earlier, the board of managers had financed a renovation of the basement kitchen, where the annual turkey suppers, as well as the food for wedding and funeral receptions, were prepared. But the church women's group—the "Holy Hens"—resisted any modernization of this space and its dirt floor, saying it was the ideal cold cellar for the preserves and jellies they sold at their bi-annual craft fairs.

McAllister swept past shelves of raspberry jam, zucchini relishes, and chili sauce, headed for the back of the storage area, where a sole lightbulb in the ceiling illuminated the original floor and walls. He ran his gaze over the loose stone pavers that lay over most of the floor, probing the murky corners of the room until he found what he was searching for.

He walked over and bent to pick up the candlestick. It was sticky in his hand. Grimacing, he hunted for a rag and found one on the ancient wood workbench, among the rusted tools and half-empty tins of paint. The rag came away stained with rusty brown streaks when he wiped the end of the candlestick on the cloth. Setting down the candlestick, he ran the rag across the paving stones. He frowned as more stains appeared on the cloth. A few pavers were loose, and he did his best to tamp them down with his foot. He picked up the candlestick and the rag, and then left the room, closing and latching the door.

Back in the vestry, he took the candlestick to the sink and scrubbed it with the oatmeal hand soap that Isabelle insisted on buying for his dry skin. He appraised the results, his heart sinking. He'd watched enough *CSI* to know it was impossible to scrub away blood. There'd always be traces.

After drying the candlestick on the inside of his jacket, he took it into the chancel and replaced it on the communion table. He stepped back to check its positioning. When he glanced up, the figures in the stained glass window's Gethsemane tableau were pointing the usual accusing fingers. At him, this time.

On his way out of the church, he threw the soiled rag into the compost heap behind the manse, digging it in with the toe of his shoe. Out of the corner of his eye, he saw Isabelle head down the front sidewalk to the road. He ducked, hoping she wouldn't see him. Hunched over, he scuttled to the back door of the manse.

In the kitchen, the iced tea glasses were drying on the drainboard, and the harvest table gleamed. The television was still on, but Isabelle had muted the sound.

He reached for the cell phone on the counter and dialed.

After that, he sat at the table, made a pillow of his arms, and sank his head onto them. The tap in the sink dripped. A bird fluttered in the vine outside the window. The clock on the wall ticked over. McAllister ignored it all.

He jumped when the doorbell sounded, but then he rose slowly to his feet. He tucked his untidy shirt back into his waistband, smoothed the front of his jacket, and took a deep breath. He walked to the door and threw it open.

Detective Constable Jeff Katsuro stood on the threshold.

"It's my fault," McAllister said. "I killed him."

CHAPTER TEN

I DROVE my aunt's truck down the hill into the village and along Main Street, parking in front of the 5X Bakery. After dropping a quarter into the meter, I strolled in, pausing to inhale the enticing aromas wafting from the kitchen. I stopped and sniffed again.

Nothing. No smells of cinnamon rolls baking or lavender-glazed scones cooling. Not even a hint of burnt-sugar crumble. My world shifted on its axis. What the heck was happening here?

"Emy?" I called, walking through the tiny shop to the back. I paused at the bottom of the stairway that led to her apartment on the second floor, leaning over so I could see to the top of the staircase. "Emy?"

Her black curls appeared over the railing. "Verity," she shrieked. She thundered down the stairs, holding her long, white apron up with one hand so she wouldn't trip over it. "Wait here," she whispered in a breathless tone when she reached the bottom. "You'll never guess what's happened." Emy turned and raced back up, at a pace almost as rapid as her descent a moment earlier, and disappeared around the corner.

No wonder my bestie was so slim, despite the multi-caloried treats she loved to foist on an eager public. I waited, one hand resting on the newel post, tapping my foot.

Seconds later, Emy reappeared. This time, she was tugging Isabelle Yates behind her. At the bottom of the stairs, Emy gently shoved Isabelle in my direction.

"Tell Verity what you told me." Emy stood with her hands on her hips, nodding. "You'll never believe this. It's astounding."

Even discounting Emy's flair for the dramatic, something was up. A glance at Isabelle's puffy eyes and reddened nose showed that she'd been crying—again. I wondered if being a bit damp was simply her default state.

"What?" I asked, trying to hasten the narrative along.

"Daniel"—Isabelle paused, swallowing hard—"Reverend McAllister, I mean, has... He has..." She clasped a sodden tissue to her face, unable to speak. Then she straightened up, blew her nose, and smiled weakly. "I'm making a spectacle of myself. Forgive me."

Emy reached an arm around Isabelle's shoulders and squeezed. She shot me the sort of triumphant look that indicated a really juicy bit of gossip lay ahead, so I'd better pay attention. "Reverend McAllister"—Emy paused to let the full impact sink in—"has confessed to Nesbitt-Cavanagh's murder."

With a wail, Isabelle dropped into a chair by the table at

the back of the shop. She lowered her face into the tissue and mumbled something that sounded like *mmhhhooollpp*. Or it could have been a gall bladder attack. Hard to tell.

My eyes widened. "You're joking. The minister did it?" I reviewed the scene at the village hall a day earlier. McAllister had been upset, yes. But murder? I shook my head. "That doesn't seem possible."

Emy spread her hands, nodding vigorously in agreement. "That's what we think." She gestured to include her cousin.

Isabelle raised her wet face and sniffled. "Sorry."

I rummaged through my purse and fished out a packet of tissues, which I handed to her with a sympathetic glance. "Then why did he confess?"

Emy shrugged.

Isabelle wiped her nose. Now that the worst was over, she was able to compose herself and relate her tale. She had been leaving the manse that morning when Jeff Katsuro pulled up in his squad car and knocked on the door. The minister opened it.

Isabelle paused at this point in her narrative, giving us an anxious glance. Surely we couldn't blame her for listening in?

Noooo, we mimed forcefully. "Perfectly understandable," we murmured in unison.

Bolstered, she went on. "Daniel said, 'I killed him'."

I drew an involuntary breath and forgot to let it out.

"Jeff went inside," Isabelle continued, "and they shut the door. A few minutes later, they came out and walked over to the church. I... followed." She raised a hand to her throat and pointed weakly at the bakery counter. "Could I have a—"

Emy hustled over to the sink behind the counter and

filled a glass with water, returning to hand it to Isabelle. "Go on," she urged.

Isabelle took a few swallows, then set the glass on the table. "They left the vestry door unlocked, so I went in after them. Daniel took Jeff into the basement. They were downstairs for ten minutes or so. I think they went into the storage area, although I can't imagine why. There's nothing important in there. A few tools and the jams and jellies that belong to the Holy Hens."

At my puzzled look, she added, "The women's group. They use it as a cold cellar."

I nodded. "Continue, please."

"Anyway, when they came back upstairs, they stopped at the chancel to examine the communion table."

"The chancel?" I asked.

"The part of the church that's nearest the altar. It's where the choir sits."

"Did they know you were there?" I asked.

"It felt wrong to be spying on them, so I hid in the vestry —you know, the room on the side of the church nearest the manse where Daniel changes into his robes? I was in the vestments closet."

I tried to keep my eyebrows from hitting the ceiling. "What if the police had searched the place and found you in the closet, among the... vestments?"

Isabelle bit her lip, wincing. "I planned to tell them I was picking up the minister's stole for dry cleaning."

I opened my mouth to debate this questionable strategy, but Emy poked me with her elbow and shot me a warning glance.

"Never mind that, Izzy," Emy said, leaning in. "What happened next?"

"Jeff radioed for support. I heard something about a forensics team coming to pick up a candlestick from the church."

Emy and I locked glances, obviously thinking the same thing—*murder weapon.*

I cleared my throat. "But why did they go down to the basement?"

Isabelle shook her head, looking grim. "I don't know. It was hard to hear in that closet. Everything was muffled. But I heard Daniel say, 'That bloody historian'." She shot me a worried glance and added, "The minister rarely swears, I hope you realize. Anyway, he said, 'That bloody historian had no business mucking around down there'." She lowered her voice to a stage whisper. "I think Nesbitt-Cavanagh was trespassing."

"Hardly reason to kill him," I said.

"Well, of course not," Emy blurted. "This is some huge misunderstanding."

I pulled out the remaining chair and sat down, stumped. "It's certainly odd."

"And then," Isabelle continued, "they went back out the vestry door. I watched them through the window. The officer put Daniel in the backseat of his cruiser—"

I broke in. "Did he do that thing where they put a hand on the suspect's head and push down? I've always wondered what—"

Emy shot me a look of astonishment.

"Forget it," I hastily said. "Not relevant."

Isabelle, intent on her tale, hadn't noticed my non sequitur. "Jeff left Daniel in the cruiser and headed back to the church. That's when I decided to hightail it out of there. I went out the front door as Jeff was coming in the vestry door." She stopped for a deep breath and a sip of water. "And then I came straight here."

Emy patted her on the shoulder. "Don't worry. We'll get to the bottom of this. Verity will know what to do."

I stared at Emy in astonishment. "How's that?"

"I told Izzy that with your experience of murder scenes, you can help us figure out what happened. Then we can get the minister out of jail."

I drew myself up, opening my mouth in a perfect portrayal of a person with something significant to say. Nothing happened. Whatever pearls of wisdom I intended to impart had rolled away. I closed my mouth and stared at her instead.

"Where should we start?" Emy asked.

Isabelle regarded me in anticipation.

Seeing the look on my face, Emy worked her lips a bit, and then turned to her cousin. "Izzy, why don't you go upstairs and freshen up while Verity and I talk strategy?"

With a grateful look in my direction, Isabelle got to her feet and started up the stairs.

Emy said nothing until Isabelle's footsteps reached the top and softened, indicating she was walking along the carpeted hallway. Emy reached out to gently close the door.

She pulled out the other chair and sat opposite me. "I'm sorry I threw that at you without warning," she said, her voice low. "But you have no idea what's been going on here. When

Izzy showed up on my doorstep today, she was nearly hysterical."

I considered disputing the *nearly* part but decided not to chance it. Leaning over the table, I kept my tone low to match Emy's. "Isn't that a tad over the top? I know her employer has been fingered for murder, but why the tears? And why did you call her a 'poor woman' yesterday?"

Emy looked grim. "Because of Nick. Her husband."

I remembered Nick Yates heaving that cupcake at Nesbitt-Cavanagh in the village hall. And before that, pulling at Isabelle's arm, arguing with her, and snapping at me. Flinching, I said, "I noticed."

"I don't think he hits her," Emy hastened to add. "But he's controlling. Always wants to know where she's going, who she's meeting, even what she's wearing. It drives her crazy and now—well, she's determined to end it."

"The marriage?"

"Exactly."

"So, what's the problem?"

"Nick's fighting it. He can't accept that it's over. Izzy is his whole life. He doesn't want to let her go. That's why she was here yesterday morning. To ask my advice."

We heard water running upstairs, a sudden bang in the pipes as the flow was shut off, and then footsteps. Emy cast a wary glance at the stairwell door. "And the minister..." She bit her bottom lip.

I gasped as awareness hit me. "They're involved?"

Emy made a wry face. "I don't know, to be honest. But she's been so happy. Until this, I mean."

"Is that unusual?"

Emy glanced up at the ceiling. "You have no idea."

"Does Nick suspect that something is going on?"

"I don't know, but he might be following her around on the sly."

"That's stalking."

"Nick would disagree. He says he has a right to know what his wife's up to."

"He's a jerk."

She raised her eyebrows. "No argument here."

"I understand why Isabelle is... upset by Reverend Daniel's arrest," I said, choosing my words carefully. "But I don't see what I can do about it."

"She's my cousin, Verity. I'm worried about her. Please help her."

"I'd like to, but—"

"Remember when the police suspected you of murder?"

I narrowed my eyes. "Are you reminding me of the time we broke into the victim's apartment to search for clues?" I had a flashback of Emy wearing a deer's head balaclava with a button nose. She would never be so crass as to imply that I owed her for that. But I did—big time.

"No. I would never. I was simply thinking that before *that*, we tried to come up with other suspects to take the heat off you. Maybe we could do the same for Reverend Dan."

I cast my mind back to the list of suspicious individuals I'd worked up at the cemetery. But those were hypothetical. Besides, the police already had a confession. "I'm not a detective, Emy."

"Nobody's saying you are. But you did solve a murder."

This conversation was eerily reminiscent of the one I had

with Zander and Terry. When did everyone in Leafy Hollow decide that an anxiety-prone, accidental landscaper could solve homicides? "Look, I'd like to help—"

"Then *help*," Emy hissed as Isabelle's footsteps sounded on the stairs. We fixed our smiles and turned to face her as she pushed open the door.

"How about a cheddar-bacon scone, ladies?" Emy asked, rising to her feet.

I brightened, but then my face fell as I recognized the obvious bribe. *Oh, what the heck. I never said I couldn't be bought.*

"I'll take two."

CHAPTER ELEVEN

VISITING Reverend Daniel was the next logical step, even though I had no idea what to ask him. He'd been released on his own recognizance that morning, so he would be at home.

By the time I reached the manse, I was already regretting my promise to Emy. A police car was parked down the lane, its young male driver bent over paperwork—or possibly word games on his phone. Occasionally, he glanced up at the television news van across the street.

The van's driver buzzed down the window and hoisted his camera when I emerged from the truck, so I retrieved gardening tools from the back to make this look like a land-scaping call. I left behind a bag of tinned cat food and a wrapped sandwich from Tim's for the next call on my to-do list.

I made my way up the cracked sidewalk to the front door of the white-clapboard bungalow. My knock went unan-swered, so I followed the walkway that curved around the side of the manse, hoping to catch the minister in the back garden.

As I passed the kitchen window, I peered in. He was seated at the table, staring glumly at a mug of what I assumed was coffee—until I noticed an unstoppered bottle of Scotch on the counter. McAllister was in short, black shirtsleeves, an unfastened end of his clerical collar sticking up under his chin.

He looked up at my rap on the glass and shot to his feet, smoothing back his hair. Then he pointed to the back door. I walked around and mounted three steps to the small porch.

"Verity," the minister said with forced gaiety as he threw open the door. "What brings you here?"

There were bags under his eyes, a day's worth of stubble on his chin, and his shirt was partially untucked. I got the impression he'd been sitting at that table since arriving home from the station.

He ushered me through the mudroom and into the kitchen.

I pulled out a chair and sat down. "I dropped by to tidy up the perennial garden," I lied. "The crowd made quite a mess of it the other day. I also wanted to see how you were feeling."

Before he could answer, there was a tap on the window. We turned. Isabelle's face was inches from the glass. She mouthed something inaudible, gestured to the back door, and disappeared.

Daniel walked through the mudroom to open the door. Murmurs followed, which I couldn't make out. They came into the kitchen, and the minister slumped back into his chair.

Isabelle placed a cardboard box on the counter that I recognized as having come from Emy's bakery. "I saw your truck outside, Verity," she said. "Have you discovered anything new?"

"Not yet. I thought I'd tidy up those footprints in the perennial bed. Somebody with big feet has been trampling about in there." I flexed my eyebrows at Reverend Dan's Hush Puppies. Daniel and Isabelle only stared at me. My attempt to lighten the mood wasn't working.

Isabelle filled the teakettle, placed it on the stove, and flicked on the burner.

I shifted on the hard wooden chair. "I thought I would begin by asking you a few questions. About what you told the police."

Daniel jerked back in his chair. "Excuse me?" he asked.

Isabelle pulled out a chair beside Daniel, sat down, and patted his hand. "Verity has offered to look into your case, Daniel. Obviously, the allegations against you are ridiculous, and she's going to discover who killed that odious man."

"I wouldn't go that far," I said, flustered. "I'm not an investigator."

"Maybe not, but you know how these things are done."

Daniel appeared bewildered. He reached a trembling hand for his mug, but not fast enough.

Isabelle grabbed the mug and rose to empty it in the sink. "Tell Verity what you told the police, Daniel." Her voice was surprisingly firm.

He tugged at the loose clerical collar at his throat, glancing around the room. "The lawyer said not to..."

I grabbed at the chance to abandon my hasty promise. "I don't want to intrude, Reverend Daniel. I understand if you don't want to talk about this." I rose to go.

Isabelle clapped a hand on my shoulder with an iron grip, once more transforming from teary-eyed wimp to warrior princess. It was a bit scary. "No," she said. "Stay, please." Her grip loosened into a friendly pat as I sat back down, and then she turned to Daniel. "Your lawyer won't mind if you talk to Verity. She's a friend." Isabelle rested one hand on Daniel's shoulder as she leaned over to place a plate of bran muffins on the table in front of us.

"Well, if you think so..."

Isabelle filled the teapot and placed it in the center of the table, next to the muffins. "I do." She sat down opposite me and trained her gaze on Daniel. "Go ahead."

"Well... after that palaver in the village hall, I couldn't sleep that night," he said. "I got up for a glass of... milk."

I tried not to glance at the Scotch on the counter.

"But when I was in the kitchen, I looked out at the church and noticed a light on in the vestry. I thought it was odd, so I went over to check. The lock on the door was broken, so I knew someone was inside."

"Why didn't you call the police?" I asked.

"I thought it might be Ford. He gets confused sometimes, and we let him sleep in the church during bad weather."

"But it was a beautiful, clear night."

Daniel fingered his collar again in a half-hearted attempt to get it under control. "It didn't seem necessary to call anyone." He shrugged. "I suppose I also thought it might be village kids, fooling around."

Isabelle placed a filled mug of tea in front of him, and he took a sip before continuing.

"Once I got inside, I heard noises from the basement. Like somebody in the storage area. There's paint in there, and if the kids got into it, they'd really make a mess. So on my way through the nave, I picked up a candlestick from the communion table. I wouldn't have used it," he added hastily. "I thought it would make me more imposing or something. It was silly, really."

"No, it wasn't," Isabelle snapped. "You didn't know who was in the basement. Obviously, you needed a weapon."

Both Daniel and I stared at her. Isabelle sipped her tea, seemingly oblivious to our surprise.

The minister nodded slowly. "Yes. Well, when I pushed open the door, there was Nesbitt-Cavanagh. He had a shovel in his hand. He'd pried up several of the paving stones and was starting in on the dirt floor. I said, 'what on earth are you doing?'" Daniel raised both hands incredulously as he continued. "And he said, 'I'm looking for buried treasure.' *Buried treasure.* In our church basement."

"Ridiculous," murmured Isabelle.

"I assured him there was no treasure and told him to leave. He insisted there was Loyalist gold in our floor and refused to go. He was obviously drunk. And then..." Daniel grimaced. "There was a shoving match."

I tried to picture the scene—the pudgy, inebriated historian grappling with the bespectacled, pajama'd minister on the muddy floor of the cold cellar. Xavier would be sorry he'd missed that.

"He tried to whack me with the shovel, so I swung the candlestick at him," Daniel said. "I swear I didn't hit him. But when he tried to get out of the way, he tripped and hit his head on the floor."

I gasped. "Was he dead?"

"No! I swear. I dropped the candlestick and went to help him. He had a cut on his forehead, so there was blood everywhere. He was a little groggy, but I got him to his feet without much trouble. I told him I'd call an ambulance. He refused and insisted on leaving."

"We went upstairs, through the front door, and outside. That's when I realized he still had the shovel. I took it away from him and said I'd order him a cab. He was fine, I swear, so I returned to the manse. I called a taxi and went to bed. The last I saw of Nesbitt-Cavanagh, he was standing in the cemetery, in the moonlight, staring at the Bannon crypt."

The reverend lowered his head into his hands with a groan. "I never should have left him. He must have had a concussion. I should have insisted on medical aid."

"You offered, and he refused," Isabelle said. "What else could you have done?"

"I killed him," he mumbled. "That's what the police think."

"I don't see how," I said.

Isabelle turned to face me, a sliver of hope glinting in her eyes. "What do you mean?"

"Well, how did his body get into the crypt? If Daniel left

him in the cemetery, then somebody else moved him. And only the killer would do that."

There was an obvious flaw to this theory since we all knew Reverend Daniel had a key to the vault. But I thought it best not to bring that up.

"There's more," he said. "I went back to the storage area the next day to retrieve the candlestick and clean up the blood."

"Why?"

"I don't know. Panicked, I guess."

I pursed my lips, trying to think of something reassuring. It was clear why the police arrested the minister. His story about buried treasure was intriguing, but ridiculous. They probably thought he concocted it to explain why a shovel from the church basement was found in the cemetery. Coupled with traces of the historian's blood on the candlestick, plus Reverend Daniel's animosity toward Nesbitt-Cavanagh, it was almost an open-and-shut case.

Almost.

"What about the key to the crypt?" I asked. "Could there be other copies? Besides the one Isabelle has, I mean?"

Daniel looked thoughtful. "When I took over in Leafy Hollow, I asked the previous minister why there were three large hooks on the keyboard in the vestry, but only two sets of keys. There was a third set, he said, but it disappeared. No one knew where."

That was weak evidence, but still. "Did he say when the third set went missing?"

"I don't think so. I can't recall."

Isabelle's forehead wrinkled. "What about asking him?

Reverend Doctor Abbott is well over eighty by now, but he might remember."

"Does he live in Leafy Hollow?" I asked.

"No, but I can get his current address from the church head office. I'll find out and call you."

"I'll wait to hear from you, but until then..." I had a thought. "Daniel, did you ever discuss the contents of Nesbitt-Cavanagh's book with him?"

"We talked about it, yes, before the unveiling, but obviously he didn't tell me the truth."

"Did he mention anything else that might be in the book, besides Prudence Bannon? Say, cocoa-growing in West Africa?" I mentally crossed my fingers.

Isabelle looked askance. "What on earth would—"

Daniel looked surprised. "How did you know? We chatted about family farms in The Ivory Coast because I've seen them."

"Seen what? The cocoa farms?"

"Yes. I spent time in Abidjan as a youth. The church had a mission there."

"I never knew that," Isabelle said, frowning.

"It was a long time ago, before I entered the ministry."

"Did Nesbitt-Cavanagh say *why* that was in his book?" I asked.

Daniel shook his head. "No. I thought it was odd, to be honest, but I assumed he had some historical records that shed light on the colonial era." He snorted. "Of course, that's when I believed he was a real historian, not the charlatan he turned out to be."

I wondered idly if Daniel had shared that perspective with the cops.

"What about the storage area, then? Can I see it?"

"The police have cordoned it off as a crime scene. We're not allowed to go down there," he said.

Too bad. I would have liked to take a look. How many times did you get the chance to dig for buried treasure?

I went back to the truck, waved at the news crew, and retrieved the wrapped sandwich and the cat food from the cab. By the time I'd navigated the footpath to the river, it was mid-morning. Ford was sitting by a camp stove, eating beans from a can. Stones surrounded a campfire pit that held only ashes. He rose, setting down the can, when I approached.

"Hi, Ford. I'm Verity. We met in the churchyard the other day."

I thought he might object to my intrusion, but he merely nodded.

"I remember."

"I brought you a sandwich," I said, holding up my two bags. "And some cat food." When he didn't move, I set both down on a rock by the campfire. "I'll leave them here." I pointed to another boulder. "May I?" At his nod of consent, I sat down, trying not to stare at the grubby one-man tent and its even grubbier sleeping bag.

He shuffled over to the rock and bent to pick up the sandwich. The white hair that cascaded to his shoulders was clean, even if his olive-green nylon jacket was not. I recalled

Isabelle saying the minister let Ford shower in the church. He sat on his rock and placed the sandwich beside him. "Thank you," he said, not looking at me.

We sat silently, listening to the river rush and tumble over rocks a few yards away. Birds chattered in the birch and cedar trees. Sitting on that peaceful riverbank, I relaxed for the first time since the dreadful scene in the cemetery. With a blissful sigh, I leaned my head back and closed my eyes.

A jay's sudden cry of alarm was echoed by others. I snapped to attention, nearly falling off my boulder. A bedraggled brown tabby slid out from a clump of tall grass at my feet. The cat rubbed up against Ford.

"Is this one of yours?" I asked, regaining my balance.

He extended an arm to scratch her back. "Sorta." His gruff voice was soft as he addressed the tabby. "Time for dinner, Diana," he murmured, and then rose to his feet to unlatch and open a battered plastic cooler. "Keeps out the raccoons," he said, gesturing at the cooler while he tugged out a bag of kibble.

I watched as he gathered up an assortment of battered metal and plastic bowls and dropped kibble into each. No sooner did the hard bits rattle onto the metal than there were eight cats seated nearby, chowing down.

Ford pointed to them, one at a time, with satisfaction. "Minerva. Mercury. Bacchus. Persephone. Aphrodite. Cronos. And Ceres."

My eyebrows rose. Greek and Roman gods?

"Interesting names," I said.

Ford dropped the wrapped sandwich into the cooler,

latched the lid, and swiveled his head to face me. "Want to see?" He tilted his head toward a little path through the grass.

"The kittens? Yes." I rose to my feet.

"This way."

The path led through a stand of tall grass along the river's edge, into a clearing about twenty feet from Ford's camp. Wooden packing crates were nailed together in bundles reminiscent of those tiny, stacked hotel rooms in Japan. Tarps covered their tops. One crate was separate from the others, and Ford bent to pick it up. "I take them in the tent at night," he said. "Because of raccoons."

I nodded knowingly. At Rose Cottage, Carson had warned me about raccoons when he suggested my aunt's ruined Ford Escort would make a safe nighttime coop for Reuben. According to him, Leafy Hollow raccoons were not the endearingly curious creatures of the cartoons, but deadly killers. Which made sense. I'd already discovered the village's human inhabitants weren't all that peaceful, either.

The scruffy brown tabby—a.k.a. Diana, Roman goddess of the hunt—followed Ford, meowing, but didn't object to the viewing of her kittens. She followed us back down the path, tail erect. When Ford placed the crate down outside his tent, she jumped into it and settled down, wrapping herself in a semi-circle around five of the cutest fur babies I'd ever seen. I watched as the tiny blind kittens snuggled and sucked. Two of them were brown tabbies like their mom, and the other three... I bent for a closer look at their beautiful gray-tabby coats. I recognized that color. I straightened up with a studied air of nonchalance. "Have your cats been neutered?"

"Most. Diana is a new arrival."

I bit my lip, eying the kittens again before I replied. "So the father of these little guys is?"

Ford shrugged. "He hasn't been around much lately."

I wondered what General Chang's name had been—Eros? When I got back to Rose Cottage, he and I would have a talk.

Ford and I settled back on our boulders, listening to the birds. I broached the topic I'd come here about. "When Lorne and I met you in the churchyard, you told us you'd seen someone there the night before. Do you remember who that was?"

"In the cemetery?"

"Two nights ago."

He looked confused. "Dunno."

We listened to the birds for a while longer. I hoped the police didn't need to question Ford—they'd be at it for days. My gaze drifted over to the river. "We're not far from Paradise Falls, are we?"

"'Bout a hundred meters."

"It's nice you're so close to the water," I said. "Do you take a dip now and then?"

"Never go in there." Ford shuddered. "Can't swim." He drew a noisy breath. "I can't help him," he said, shaking his head at the nearest cat. The straggly black feline—Cronos, I thought—absorbed this information with a beady stare, and then curled around to check his butt.

"Who couldn't you help, Ford? Who did you see in the cemetery?"

"Did this," he said, gripping his neck with both fingers and squeezing, his eyes wide. He made a strange gurgling sound. Then he lowered his hands, mumbling under his breath.

I couldn't tell if he was talking to me or to himself. But I'd seen Nesbitt-Cavanagh's body and there were no bruises on his neck. "Who did that?" I asked, confused.

"I can't help him."

"Help who? Ford, tell me—who couldn't you help?"

No answer.

"I think it's time to go to the police, don't you?"

He leaped to his feet and took several steps back. "No. No."

"I'm sorry. No police."

With a suspicious glance, Ford returned to his boulder.

I pulled a pencil and my Coming Up Roses Landscaping receipt book from my purse, then tore off a sheet. I placed the sheet on the flat rock in front of him and drew squares to mark the church and its surroundings. On the largest square, I penciled in a cross.

"There's the church," I said, pointing, "and that's the manse. This is the path to your campsite, past the cemetery." I added a few tombstones and a wavy line for the path. "And this"—I added a smaller square, with crosshatching—"is the Bannon family vault." I considered drawing in the flowers, but decided against it. With my artistic skills, they might look like an army of stick men. I didn't want to alarm Ford any further.

Tapping the paper with one hand, I handed him the pencil. "Show me what you saw."

He licked the pencil's lead tip, and then laboriously drew

a stick figure lying on the ground beside the vault. After a moment's consideration, he added Xs for eyes.

"A man?" I asked.

He nodded. Then he drew a second figure, bending over the first, its little stick arms dragging the first figure toward the vault.

"Another man?"

He nodded again and put down the pencil.

"Who was it?"

Ford shrugged. It was possible he saw nothing in the cemetery that night, and this stick-figure account was the invention of a confused mind. And it wouldn't help clear Daniel since Ford didn't seem to know the identity of either stick figure.

I picked up the paper, folded it carefully, and put it in my purse. After swinging the purse over my shoulder, I got to my feet. "I'll bring more cat food tomorrow, Ford."

He grunted and picked up his half-eaten can of beans.

"By the way," I asked. "Would these cats go after a rooster?"

He shrugged, the spoon in his hand. "Maybe."

I sat in the truck for a few minutes, pondering what to do next. I had two landscaping appointments today, but this afternoon would be plenty of time to get to them. Carson was busy at the cottage, Lorne was at his literacy lesson, and it was too early for lunch—I double-checked the time before conceding that—so there was nothing to draw me away from my quest to help Isabelle and Emy clear the minister's name. If Reverend Daniel was telling the truth, then someone else attacked Nesbitt-Cavanagh in the cemetery and dragged his body into the crypt.

But who in Leafy Hollow hated the annoying, smug British historian enough to kill him?

There was another possibility—that Nesbitt-Cavanagh was fine when he left the cemetery after his encounter with the minister and was lured back later. I recalled Jeff's words.

A woman could have led him there.

There was a woman in Leafy Hollow who knew the annoying historian well, according to Zander and Terry—the artist, Madeline Stuart. I put the key in the ignition and turned it.

CHAPTER TWELVE

"EMY, calm down. Tell me that last bit again." I held the cell phone to my ear, biting my lip, as I waited with the truck pulled over to the side of the road.

She gulped air before continuing. "Nesbitt-Cavanagh's blood was found on the candlestick and in the basement storage area. A blow to the head killed him. And Daniel's fingerprints are on the candlestick. The results came back from the lab this morning. Jeff showed up at the manse half an hour ago to take him in for more questioning."

"That's not good," I said.

"Izzy is here"—Emy's voice dropped to a low murmur —"and she's... upset." By the way she stressed *upset*, I figured her cousin was frantic. "I don't know what to tell her."

"Do you need reinforcements?"

"Please?" She lowered her voice again. "In fact, I'm begging you to get over here. And bring a box of Kleenex—

super large." I heard wailing in the background, and then Emy clicked off the call.

By the time I'd stocked up on tissues and walked into the 5X Bakery, Emy had persuaded Isabelle to settle down long enough to drink a cup of tea. It was only the calm before the storm, because the next person to walk through the front door was Wilf Mullins.

"Ladies," he said, shuffling to the table and resting his hands on the back of my chair. "I understand there's been a development?" Wilf took a step back and rubbed his fingers together, giving us an inquisitive glance. For some reason, I was reminded of a character from Charles Dickens. Maybe a lawyer from *Bleak House*—only much shorter. Emy pulled out a chair for him, and he hopped up.

"It's the minister," Emy said with a sidelong glance at Isabelle. "He's at the station again."

"I heard," Wilf said, nodding sagely. "Looks like they're charging him with manslaughter. Maybe worse. I hate to think what this will do to his career. Has the church lined up a replacement yet?"

Isabelle burst into a renewed fit of wailing. Emy grabbed the teacup from Isabelle's hand and replaced it in the saucer. She patted her cousin on the back while shooting Wilf a furious glance.

"Sorry," he said. "I'm being too negative. The police will probably just send him home." Wilf was a master of optimistic legalese, but this whopper stretched even his elastic face into a parody of sympathy.

"And if they don't?"

"I'm heading into town now to see if I can be of assistance. Put up his bail, perhaps."

That was a surprise. Wilf was my aunt's lawyer—and mine by default—and I knew he meant well, but for him to cough up money would be unprecedented. "That's kind of you," I said.

"It's a loan," he said, sensing my confusion. "I'm sure the minister's good for it. I'm also going to contact a criminal law specialist in Strathcona." He nodded briskly. "Same one your aunt always uses, Verity." For some reason, the word *kickback* echoed in my head. Wilf had mentioned this lawyer before with regard to my aunt, but I'd yet to learn why Aunt Adeline needed a criminal lawyer on speed dial. Although, she had insisted I learn the defensive martial arts techniques of her own discipline, Krav Maga, so I suspected my aunt was no stranger to conflict. I'd done my best to master the moves, but I imagined Aunt Adeline could still beat me—even at sixty-five.

"The minister is the obvious suspect," Wilf continued, ignoring the glances exchanged by Emy and me, and Isabelle's horrified stare. "After all, who else had access to the crypt? Because if you think about it—"

I blurted an interruption. "Say, Wilf—how are the water-park plans going?"

Thank you, Emy soundlessly mouthed at me.

He frowned. "This unfortunate incident has halted the entire development in its tracks. The investors stand to lose thousands. All because of those ridiculous notions of that Nesbitt-Cavanagh person."

"You mean the murder victim?" I asked.

Wilf snorted in disgust. "I bet he had high blood pressure. Diabetes, even." He narrowed his eyes. "Could have been a stroke. Did you notice at the village hall how red his face was? Metabolic syndrome, definitely. So he was almost dead, anyway."

I stared at him. "That blow to his head probably didn't help."

"Well, it's always something, isn't it? Frankly, whoever delivered the coup de grâce did the world a favor. Less bloviating is always a good thing."

Really? I nearly bit the end off my tongue to keep from jumping to that bait.

Wilf hopped off the chair and straightened to his full height. "The Prudence Bannon Waterpark will be built," he proclaimed, hoisting an emphatic finger in the air. "And the public will come. Mark my words." After letting that sink in for a few seconds, he glanced over his shoulder at the bakery's glass-fronted counter. "Can I get a buttermilk-lemon scone to go?"

As the bells over the front door jingled to announce Wilf's exit, I pondered his statement about the investors and wondered who they might be. I suspected the only person who stood to lose "thousands" was Wilf himself. Public accusations of fraud surrounding Leafy Hollow heroine Prudence Bannon might sink his ambitious waterpark plan. But now that the man who made those accusations was dead... No, impossible. Wilf wasn't tall enough to whack someone of Nesbitt-Cavanagh's height on the head with a candlestick.

But what if the historian had been bending over?

I ducked down about a foot. "Emy, hit me on the head

with that fork." She complied—a little too eagerly, I thought. But as remnants of buttermilk scone crumbled over me, I had to admit that even tiny Emy was more than a foot taller than Wilf.

"Should I hit you again?" Emy asked, the fork poised in her hand.

"No thanks." I slumped into the last chair.

"Well, good, because Izzy has something to tell you."

Isabelle started at the mention of her name, and then plucked her handbag from the floor. She pulled out a rumpled piece of paper and smoothed it on the table. "I have Reverend Doctor Abbott's contact information." She pushed the paper over to me.

I picked it up and read, *Golden Legacies Rest Retreat* and an address in a small town about two hours away. "Did you try phoning him?"

"I did, but the reverend is eighty-five. They told me his hearing is so bad that telephone conversations are out of the question. And no one seemed to have time to write out a few questions for him." She frowned, and the warrior princess persona I'd glimpsed in Daniel's kitchen reappeared. "Even when I emphasized how important it was."

I tapped the paper. "You were discreet, right? You didn't mention anything about tracking down keys to the crypt where a murder victim was found, did you?"

Isabelle bristled. "Certainly not. I had a cover story. I said one of the minister's former parishioners was dying and had something to tell him before it was too late."

I stifled the urge to roll my eyes. *Yeah, a deathbed confes-*

sion wouldn't get anybody's attention. "Isabelle, can I see your key chain again?"

She fished it out of her purse and plunked it on the table. The skeleton key for the crypt was the biggest one on the chain. I separated it out, placed it on the back of the paper with the address, and traced around it with Emy's pen. I handed the key chain back to Isabelle. "It's hard to believe you couldn't get some kind of antique key to fit an old lock like the one on the crypt."

She shrugged. "Maybe somebody did, because I swear that key has never been off my chain. I haven't misplaced it, either. I would never be that careless with church property."

"But the location of the third key is worth following up, isn't it?" Emy asked.

I folded up the paper with the minister's address and the traced outline and slid it into my purse. "Let's visit Reverend Abbott and ask him. Maybe he'll remember when it disappeared and who might have taken it."

"I can't leave the bakery," Emy said.

"And I have to stay in case Daniel calls," Isabelle said, eyes wide.

I sighed. "Which means I'm driving to the"—I re-read the name on the paper—"*Golden Legacies Rest Retreat* by myself. I'll call Lorne and ask him to do our afternoon appointments alone." I fished my cell phone from my purse.

"Where is Lorne, anyway? Why isn't he with you?" Emy asked.

"He's busy."

"He seems to be busy a lot lately." She looked away, a finger tapping on the tabletop.

I couldn't tell Emy about Lorne's literacy lessons, since I was sworn to secrecy, so I merely shrugged. "Maybe he's helping out at home."

I had plenty of time to think during the two-hour drive to the small town that housed *Golden Legacies*. And one of the things I pondered was how I'd gotten involved in another murder investigation. My sojourn in the village had been an endless hassle of home renovations and backbreaking gardening, interrupted by cryptic clues to my aunt's whereabouts that led nowhere. It wasn't too late to give up the whole idea and fly back to Vancouver and my snug little apartment. I remembered strolling through Stanley Park with Matthew and watching the giant cruise ships glide into the Vancouver port. Living in this quiet village allowed me to finally accept that Matthew was gone, and I was grateful for that, but I missed the West Coast. I even missed my high-rise neighbor, Patty, who made some of the weirdest baked goods in the Western Hemisphere. I smiled at thoughts of her mustard jelly roll and three-alarm chipotle brownies. Patty was one of the few friends I didn't push away after Matthew's death. Or maybe—I smiled again—she simply didn't know the meaning of no.

The staff at *Golden Legacies Rest Retreat* directed me to a bench under an enormous elm tree on the front lawn.

Reverend Abbott sat in a wheelchair with an oxygen tank strapped to its back. A paltry fringe of white hair brushed his earlobes, and his belt was closer to his armpits than his waist, but his eyes twinkled behind broad-rimmed glasses.

"What did you say your name was?" Reverend Abbott leaned forward in his chair, tilting his head to the side.

The nurse at the front desk had warned me that the elderly minister often didn't wear his hearing aid. "So speak up," she said.

I sat on the bench beside him. "Verity Hawkes," I answered in a tone so loud that three startled sparrows burst from the branches above. "From Leafy Hollow." I told him what sparked my visit. He appeared delighted at the mention of his old parish, but showed signs of agitation when I related my tale. However, it wasn't the murder that concerned him.

"A bawdy *what*? At Leafy Hollow Community Church?" He shook his head. "Things have changed a lot since my days. Although we did bring in folk singers once. The young people seemed to appreciate it."

"No, a body. A *body*. In the crypt behind the church."

"Who crept behind the church?"

I tried again, even louder. "There was a dead person in the crypt."

He squinted at me. "Isn't that where they normally keep them?"

"This one hadn't had a funeral yet."

"Ah. Why didn't you say so in the first place? I can't follow when you mumble."

"Sorry. If it's any consolation—"

He lifted a hand to stop me with a disgusted shake of his

134

head. "Please don't. That is *the* main topic of conversation here. Just take the darn Metamucil and stop talking about it, I say."

I looked around for a nurse. Or one of those Victorian ear trumpet thingies. Raising my voice by tens of decibels, I asked, "Reverend Abbott, when you were at Leafy Hollow, how many keys"—I inserted an invisible key into an invisible lock and twisted my hand—"did the Bannon family crypt have?"

He brought a hand to his chin, thinking, and then lowered it. "Three."

My heart soared. Finally, a break in the case. All we had to do was find out who had the third set of keys and we could divert suspicion from Daniel and Isabelle. Maybe even get the pending manslaughter charges lifted.

And I could resume the search for my aunt. Or go home to Vancouver.

He pointed to the lock on his wheelchair. "Release that, and we'll go upstairs and get them."

"Get what?"

"You came here to collect them, didn't you?"

A prick of foreboding threatened to burst my happy-ending balloon. "Collect what?" I asked.

"The third set of keys. I took them with me by mistake all those years ago, and I've had them ever since. I phoned several times, but nobody seemed interested. Come on"—he pointed to the main building like the leader of a wagon train—"this way."

Once we'd reached his second-floor room, which over-looked the lawn, the minister plucked a hearing aid off the bureau and fitted it into his ear. Then he opened a sock drawer and felt way in the back. He fished out a yellowing envelope and handed it to me.

I drew open the flap and looked inside. The old skeleton key on this chain looked identical to the one I'd seen on Isabelle's key ring. I pulled out the tracing from the bakery and compared them. Yep. Same key.

"Did anyone else know you had this?"

He shrugged. "They knew at the church. But it was a busy time."

"In what way—busy?"

"They were painting the basement to prepare for the Easter events. We did it every few years because it was damp down there and the condensation was hard on the paint."

"When was that?"

"The last time would have been... Let's see"—he counted down on his fingers—"twelve years ago."

Twelve years? I wracked my memory. That was about the time Isabelle's former beau disappeared.

"Do you remember a young man, Charlie Inglis?"

He brightened. "Charlie... yes, I do remember him. He helped with the painting." His expression darkened. "Until he ran off, that is. We had to find someone else to finish it." He shut the drawer and wheeled his chair around. "You know, that may be why no one ever called me about the key. Maybe they thought Charlie took it with him."

"Why would Charlie have a key to the crypt?"

"There was a lot of rain that year, and the basement flooded. We moved the paint cans, and everything else, upstairs while we waited for the board of managers to approve the expenditure required to dig up the weeping tiles outside the church. But there wasn't enough space in the nave, so we stored a number of items in the crypt." He made a face. "Probably not the best place, but there was a fair bit of room in there, and the last of the Bannons died off after the Great War. There hadn't been a Bannon in Leafy Hollow for generations."

I assumed he meant the First World War, which meant there hadn't been a Bannon living in Leafy Hollow for nearly a century. "No one to complain about a little overcrowding, then?"

He smiled. "That's right. Anyway, Charlie moved everything in and out, so he might have had a key."

"Although he must have returned it, or you wouldn't have it now."

"Yes," he said thoughtfully, contemplating the key ring in my hand. "Charlie must have replaced it on the vestry keyboard before he left. But I couldn't swear to it. The new minister had arrived by that time, and I spent that summer visiting parishioners and saying my goodbyes."

"You mean Daniel McAllister?"

"Yes, nice young man, but he didn't get on with Charlie all that well."

"Why was that?"

He wrinkled his already furrowed brow. "I'm not sure."

"Why did Charlie run off, anyway?"

"He had trouble finding a job. That's why he helped with the painting—to use the church as a reference on his résumé. I think we found a little money for him in petty cash, too. I remember he talked about oil jobs out West and how much they paid. So it wasn't a surprise. Although..." His brow wrinkled. "I thought he really loved that girl—what was her name?"

"Isabelle—" I started to add "Yates" before realizing I didn't know her maiden name.

"That's right. Isabelle Gagnon." He smiled. "She used to teach a Sunday school class."

"She still does, although she's married now, to Nick Yates."

He gave me a quizzical glance. "Is she? Odd choice."

"Why?"

"Oh, no reason. I don't know why I said that." He pointed to the antique pendulum clock on his bureau. "Lunch in fifteen minutes. Care to stay? Shepherd's pie today. With bread pudding."

"No, sorry. I have to get back." I was hungry, but given that I still had all my teeth, nursing home fare held little appeal for me. "Thanks for the offer."

CHAPTER THIRTEEN

IT WAS some of her finest work, and now no one would see it.

Madeline Stuart sank to the floor on trembling legs. She sat, cross-legged, staring at the open grate of her fireplace. With a quivering hand, she scraped a match against the box and watched it flare. She held it, wavering, until the flame bit at her thumb. Madeline dropped it with a wince onto the grate. She lit another and touched the flame to the bottom of the first drawing—a pen-and-ink depiction of Prudence Bannon waving from a hilltop to a group of soldiers in the valley below. The wind caught Pru's hair, blowing it back.

Madeline had worked hard to make Pru's expression exultant, but tired. Determined, yet weary. A little pooped, in fact—it would have been a long and arduous journey from Leafy Hollow to the military camp. The troops below greeted the child with enthusiastic waves and a few shouts—depicted by hands cupping their mouths. Pru stood resolutely against the horizon, framed by blue sky and fluffy clouds.

Madeline watched as flames consumed the soldiers, the hill, and, finally, Prudence. As her heroine's face crumpled and flared, Madeline shed a tear. She dropped the ruined drawing into the fireplace.

The second one was even harder—her sketch of the troop commander. There was no existing portrait of him, but Madeline had portrayed him with a noble brow and countenance, a hand pressed against his chest. The brass buttons on the red flannel of his uniform glowed in a beam of sunlight. She'd even added a few anonymous medals. That was before she heard Edgar's description of him as an out-of-his-depth vegetable farmer pressed into duty to lead a ragtag band of local militia. The great general, Isaac Brock, preferred not to arm the colonists, fearing there were concealed American sympathizers among them. Instead, he relied on well-trained volunteer forces to augment his own troops and the First Nations warriors who fought beside them. Even so, Madeline had opted to leave the portrait as it was. Edgar was a historian, but history wasn't always truth.

She studied the next drawing, which depicted the burning of the White House in 1814—the only time in U.S. history that a foreign force occupied Washington, D.C. That went into the flames, too.

Her sketch of the Bannon family crypt sparked a flashback of that terrible discovery in the cemetery. And only hours earlier, Edgar had been so... alive. She felt her cheeks flush at the memory. Or was that reflected heat from the fire?

Madeline picked up the rest of her drawings and threw them into the fire.

CHAPTER FOURTEEN

LORNE and I had heaved the last of the landscaping equipment back onto the Coming Up Roses truck and were on our way home when he turned to me with an unusually serious expression. I braced myself, hoping he wasn't about to quit.

"Verity, I'd like to thank you."

"What for?"

"For hooking me up with Thérèse's reading lessons."

"You're very welcome. But I thought we agreed not to talk about it."

"I still don't want Emy to know, but Thérèse says I'm doing great, and I wanted to tell you. And to say thanks."

I flicked on a turn signal and pulled out onto Main Street, grinning. "I knew you'd do great. I bet you're burning up those workbooks. Those invoices you wrote were perfect."

Now it was his turn to look embarrassed. "Thanks. We've been concentrating on business correspondence lately."

"Good idea." We traveled in silence for a few blocks.

"I'm going to start my own business."

"That's a great idea." I slapped his hand in a high five. "Congratulations."

"Thérèse suggested classes at the community college in Strathcona—spreadsheets, business plans, that kind of thing. I'm not ready yet, but she says I can enroll in courses this fall."

"She wouldn't say that if it wasn't true. What kind of business are you thinking of?"

"Well..." He contemplated the shops on Main Street as we drove past, his elbow resting on the window frame. "I thought maybe a chain of bakeries."

Bakeries? I stifled my smile. "That sounds like an excellent idea. You wouldn't do the baking part, would you?"

"Of course not." He laughed. "Just the business stuff. Sourcing, managing, and marketing. But I won't leave you in the lurch. I like landscaping. Besides, I need the money to pay for my classes." He pointed out the window. "Here's my street. I'll drop off a few things and catch up to you."

I pushed open the red door of the 5X Bakery, setting off a tinkle of bells overhead, and strode in. "Emy, you'll never guess where Nesbitt-Cavanagh—" I stopped in mid-sentence.

Emy wasn't alone.

A trim man with short reddish hair, rimless eyeglasses, and two days' worth of stubble sat across from her at the tiny table at the back of the bakery. A dozen dessert plates were laid out between them, and Emy was offering him a bite of something—possibly lemon meringue—on a fork.

He bit down, chewed for a second or two, and then winked. "Fantastic," he said.

Emy blushed crimson and put down the fork.

Well, that was new. Not a handsome stranger loving Emy's lemon meringue pie—that was routine. Patrons always praised her baking. But that was the first time I'd seen her embarrassed about it.

The stranger placed his hand on Emy's arm and leaned in to speak.

I cleared my throat, and they turned.

Emy leapt to her feet. "Verity. Hi. Come in."

Since I was already in, that seemed redundant, but I walked to the back of the bakery and extended my hand. "I'm Verity Hawkes."

The handsome stranger rose, laugh lines crinkling around his hazel eyes, and grasped my hand. Freckles spotted his skin. There was a touch of gray in his hair, so he was exactly Emy's type.

"Fritz Cameron. I'm new here."

Well, of course he was, because news that a man this intriguing had moved into the village would have made the rounds in minutes.

"Are you visiting, or—"

Emy broke in. "Fritz is a chef, Verity. He's hoping to open a restaurant on Main Street, in the old Chinese food place. Everything will be locally sourced."

"Especially the desserts," Fritz said, grinning at her. "I've found my source for those."

Emy blushed, and, for a moment, I felt like the third wheel on a canoe. If this were a movie, right about now the music would swell and the focus blur while they stood, looking at each other.

I cranked the imaginary medley to a halt by gesturing over my shoulder at the door. "Why don't I—"

"No," Fritz said. "Don't leave on my account. I have to go. Thanks for the organic farm recommendations, Emy. I'll be in touch. In fact"—he looked at his watch with a sly grin —"are you free for dinner tonight, by any chance?"

Behind his back, I shook my head and mouthed *No* at Emy.

Her brow wrinkled slightly when she noticed my expression, but she reacted smoothly. "Not tonight, sorry. Maybe another time?"

"Count on it." He turned to the door.

"Wait. Let me pack up a few samples for you." Emy hurried behind the counter for a white cardboard box. She swept into it what in many countries would have been a week's worth of food and tied the box with string before handing it over. I eyed it ravenously, hoping that wasn't the last of the maple-pecan butter tarts.

Emy walked Fritz to the door and stood in the entrance, waving, as he strode off up the street.

I plunked myself into his empty, but still warm, seat. "New business opportunity?" I asked casually, stretching my arms overhead as Emy closed the door.

"Fritz's restaurant is going to be fabulous," she said, hustling back to join me. "He's calling it *Anonymous*. Isn't that clever? It's a play on the pervasive nature of social media, and how everybody knows everything about everybody else. He told me about the menu, and I promised—cross my heart —not to divulge any of the details, but..."

I nodded as Emy related every possible aspect of the new eatery, including the number of Irish linen hand towels in the bathroom. For someone new in town, Fritz had a shrewd sense of marketing. Tantalizing news of *Anonymous* and its "locally sourced" menu would be all over the village within the hour. Possibly as far as Strathcona by dinnertime.

"Well, if he's serving 5X Bakery desserts," I said, "the place can't fail. Especially with your new butter tarts."

Emy paused in her praise of the fabulous new restaurant and grinned. "You could have just asked." She got to her feet, plunked the last maple-pecan on a plate, and set it before me.

"That wouldn't be any fun," I said, tucking in. After one or two glorious sugar-soaked nibbles—okay, I inhaled the whole thing—I remembered my purpose. "Is Isabelle here?"

"She's at the church. Wilf got Daniel off on bail. She's helping Daniel tidy up after the police search." Emy narrowed her eyes at me. "Aren't you supposed to be having your bowling lesson with Jeff tonight?"

I gave an embarrassed flick of my hand. "He's been busy."

Her lips twitched. "We'll have to see about that."

"Don't even. Besides, I have news," I said, anxious to change the subject.

"Did you find something?" Emy pulled up a chair and rested her arms on the table. "Tell me."

"It may be nothing. Let's wait for Lorne, and I'll tell you both at the same time."

"Lorne?" Emy slumped back in her chair. "What makes

you think he's coming? I've hardly seen him these past weeks." She reached out a finger to push the sugar bowl into the center of the table, aligning it precisely. "If I didn't know better, I'd think he had a girlfriend." She uttered a slight laugh. "Not that it matters. He's free to do whatever he likes."

Now what? I couldn't tell her the truth, but I hated to see her give up on Lorne—no matter how many handsome, graying-at-the-temples foodies blew into town. "I'm sure it's not a girlfriend. He would have mentioned her."

She shrugged, pushing the sugar bowl a fraction of an inch to the right.

My mind spun through possible exits from the corner I'd painted myself into. "Maybe... maybe he thinks you take him for granted. A bit."

Emy looked up, startled. "Did Lorne say that?" She straightened up. "What gall. I mean—"

"No, no," I blurted. *Good work, as always, Verity. Now you've made it worse.* "He never said anything like that. That was totally my own observation."

Emy studied my face. "You know that Lorne and I are only friends, right?"

"Why is that?"

Now she looked embarrassed. "Well, for one thing, he's three years younger than me."

"So?"

"Well, that's a lot."

"Three years is nothing. And the older you get, the less important it will be. Look how old Fritz is, and he's still reasonably attractive." I mulled it over. "For such an old guy."

Emy looked suspicious. "What are you getting at?"

147

"Nothing. Except maybe your taste in men needs adjusting."

"My taste in—" Emy leaned back in her chair with an incredulous look on her face. "Explain yourself."

"I only meant that you seem to like men a lot older than you," I said, squirming. "How's your relationship with your father?"

"Fine. How's yours?"

"I think it would be fair to call it... sub-optimal."

Sub-zero was more accurate. In fact, I hadn't talked to my dad in months. Or to wife number three, who lived with him in Australia. Nor did I want to.

But at my mock-serious tone, Emy burst into laughter, leaning over her bent arms. She straightened up, attempting a solemn tone of her own. "And yet, you're not lusting after older men. So maybe your hypothesis is faulty."

I glowered at her. Time to change the subject.

"Listen, about Reverend Daniel. The third key was a dead end, as you know." I had texted Emy before driving back from the unfortunately named *Golden Legacies*. "But I've been thinking."

She leaned in, the sugar bowl forgotten. "Go on."

"It may be nothing, but the minister said he argued with Nesbitt-Cavanagh because the historian was mucking about in the church basement, in the storage area."

"Yes, so?"

"Well, what was he doing there? What did he hope to find? It's a cold cellar for jam, right? Along with a workbench and some gardening tools. They don't keep anything important in there, according to Isabelle. Even the floor is unfinished."

"And I say again, so? Maybe he was looking for a flashlight to help him break into the crypt."

"The power's always going out in Leafy Hollow. There must be a flashlight in the vestry. That's not it." I raised an eyebrow, waiting for her to clue in.

Emy nodded, looking thoughtful. "Then what—"

I mimed shoveling and raised my eyebrows.

Her eyes grew wide. "Daniel said Nesbitt-Cavanagh had a shovel."

I nodded. "That's right."

We stared at each other until a tinkling of bells at the door made us jerk our heads around.

"Hey," Lorne said. He closed the door and walked toward us, glancing at the bakery counter on his way past. "What happened to all your stock? Did one of those tour buses go through the village today?"

"You'll never guess," Emy said. "The old Chinese-food place has been sold and a new restaurant is moving in. They're going to serve my desserts." She clapped her hands together, grinning. "Isn't that amazing?"

"Nope." Lorne stood before her, grinning. "You make the best desserts for miles. What else would they use?"

Emy told him about *Anonymous*. I stopped her before she got to the hand towels.

"That's all very fascinating," I said. "But we have work to do."

Lorne swiveled his gaze to me. "Like what?"

I eased the third chair out from the table with my foot. "Sit. We're planning a clandestine operation."

Emy raised her eyebrows. "How clandestine?"

"Well..." I pondered her query, wondering how best to phrase, *an illegal break-in that might land us all in jail.* After a moment I settled on, "Hardly at all."

"Cool." Lorne plunked his lanky frame into the chair, stretching out his legs so that the heels of his work boots rested on the floor, and looked at both of us in turn. "Where?"

"The Leafy Hollow Community Church."

"But we can walk in there any time," Emy said.

"Not in the basement storage area. The police closed that off as a crime scene after Daniel told them he confronted Nesbitt-Cavanagh down there."

"Still not getting it."

"Daniel claimed the historian was looking for buried Loyalist gold. I'm sure the police don't believe that, so they won't look for it. But if we can find evidence that it exists, they'll have to believe at least part of Daniel's story."

"Whoa," Lorne said. "We're digging for treasure? Do we get to keep it?"

CHAPTER FIFTEEN

IT WAS WELL past midnight when I parked my aunt's truck in the parking lot of the Pine Hill Conservation Area. A pickup with *Coming Up Roses Landscaping* blazoned across the door panel wouldn't have been my first choice for a covert operation, but Emy's tiny car was in the shop. It was there so often that the mechanics had installed a sign over one bay, *Emy's Fiat Goes Here*. The mechanics all loved Emy.

"We'll go into the churchyard through the back way, up the path that leads from the river," I said. "Keep an eye out for Ford. Make sure he doesn't see us."

Lorne tumbled out of the front seat and onto the gravel lot, followed by Emy, who'd been sitting between us. Three in the front cab was a tight squeeze, but I didn't think Lorne minded. Once out of the truck, we heard Young River Creek below us, surging past on its way to Paradise Falls.

We gathered by the tailgate for our pre-op briefing.

"Equipment check," I said. "Emy?"

She held Isabelle's key chain aloft, keys clinking, and, in her other hand, a flashlight. "Check."

"Batteries?" I nodded at the flashlight.

"Fresh today. I mean—check."

"Lorne?"

He held up a shovel and a pickaxe, one in either hand. "Check."

As expedition leader, I had to keep my hands free for emergency maneuvers. That didn't mean I was unprepared. I rummaged in my hoodie pocket, half-drawing out a parcel. Moonlight glinted off its aluminum foil wrapping. "And I have the brownies. So, we're good to go."

"Copy that," Lorne said in a clipped tone.

I narrowed my eyes at him. "Not necessary, Lorne."

"Right," he whispered, nodding.

I peered at him in the moonlight. "What have you got on your face?"

"Eye black. In case of surveillance."

We crossed the road and set off for the path that led through the fields behind the church, with Emy in the lead. At the outskirts of Ford's camp, she held up a hand. We halted. Emy performed one of those "visual signs" from the armed forces field manual we'd studied online before embarking. We stared at her, foreheads furrowing.

"What? I didn't get that. Did you get that, Lorne?"

"Nope. What are you trying to tell us?"

Emy signaled furiously, her lips pressed together in a grimace.

We shook our heads. "No, not getting it," I said. "Is that—"

"Oh, for heaven's sake," she hissed. "I'll check on Ford and signal if he's out of the way." She crept off.

I made a mental note to delete the army field manual from my aunt's laptop as soon as I got home.

A few seconds later, Emy returned. "All clear."

As we tiptoed past, I turned my head. Ford's campfire was doused, and the flap to his one-man tent was zipped shut. I assumed the crate with the kittens was inside. I pursed my lips. I still hadn't had that talk with the General. Or made the inevitable appointment. I felt a twinge of conscience. Poor General Chang. He would not be happy about his upcoming encounter with the vet.

After negotiating the rocky path and brushing past drooping branches—I hoped none of them were nettles—we reached the cemetery. We huddled next to the fence at the far side, studying the church that loomed before us. The gravestones seemed to tilt toward the Bannon family crypt in the center, which was wrapped stem to stern in yellow police caution tape.

Spotlights shone over the church's front and side doors, but the rest of the yard was in darkness. The manse beside the church was also dark. Reverend Daniel must be in bed, exhausted after his enforced stay at the police station—and all the questioning. So it was essential to maintain silence.

"Remember our cover story," I whispered. "We're retrieving Isabelle's paperwork from the vestry."

Emy screwed up her face. "What if they ask us why we're doing it at two a.m.?"

I mulled it over. "I'll get back to you on that. Let's go. And no talking until we're inside."

We threaded our way through the tombstones and halted at the vestry door. Emy handed the flashlight to Lorne and wielded Isabelle's keys, trying one after the other. They huddled over the lock while I served as lookout. Within seconds, we were inside.

Emy took the flashlight back and switched it on, aiming it at the floor. "Isabelle said to go through the church, down the stairs, and then through the finished part of the basement to the storage area." She indicated the way. After brushing stray dirt from our shoes, we followed.

There were no lights on in the nave, but the stained glass windows flashed whenever the moon came out from behind the clouds, illuminating the figures' pointed fingers. Their eyes tracked us down the aisle until we entered the lobby and turned right to descend the stairs. In the basement, we negotiated a sea of folding chairs, tables, and whiteboards. Lorne and I knocked into a few, followed in each case by a muffled "*blast*" and a quick massage of the relevant body part. Emy, showing off the former-gymnast agility that I'd admired on a previous rooftop raid, didn't run into anything.

Eventually, we reached a broad door at the far end of the basement. The door was easy to spot since it was crisscrossed by two strips of yellow caution tape. It also presented our first obstacle—a padlock. Emy tried several of the keys on Isabelle's ring without success.

"Do you think this is new?" I asked.

"Maybe the police added it?" she suggested.

"Stand back," Lorne said, brandishing the pickaxe.

"No, wait," I said. "There must be an easier—"

Too late.

Lorne grinned as the shattered padlock hit the floor.

"Well, that's one way to do it," I said.

Once we'd closed the door behind us, I flicked on the light switch. The air was damp and musty. A bare bulb overhead lit up the windowless area. An ancient wooden workbench lined one wall. Woodworking tools hung from hooks on a plank attached to the stone foundation wall above it.

"I wonder what the police did with Nesbitt-Cavanagh's shovel?" I said as I surveyed the brooms, pails, and mops beside the workbench. "Do you think they took it as evidence? I don't see it anywhere."

"I don't know, but look at this." Emy was several feet away, examining the contents of two rows of shelving units that extended out from the workbench. She ducked her head to peer at me from under a shelf. "Blackcurrant jelly. I'd love to have some of this at the bakery, for the scones. It's a pain to make. Takes forever. Ooh," she said, her attention drawn to an adjacent display. "Pear jam with artisan sherry. Amazing."

Normally, I shared Emy's enthusiasm for delectable handmade treats, but we had a job to do. Preferably as quickly as possible. I studied the floor. Daniel had been wrong about one thing. It wasn't bare dirt. Patio stones were laid over it, abutting each other. There was no sign of mortar, so I suspected the pavers weren't permanent, but intended to provide firmer footing if water breached the weeping tiles. With the church so close to the river, that was quite possible.

I turned to the second shelving unit, which was stocked with more prosaic items—turpentine, stiff brushes, soiled rags, and ten half-empty cans of blue paint, all different shades.

Lorne brushed past me. As I ducked to get out of his way, I slipped and jostled the shelving unit in front of me. The cans of paint slowly slid forward.

"Jeez," I blurted, spreading my hands to keep them from falling off. "That was close." I examined the cans while I lined them up on the shelf. They'd been hammered shut, but one lid was loose. I shoved it to the back, behind the others.

My attention was caught by the pavers that ran directly underneath the shelving unit. "Emy, shine the flashlight over here." When she complied, I crouched to tap them with my fingers. "This one is loose, while those over there"—I pointed at the doorway we'd walked over—"are embedded in the ground." I stood up and tentatively tapped my foot on the nearest pavers. They were also loose. "Somebody's taken these up recently."

We exchanged glances. Lorne handed me the shovel and went back to the door for the pickaxe.

First, we pried up the pavers and stacked them by the workbench. Then we started to dig. Lorne swung the pickaxe to loosen the hard-packed soil, and I followed with the shovel.

"Be careful," Emy said. "There's not much room in here."

Lorne adjusted his backswing to clear the shelving unit by a wider margin. We worked until sweat trickled down our backs.

"Look," Lorne said, lowering the pickaxe. "The ground is softer here." Emy shone the flashlight where he pointed, and we bent over to take a look.

"You're right," I said. "Somebody's been digging here recently." I removed three careful shovelfuls of dirt, and then bent to scrabble in the soil with my hands. I hit an obstacle and my breath caught in my throat.

I looked up at Lorne and Emy's serious faces, lit by the flashlight. "There's something here."

I bent, scrabbling more furiously, my heart pumping. Could this be Loyalist treasure, hidden during the war? "Lorne, check the workbench for garden tools. A trowel would be good."

Emy leaned in with the flashlight, her rapid breathing warming my ear.

Something crunched under my hand. Carefully, I brushed away the soil to get a better look, then halted. "Uh-oh," I muttered. I sat back on my haunches, my gaze riveted on the hole we'd made in the ground. Buried treasure was one thing, but this—I tried to swallow, but my mouth was too dry.

"What is it?" Emy bent forward with the flashlight.

The beam picked out the grayish bones of a human hand.

Emy shrieked.

Then she jumped to her feet, dropping the light. She jerked back and bumped into the shelving unit, which wobbled under her weight. Jars slid past her, smashing on the floor.

"Yikes! The jam!" Emy twisted around with her arms spread to stop the shelving unit from toppling.

At the sound of her voice, Lorne raced back from the workbench. "What happened?"

"Stop," I shrieked. "Watch out for the—"

Lorne's feet hit the slippery preserves and slid out from under him. He flung out his arms, trying to break his fall.

One hand connected with the second shelving unit. It rocked.

Half-empty cans of blue paint slid off the top shelf and hit the floor, one after the other. One bounced off Lorne's head. "Ow," he said, grimacing and rubbing his forehead.

Fortunately, the lids stayed on. I turned to face the shelf as the last of the cans slid forward. My eyes widened. It was the one with the loose lid.

I reached out a hand to stop it, but it slid past, just out of my grasp. As the can bounced off my arm, the lid flew off. A stream of blue paint flew through the air, splashing off me, the shelving units, Emy, and Lorne. The can hit the floor and spun around, the last drops of paint spilling out. Finally, it stopped moving.

Emy stood motionless, dripping paint.

Lorne wiped a hand over his mouth. It came away blue.

I finished my sentence. "—jam."

The more we tried to wipe off the sticky blue paint, the more it smeared. Before long, our hands, faces, and hair were blue.

"We can't walk through the church like this. We'll leave paint stains everywhere," Emy said. "Even if we take our shoes off, our clothes are covered in it."

"We could wait for it to dry," Lorne offered.

Emy fingered the sleeve of her shirt. "This is oil paint. It'll take hours even to reach the tacky stage. We can't wait that long. We have to call the police and report the body."

"Agreed," I said. "What should we do?"

Emy ran her eyes over my paint-stained jeans and T-shirt. My hoodie, flung over a nearby shelf, was also splattered with paint. We exchanged glances.

"Why can't we wait here?" Lorne asked from behind us.

We turned to look at him, our muscles rigid in disbelief. He shrugged, gesturing at the skeletal hand in the ground. "That guy's been dead for a while." Lorne bent over to peer at the uncovered hand. "Maybe we should dig the rest of him out."

I glanced at the gray-white finger bones and shuddered. The flashlight—which had rolled into a pool of paint under the shelving unit—projected strange shadows on the far wall, and the corners of the storage area were in darkness.

"I'm not hanging around. This place is too creepy." I plucked at my shirt with a sigh. "We'll have to take off our clothes and carry them. We can phone the police once we reach the truck. I have a couple of sweaters behind the front seat." With a nod of gratitude to the god of inept burglars—my favorite—I remembered leaving my cell phone in the glove box. At least it wouldn't be covered in sticky blue paint.

Emy nodded. She pulled her T-shirt over her head, revealing a leopard-print demi-bra. After using her shirt to wipe paint from her arms and hands—which only smeared it further into her skin—she dropped it on the floor and unzipped her jeans, revealing a matching leopard-print thong. I wondered where she'd been planning to go after our late-night expedition—a strip bar?

"Are there any garbage bags on the workbench, Lorne?" I asked while I tussled with my own shirt, trying not to smear more paint in my hair. No reply. I raised my voice. "Lorne!"

He tore his bedazzled gaze from Emy's thong and swiveled to face me. "Sorry. No garbage bags, but there's a pail. Will that do?"

"Get it, please."

We stripped down to our underwear and bare feet, stuffing our clothes and shoes into two grungy plastic pails. I reached for the paint-covered flashlight and jammed it into the pail next to our clothes, conscious of the skeletal hand behind me. I imagined it coming to life, flexing those fingers, reaching out... I shook my head to clear the image, refusing to look back.

When we left the storage area, I kicked the broken padlock out of the way and closed the door. I wasn't sure why I bothered, but it seemed like the thing to do.

We tiptoed up the stairs, through the nave, and into the vestry.

At the exit, Emy stopped, giving the pail in my hand an anxious glance. "The church keys are still in my jeans pocket," she said.

"Doesn't matter. We don't need to lock it."

As Lorne reached to open the door, I noticed a bright light coming in the window to our left, almost two meters above the ground. "Wow. Is that the moon?" I asked. "It seems awfully—"

Too late. Lorne had already swung the door open.

We stepped outside, squinting against a painful white light.

"Stop right there," a familiar voice boomed.

Lorne dropped the pails. With a hand shading my eyes, I made out the flashing blue-and-white light bars of two police cruisers. Over to our right, Xavier Roy had set up a reflective silver umbrella and a spotlight. His video camera was slung onto his shoulder, and he was squinting into the viewfinder.

With a sinking feeling, I glanced at Emy and Lorne. My eyebrows rose. In the dim light of the basement storage area, I hadn't realized how much we resembled Smurfs. And not Brainy Smurf, either.

Jeff Katsuro stepped into the circle of light and glared at us.

Instinctively, we raised our hands over our heads.

CHAPTER SIXTEEN

WHAT KIND of society did we live in when even churches had silent alarms? What if a parishioner had a spiritual crisis? A dark night of the soul? Would he be denied solace just because it happened after hours?

I considered these questions as Emy, Lorne, and I stood in the churchyard, squinting against the light. While it was a legitimate line of enquiry, I decided to keep it to myself for the time being. My first priority was to find some clothes.

"Turn that light off," Jeff barked. With a snap, Xavier complied. Even without the filmmaker's added glare, we were still visible in the beam from the bulb over the vestry door. Not to mention the moonlight and the light bars on the cruisers.

Thankfully, I'd chosen to wear a bra today, in a fairly demure shade of navy. Most of the time, I considered it optional. Lorne's tighty whities glowed almost neon in the moonlight. And Emy's leopard prints—well, let's just say none of the onlookers were ogling Lorne or me.

Jeff's stern gaze swept from Emy to Lorne, and, finally, me. His lips twitched. He pressed a hand to his mouth and turned away. I swear his shoulders were shaking. He waved at a constable, who hustled over to a cruiser and returned with three blankets, which we gratefully accepted.

Someone beyond the circle of light snickered.

Jeff straightened up, his face set in that *don't mess with me* expression I knew all too well. "Care to tell me what's going on here?"

We all talked at once.

"We were looking for buried gold—"

"It's not our fault—"

"There's a body, in the church—"

Jeff raised both hands in a gesture of resignation. "Stop. What's this about a body?"

We opened our mouths.

"One at a time," Jeff barked. "Verity, you first."

I explained about the skeleton in the storage area. Jeff called over two constables, and they conferred in low tones. One jogged over to the vestry door and disappeared inside the church.

We waited, our bare feet sinking into the grass, until the constable returned and stuck his head out the door. He nodded at Jeff, who stepped away and spoke into his radio. We heard a burst of static. He marched back and glared at us.

"What on earth possessed you?" he asked. "You three have done some dumb things, but this..."

I tuned out the rest. I'd heard it before. We'd uncovered valuable evidence, and you'd think that would garner a thank you, at least. But no... Instead, we had to listen to a boring lecture on civic responsibility. Although—I contemplated Jeff's face as he droned on. He was criminally good-looking, and that stern expression of his as he scolded us only added to his appeal.

An ambulance pulled up. Two medics emerged and walked over to us.

It wasn't clear why we needed an ambulance. Other than Lorne's battered forehead, our injuries were mostly sartorial. I clutched the blanket wrapped around my shoulders, waved away the nearest medic, and tried to focus on Jeff's lecture. Apparently, we had jeopardized an ongoing investigation. Evidence may have been irreparably damaged. We could be charged with breaking and entering. Blah, blah—

"Wait a minute. That's not fair," I said, backtracking. "We didn't break in. We had keys. It was perfectly legitimate."

"Uh-huh. So that's why you did it at two a.m.?"

Emy shot me her *told you so* glance.

"And that's another thing," Jeff continued. "Why am I only now learning that Isabelle Yates had a set of keys to the church?"

"That's my fault," Emy said. "I was afraid it might incriminate my cousin if you knew about the other key to the crypt. I'm sorry. It was wrong not to tell you."

"You can buy replacement skeleton keys online. It wouldn't be hard to find one to fit that old lock," Jeff said.

I grimaced, mentally kicking myself. Why hadn't I thought to check with Carson, my own personal antique-hardware specialist, before driving all the way to the *Golden Legacies Rest Retreat* in search of a useless third key?

"Can we go home?" I asked.

"Please?" Emy pleaded. Her heart-shaped face was as earnest as I'd ever seen it, made only slightly less pathetic by a coating of vivid blue paint.

But I was exhausted. Before I could stop it, one of those *I'm-so-tired-I-can't-help-it* chuckles burst through my lips.

Jeff uttered an exasperated sigh. "There's nothing funny here, Verity."

"No, of course not." I looked down at the ground and gave my head an emphatic shake. Drops of paint flew off my hair and hit Lorne's blanket.

Lorne nudged me with his elbow, and I chuckled again. Since my lips were firmly shut, my giggles sounded more like hiccups. "Sorry," I said. Emy poked me with her elbow, but not in a friendly manner. "Ow," I said.

Jeff shook his head, but I could tell he was suppressing a smile.

Judging by the chatter coming from his police radio, the coroner was on her way.

"What happens next?" Lorne asked. "Are you going to dig up the body?"

Jeff had no chance to answer.

With a rattle, the news van for the local television affiliate roared up the road and onto the shoulder, flinging gravel as it shuddered to a halt. The anchor with the big hair jumped out, followed by a cameraman, who started filming even before they'd rounded the fence corner and barreled into the churchyard.

I tucked my blanket higher around my neck and considered wrapping it around my face.

Jeff motioned to the nearest constable. "Take these three home." He turned to face us. "Someone will come by tomorrow to get full statements. And fingerprints. Don't go anywhere."

We nodded. I wondered where he thought we'd go, covered in blue paint. We followed the constable to the curb.

"And don't smear any of that on the cruiser," Jeff called after us. He strode away to head off the television film crew. Xavier followed, filming the film crew.

The three of us hunched over in the backseat of the cruiser, trying not to touch anything. At least we didn't have to worry about the door handles, since there weren't any. I'd finally learned the answer to a question I'd pondered as a child, watching *Cops* with my auto-mechanic dad—why didn't the bad guys just get out of the police car and run away?

"Do you think we found the body of a United Empire Loyalist?" Emy asked.

"That would mean the skeleton was two hundred years old," I said. "Did it look that old to you?"

"How would I know? I've never seen a skeleton, except for the one in our high-school biology class. And that was a plastic replica, like those ones you buy online."

"Well, that hand in the basement wasn't plastic, I guarantee it." I shuddered, remembering the disjointed, grayish-white finger bones.

"Maybe the gold was underneath the body," Lorne said. "We should have kept digging."

"I don't think there's any gold," I said. "Someone would have found it by now."

Emy drew in a quick breath. "Maybe that was Prudence Bannon's body."

"So you believe Nesbitt-Cavanagh's story? That the coffin in the Bannon family crypt is empty?"

"I don't know," she said. "It's possible, isn't it?"

We exchanged glances. "That's a little creepy," Lorne said.

We drew our blankets closer.

"What happened to the exhumation, anyway?" Lorne asked. "Are they going to go ahead with it now that Nesbitt-Cavanagh's dead?"

"I don't think so," I said. "He was the only one who wanted it. Wilf would know." I made a mental note to ask the lawyer next time I saw him.

The driver's door opened and our constable escort got in. "Who's first?"

"Could you take us back to the conservation area to pick up my truck?" I asked.

"Sure thing." He wheeled the cruiser out of the church driveway and onto the road. I glanced back at the cemetery and the flashing lights of the cruisers parked by the church. Our attempt to clear Reverend Daniel's name was a bust. Worse than that, we might have turned up evidence that

Nesbitt-Cavanagh's theory about Prudence Bannon was correct.

Which would have given Daniel even more reason to whack him over the head with a deadly candlestick.

CHAPTER SEVENTEEN

AFTER DROPPING YET another turpentine-soaked rag into the garbage bag in the bathtub, I assessed my face in the mirror and sighed. The hair would be harder. Luckily, I was due for a trim. I reached for the manicure scissors.

Emy, Lorne, and I had been swaddled in blankets when the television crew arrived, so I hoped our appearance on the television news later today would be brief. Twitter, on the other hand, was wriggling with delight over the report that a skeleton had been found at the same church as Nesbitt-Cavanagh's body. "Reverend Dan" was the target of indignant rage, with the most popular hashtag being #deadlyvicar.

Fortunately, among the online photos of police officers and white-suited forensic teams going in and out of the church, there was only one blurry photo of me. I looked dazed and underdressed. The tweet beneath read, Local landscaper involved in another murder case? #deadlygardener #LeafyHollowLegend #bluepanties.

At least Emy's leopard print hadn't made it onto Twitter —yet. I set the scissors down on the counter with a frown. Xavier filmed our entire encounter with the police, starting from the time we stepped out of the vestry. I was grateful he hadn't sold the footage to the Strathcona TV station, but given that he'd been fired from the *Leafy Hollow* documentary, that only raised another question.

Why didn't he?

I awakened with bed head, a pounding headache, and a gray tomcat pawing at my face. "Whass is it?" I asked before realizing the bedroom had grown bright. I glanced at the clock, then vaulted out from under the covers and into the shower— after feeding the General, of course. Living with a cat had rearranged my priorities in an unexpected way. Lately, I'd even been wondering if General Chang would be happy in a high-rise apartment in Vancouver—which was ridiculous. Crouching beside him as he ate his *Feline Fritters*, I ran my hand down his ragged, furry back. He head-butted me once before returning to his food—an unusually emotional display for the old boy.

Checking my phone on the way out the door, I found two texts from hours earlier. One from Lorne, agreeing to my suggestion that we take the day off—no surprise there. And one from Emy, insisting I meet her at the bakery, ASAP.

My cell phone beeped again with a new text from Emy.

JEFF'S HERE. STOP DAWDLING. :)

By the time I made it to the bakery, Jeff was at the back

table, tucking into his favorite lemon cupcake. He was too disciplined to eat desserts, but for this specialty, he made a weekly exception. He nodded in greeting as I walked in the door.

"You clean up good," he said between mouthfuls.

"Very funny. Are you here to arrest us? Because we have nothing new to add to our statements."

"It's a friendly call. I thought you might appreciate an update on the body."

I slid into a chair. "Where is it now?"

"Still in the church. The coroner called in a forensic anthropologist. We're not sure if we're dealing with a recent crime scene or a long-dead Loyalist. The experts want to weigh in before we move him."

"But it is a him?"

"Apparently. That's all they're willing to say until they get the body back to the lab."

We looked up as the bell over the front door tinkled and Isabelle walked in. Her eyes were red and puffy. No surprise there. Emy hurried over and ushered her onto a seat at the table. Isabelle perched on the edge of her chair, looking wide-eyed at Jeff.

"How's Daniel?" Emy asked.

"How do you think? Devastated," Isabelle said, pulling a crumpled tissue from her pocket. "We all are. I mean, we've been walking on someone's grave all these years. Even the Holy Hens. It's horrible." She pressed the tissue to her face.

Before the waterworks could start again, I tried a counter-argument. "Isn't it possible the skeleton washed in from the original cemetery? And he died a peaceful death two hundred years ago? Maybe the most recent flooding brought him to the surface."

"I think it was your digging that did that," Jeff muttered.

I glared at him.

Isabelle brightened a bit, although she was still sniffing. "So he wasn't murdered after all?"

"Maybe not," I said. "Maybe he's just another victim of global warming."

Emy frowned and opened her mouth to say something. But her objection was lost in the crash of the front door whooshing open and banging against the wall.

Nick Yates stood in the doorway, his expression black. He stalked up to Jeff and halted inches from his face. "What are you doing with my wife?"

Jeff stood his ground. If anything, he looked bored. "I'm conducting a routine investigation. Do you have something to add?"

Nick turned away with a grimace of irritation. He crouched by Isabelle's chair, pulled a handkerchief from his pocket, and dabbed at her face. "Look at you," he whispered. "All upset. This is what comes of spending so much time at that bloody church." He raised his voice and glared at all of us in turn. "I've always said something funny's going on there. Never thought it was murder though." He snorted in disgust. "You're coming home with me, Isabelle," he said, rising to his feet and pulling on her arm.

She yanked it away. "No, I'm not. Stop doing this."

"Doing what? Comforting my wife?" He glanced around, seemingly embarrassed, unwilling to meet our gaze. "You can't stay here," he whispered, bending over her. "You need to come home, where you're safe."

"I'm safe here, with my friends."

"Friends?" He spit out the word, scowling at us. "These friends have gotten you involved in a murder investigation. None of this would have happened if you'd stayed home. Do you think I don't know what goes on at that manse?"

Uh-oh, I thought. *Here it comes.*

"What you and that minister get up to?" he continued. "And you"—he pointed at Emy—"her own cousin, are encouraging it."

"Nick," Emy said. "You're overreacting."

Ouch. That wouldn't go over well. I scrunched up my eyes, wincing.

Jeff rose to his feet.

"Overreacting?" Nick said, his voice calm. He stepped closer to Emy. They would have been nose to nose if Emy hadn't been a foot-and-a-half shorter. "Overreacting?" He shoved her. "I'll show you who's—"

Lorne barreled out of his chair before any of us could stop him. He grabbed Nick's arm and swung him around. "Leave her alone," he yelled.

I winced again, expecting to hear the crunch of Lorne's nose at any moment. But I underestimated my landscaping assistant. Before Nick could even get his hand up, Lorne spiked him with an uppercut.

Nick pitched backward onto the floor.

Emy and I exchanged shocked glances.

Jeff pulled Lorne back, holding up a hand to prevent Nick from throttling him. "That's enough. Cool off, both of you." He turned to Nick—who had scrambled to his feet with his fists up—and pointed to the front door. "Out. Now."

Sullenly, Nick obeyed. Jeff followed him out the door and onto the sidewalk.

Isabelle rose to her feet, tears drying on her face. "I better go see how Nick is," she said, her face grim. She walked out, closing the door behind her.

"Wow, Lorne. I didn't think you had it in you," I said.

Emy was still slack-jawed.

Lorne gave her a shy look. "Sorry. I don't know what came over me."

Finally, Emy regained her voice. "Don't you ever, *ever* do that in my shop again. What the heck were you thinking? This is a *business*, not a fight club."

Lorne took a step back, a shocked expression on his face. "But..."

I hastily pushed away from the table and rose to my feet. "Gotta go," I mumbled on my way out.

"And another thing—"

I shut the door behind me. Across the street, Jeff was closing the driver's door on Nick's car. Jeff thumped on the roof, and Nick drove off. As Nick passed me, his gaze riveted on the road, I almost felt sorry for him. It must be painful to have your wife reject you in public like that.

I crossed the street. "Hey there," I said, smiling at Jeff.

Jeff was watching Nick's car drive off. He turned and smiled back.

"I know we're supposed to have our bowling lesson tonight," I said, "but with all that's happened, I understand if you want to cancel. You must be busy—"

He took me by the elbow, and, for a second, I forgot to breathe. Then I realized he was guiding me out of the way of traffic and onto the sidewalk.

"Thanks," I said weakly. "Anyway, if you want to cancel—"

"No need. Until the pathologists are done and the skeleton's been identified, there's not much we can do. Besides..." The skin at the edge of his deep brown eyes crinkled. "I'm looking forward to it."

CHAPTER EIGHTEEN

GIDEON WAS WAITING for me on Rose Cottage's front porch, in a chair tipped back to lean against the fieldstone wall. His eyes were closed. I paused with my hands on my hips, pursing my lips at him, before climbing the worn steps— taking care, as always, to avoid the rotted bits. "Why are you here?" I asked when I reached the top.

"To apologize." He got to his feet and held out his hand.

Ignoring his goodwill gesture, I turned the key in the front door and walked over the threshold, head high. My attempt at haughty indifference didn't last. The moment I walked through the door, I had second thoughts, so I ducked my head back out. "Coming?"

After I closed the door behind Gideon, I walked over to my aunt's desk and picked up her laptop. While setting it on the dining table and pulling up a chair, I said, "You were right, Gideon. We should search for Nesbitt-Cavanagh's name. I'm not convinced he had anything to do with my aunt, but it would be dumb to ignore any lead, however slim." When Gideon opened his mouth to reply, I held up a hand. "Don't agree with that, if you know what's good for you."

"Don't worry. I learned my lesson." He grinned, bouncing up and down on his right leg. "The knee's almost back to normal, though."

"You've got another one." I sat down and pulled the laptop closer.

"True." He grimaced and dropped into the chair beside me.

Flexing my fingers, I typed in the password and then *Nesbitt-Cavanagh*. We watched the spinning ball until the list of results flashed up.

Three hits. All of them emails.

The first was a six-month-old message from Edgar Nesbitt-Cavanagh to Adeline Hawkes. Gideon and I exchanged glances, and then I clicked to open it.

The subject line read, *Prudence Bannon Crypt Hoax*, but the note comprised only one sentence: *Your secret is out.*

The second email was my aunt's reply.

So is yours. Enjoy your cocoa.

It included a link to Oxford University's faculty directory. I ran my eyes down the names, starting with N. "What's the point of this? Nesbitt-Cavanagh's not even on this list." I did a double-take. "He's not on this list? How can that be?"

A quick online search revealed that Nesbitt-Cavanagh had left the university in disgrace more than a decade ago —"dismissed for academic and professional reasons." So the cranky historian didn't even achieve tenure. No wonder he wanted to redeem his reputation with a big, newsworthy discovery. *The Legend of Leafy Hollow* was his attempt to do just that.

But how did Aunt Adeline learn about the Prudence Bannon "hoax" months before the historian's ill-fated visit to the village? *Enjoy your cocoa?* What did that mean?

"Could Nesbitt-Cavanagh have alerted the Syndicate to my aunt's interest in his book?" I asked. "That's crazy, right?"

"It's not crazy at all," Gideon said, frowning at the screen.

The last item on the list of results was another email, this time from Aunt Adeline to Wilf Mullins. She sent it shortly before she disappeared. The subject line was a simple *WTH?* The message read, *Nesbitt-Cavanagh is a menace. Do something.*

I closed the lid and pushed the computer away. "What secret was Nesbitt-Cavanagh talking about?"

Gideon looked grave. "No idea."

It had been two or three weeks since I'd cut Madeline Stuart's lawn. Even though the eccentric artist never paid for my aunt's services—or mine—I thought it was time to make another visit. Aunt Adeline had considered the freebie her contribution to the arts. In return, a grateful Madeline recommended Coming Up Roses to anyone who needed their grass cut, shrubs trimmed, or perennial beds weeded. So it could be considered clever marketing. Except that my aunt never did any.

I had given Lorne the day off. He wanted time to go over

his lessons, and he'd done me a favor by doing all our work himself on the day I grilled Reverend Doctor Abbott.

But the real reason I pulled up outside Madeline's and wrestled the mower off the back of the truck was my curiosity about my aunt's correspondence with Nesbitt-Cavanagh. Madeline was a friend of my aunt's. She might be able to shed light on the mysterious email messages. At the same time, I could suss out her relationship to the cranky historian. Her reaction to the discovery of his body at the cemetery was more than that of an interested bystander.

I revved the lawnmower and started on the front lawn.

By the time I made it to the backyard, the toes of my running shoes were coated with grass clippings and my neck was slick with sweat. The commercial-size mower was hard to handle and the lines I'd sculpted in the grass were far from even. Lorne usually operated the lawnmower while I trimmed around the edges. Several times, I glanced at Madeline's back windows, where a screened sunporch faced the massive weeping willow. I saw no one. I hoped I wasn't doing this for nothing.

Then, on my final pass, Madeline opened a window and leaned out. She waved at me, smiling, her brilliant red curls bobbing. I turned off the mower.

"Come in for lemonade," she called, gesturing at the back door.

I waved back before finishing the last strip of lawn. After running the mower out to the road and wrestling it onto the truck, I wiped my face and neck with a towel. I left it draped over the lawnmower handle, then walked around to the sunporch. I could make out Madeline through the screen, standing in front of her easel. I tapped on the doorframe.

"Come on in," she called, without turning.

I opened the screen door and stepped into the sunporch.

Madeline had one hand against her face with her elbow resting in her other. She was staring at the damaged Prudence Bannon portrait and muttering under her breath.

I walked over to stare at the painting with her. Cherry custard had congealed in a circle around Prudence's enormous eye, lending it a bloodshot appearance that brought to mind a particularly vivid hangover during my university days. "That's a shame," I said. "Can you fix it?"

"I suppose." Madeline's lower lip protruded sulkily. "But what's the point? Edgar's book won't be published now."

"I thought this portrait was for the Leafy Hollow Historical Society to hang in their display? What does it matter about the book?"

She straightened up, waving her hand. "Oh, it doesn't matter. Not at all. I was just... thinking out loud. How about that lemonade?" She plucked a swath of blue cloth from a nearby chair and tossed it over the painting, then turned to the kitchen. "Sit down. I'll be right back."

While Madeline fetched the lemonade, I reviewed what I already knew about her dealings with Nesbitt-Cavanagh. At the cemetery, she was distressed by the discovery of his body. And she called him *Edgar* then, too. But was she as shocked as the rest of us? Or merely faking it?

Terry and Zander said all four of them went to Kirby's for dinner and a drink the night before the village hall presentation. According to Tee and Zee, Madeline was cozying up to the historian when they left. The next day, after CakeGate, Madeline and Nesbitt-Cavanagh drove off in her car. Did they spend the night together?

More importantly, was Madeline the last person to see Nesbitt-Cavanagh alive? I shuddered, because the last person to see a murder victim alive was the murderer, wasn't it?

"Let me know if you want more sugar."

I started as Madeline set a glass beside me, ice tinkling. A delightful tart fragrance wafted from the lemon slices floating on top.

"Thanks." I picked it up for a sip, smiling over the rim. "Delicious."

"It's the least I can do, seeing as you've cut my lawn." Madeline settled into a sagging, maroon armchair opposite and set her own glass on the paint-stained table beside it. She turned her head to gaze at the waving branches of the weeping willow, looking pensive.

"What are you going to do with the portrait?" I asked. "It would be a shame if no one could see it."

"Hmmm," she said, picking up her glass for a sip.

I tried another tack. "Zander said you and Nesbitt-Cavanagh were quite friendly. Did you know him long?"

Madeline's enormous hazel eyes widened even more. "When did he say that?"

"After the... incident at the cemetery. He said you had drinks the night before the village hall meeting, and that the next day you drove Nesbitt-Cavanagh away from the crowd outside the hall."

"Well, somebody had to. That was a disgraceful event."

"Was it surprising that people were upset? That new

theory of his was a bit startling." I recalled the historian's insistence that the Bannons' "Sweet Prudence" was a family pet.

Madeline's hand trembled as she set down her glass. "It upset me, too. I have as much stake in this community as anybody. Surely no one believes I had any idea what Edgar— what that man—was intending to write."

"Did you? Know what he was writing, I mean?"

"No!" Madeline pushed off from her armchair to pace around the room.

I clutched at my glass and leaned back as she swept past. Like the rest of Madeline's bungalow, the sunporch was crowded with colorful paintings that leaned against every wall, stacks of coffee-table books teetering on sideboards, and knickknacks jamming cabinets. Two battered tables covered with water glasses, brushes, and oil paint tubes completed the decor. With all the clutter in the room, there was no telling what she might knock over. I glanced uneasily at Prudence's portrait.

Madeline dropped back into her chair, causing the old springs to twang in protest. I winced, imagining the discomfort, but she didn't appear to notice. "He did mention... something. The night before the village hall meeting."

"What?"

She drew the tips of her fingers along the chair's cut-velvet arm but did not reply.

"Did he tell you his new theory about Prudence?"

"No!" Madeline pulled her hand back sharply from the chair and pressed it across her waist. "Not in so many words."

I must have looked puzzled because her next words tumbled out in a rush.

"You don't understand. You haven't been in Leafy Hollow long enough to know that when this village turns on someone..." Her voice trailed away as she watched the swishing branches of the willow outside.

"I think I know a little about that. I was on their hit list not long ago, remember?"

She turned to look at me. We locked glances.

"You're right, and I'm sorry," she said with a sigh. "The thing is—my reputation is all I have. I'm getting older, and the critics haven't been kind. I'm running out of time."

"Good heavens, Madeline. That is so not true." I shook my head. "Women in their forties have decades in which to make their mark," I continued blithely. "Why, Emily Carr—" I halted at the look of horror on Madeline's face. *Oops.* I tried to retract. "Not that you're anywhere *near* forty." Even to me, that sounded lame. Wincing, I bit my lip. "Besides, what does that have to do with Nesbitt-Cavanagh and his book?"

"You must promise not to tell anyone."

"Tell them what?"

"Promise."

With a shrug, I said, "Okay," and crossed my chest to make it official.

Madeline narrowed her eyes at me, almost as if she was arguing with herself. Then she puffed out a breath and leaned back. "If the villagers knew I slept with him, they might think I approved of his new direction for the work."

I stared at her, blinking rapidly, refraining from the obvious comment. *You slept with that pompous blowhard?*

183

"I see," I said evenly. "But why would that matter?"

"People like Wilf, and Zander, and Xavier have a lot to lose if Edgar's book was truly as he described it at that meeting. You saw how worried they were."

"True, but you didn't stand to profit from his new approach."

"Well..." Madeline looked as if she was going to be sick.

I waited, trying not to breathe too heavily. I could sense a confession was coming, and I didn't want to upset the delicate balance in the room. Outside, the willow branches tossed in a sudden breeze, whacking against each other.

"The truth is, my portrait"—she nodded at the cloth-covered painting on the easel—"was meant to be the cover art. The publisher paid me quite a lot of money. Not only that, but Edgar also insisted they use my drawings for the interior as well." She leaned forward in the chair, her hands gripping the upholstered arms. "You can't tell anyone, Verity."

I nodded slowly. "Did you have any of this in writing?"

"No. I trusted Edgar. What are you implying?"

I held up both hands. "Nothing. I just wondered. I mean, how did he even know about your drawings?"

Madeline's face flushed red. "We met on a dating website. He told me about the cover weeks ago, when we first got together for—" Her eyes went wide as she clasped a hand to her mouth.

I zeroed in, hoping to avoid any more details. "So your meeting in Leafy Hollow was not your first?"

Her face fell, and she shook her head. "Remember, you promised not to tell anyone."

"Madeline, he was murdered. It will come out whether I tell anyone or not. If I were you, I'd inform the police right away, before they discover it for themselves."

Her eyes grew wider. "The police can't find out. Those sites are private."

"I'm pretty sure they can get a warrant for stuff like that. And they'll find it on his computer, anyway."

"Oh, no." Madeline pressed both hands against her stomach. She looked ill. "I can't go to the police. They'll think I did it."

"Did what?"

Her words came out in a squeak. "Killed him." Her eyes filled with tears.

I got up to ply her with lemonade. "Take a drink." She accepted the glass and took a sip. "And another." After her second sip, I took her glass and returned it to the paint-stained table.

She plucked at my T-shirt before I could sit down. "Verity, you have to help me," she whispered, her voice cracking. "I think I was the last person to see Edgar alive."

My neck stiffened. When did I become the go-to person for fixing murderous predicaments? Hadn't I just promised to help clear Reverend McAllister? How many suspects were there in this case, anyway?

Gently disentangling her hand from my shirt, I twisted around, slumped back into my chair, and leaned in. "Tell me what happened."

Now that the truth was out, Madeline was anxious to relate her story. Nesbitt-Cavanagh contacted her on the dating site after noticing Leafy Hollow in her bio. He was researching local history, and they'd struck up a conversation. Before long, they were meeting every week or two in a little town in upstate New York, just across the U.S. border.

"Wait a minute. He wasn't living in England?"

She shook her head. "Hadn't been for years, as far as I know."

I nodded. After his disgrace at Oxford, Nesbitt-Cavanagh probably had trouble finding academic employment in Britain.

"Anyway," Madeline continued. "Edgar was very interested in the Prudence Bannon legend, and I showed him the sketches I'd done." She fixed me with a look of regret. "I swear, Verity, I thought he understood that Pru was a real person." She glanced at the easel. "I wouldn't have been able to do her portrait if I believed otherwise. She *spoke* to me. Pru inspired me to take a whole new direction for my work. I would never betray her."

I worked my mouth a bit before deciding to leave that one alone. We had enough to contend with, without adding ghosts into the equation. I steered the conversation back to the temporal plane.

"So what happened after the village hall meeting?"

"I dropped him off at the bed-and-breakfast and went home."

"In the afternoon? But you said you were the last person to—"

"That happened later. I called Edgar and asked to meet him. I wanted to know more about his new plan for the book. I would never do anything to hurt Leafy Hollow, Verity."

"And what happened?"

"We met at the Sleepy Time motel, on the highway."

I nodded. I knew of the establishment. The villagers called it the Sleazy Time motel. I'd heard it was popular during lunch hours, despite its lack of food service, and on prom nights. "Had you been there before?" I asked.

Her eyes widened. "Never. Anyway, I said if he was going to harm the village, I wanted no part of it. And then I left."

Even accounting for my naturally cynical view, I sensed Madeline was leaving something out of her narrative. "And that's why you think you were the last person to see him alive?"

She nodded. "He was fine when I left him, I swear. I assumed he returned to the bed-and-breakfast for the night."

"Do you have any idea why he went to the church instead?"

"None. Although..." She frowned, but then shook her head decisively. "No, none at all."

"What time did you leave?"

"Ten o'clock. Well, maybe eleven."

"Did the motel clerk see you go?"

She shrugged. "I don't know."

I could check with the clerk, assuming he or she would speak to me. It was possible they saw Nesbitt-Cavanagh leave later, by himself. If that was the case, it would clear Madeline —but not Reverend Daniel. And how did the historian leave the motel? He didn't have a car, which meant he called a taxi or someone else picked him up. But who? This case was giving me a headache. If it didn't mean letting Emy down, I'd forget about the whole thing.

"You won't tell the police any of this, will you?" she pleaded. "Please, Verity?"

Whatever my involvement, I didn't work for the police. "No. But I think you should call Jeff and tell him what you told me." I rose to go. "I'm leaving it up to you."

I made a detour onto the highway and drove past the Sleepy Time motel. I slowed down outside the building to study its brown-painted doors and flickering neon sign. On impulse, I swung into the lot. I sat in the truck cab, wondering if I should simply drive away. Going into the motel would mean talking to strangers, something I still found difficult.

My curiosity got the better of me. I switched off the engine and hopped out.

An ancient electric fan whirred on a shelf in the motel office, plastic strips flapping from its spokes. A harried-looking middle-aged woman rose from a computer as I walked in.

"Hi there," I said, leaning on the counter. "Sorry to bother you, but a friend of mine stayed here the other day and thinks she may have left something behind." I realized too late that I didn't know what room Nesbitt-Cavanagh booked. My story was doomed before I'd even begun.

The clerk didn't care. "Check the lost and found," she said wearily, gesturing at a battered cardboard box sitting on the floor near the door, before sinking back into her chair.

I walked over and bent to rifle through the contents, a little surprised that she didn't ask me what I was looking for.

My surprise ebbed as I poked through the box. Among the usual single mittens, paperbacks, and worn socks, I found an ostrich feather, a silk scarf, and a pair of handcuffs—no key. I rummaged about a bit more. My eyebrows rose. *Was that a—?* I speedily withdrew my hand. "It doesn't seem to be here," I said.

"I don't know anything about it," she said, sounding a bit defensive.

"Were you working—I mean, on duty—Friday night?"

"I go home at six. You want Emil."

"Is he coming in today?"

"Nope. It'll be the owner on tonight. Emil's off on a long weekend. He won't be back for a couple of days."

"I don't suppose you could give me his cell phone number?"

"Not allowed."

I took a business card from the holder on the counter, wrote my name and number on the back, and handed it to the clerk. "Can you ask him to call me?"

With a shrug, she swiveled her chair to pin the card to the cluttered bulletin board behind her, then turned back to the computer. At the sound of her steady tap-tap-tap on the keys, I let myself out.

So far, there wasn't a shred of evidence to back up Madeline's story.

CHAPTER NINETEEN

FORD DIDN'T WANT to be in the cemetery, but it always drew him back. Even though the graveyard was deserted, he shrank into the darker shadows under the elm where he couldn't be seen. The moon slid out from under a cloud, lighting up the yellow tape on the crypt in the center. A loose bit of tape snapped in the breeze, catching his eye.

A shape appeared, coming around the edge of the vault— a man, dragging something. The man glanced up, and moonlight caught him full in the face.

Ford recognized those features. He watched, his heart catching in his throat, as the man dragged his burden through the weeds outside the crypt.

The moonlight dwindled, and the shape vanished.

Ford rubbed both hands over his eyes. Parting the branches that hung low over the fence, he tried to peer through the gloom. The tomb stood silently before him—the hush broken only by the flapping tape.

No one was here. It wasn't real.

He sank to the ground, holding his face in his hands, as another vision assailed him. Loud words. Screaming. A small boy shouting *no* and raising a hand. Ford groaned and screwed his eyes shut. The images disappeared.

But a more recent vision intruded. He slapped his hands against both sides of his skull, over and over. *Make it stop.*

Headlights flashed as two police cars sped past the cemetery and pulled into the church driveway. He rose to his feet and watched as officers emerged from the cruisers.

Ford edged closer to the fence, peering through its slats. The young woman was inside—the one who came to see the kittens, who brought the food. He had to warn her. He placed a foot on the fence's lowest rung and, with a grunt, heaved himself up.

"What are you doing here, old man?"

Ford jerked around, his heart in his throat.

The shape was behind him now, blurry in the dim light. It wavered, growing larger and then smaller as the moon swung in and out of the clouds.

"Nothing," Ford muttered. He cowered, trying to sidle past.

The man seized his arm and yanked him back. "I said, what are you doing here?"

"Police," Ford said, motioning to the graveyard.

"Police?" The man laughed. "There's no one here except you and me. Assuming you're actually here."

"I don't know what... you mean." Ford's heart hammered like a trapped bird.

The man grabbed Ford's other arm and flung him around,

trapping both arms behind his back. "No? Take a look, old man. Tell me what you see."

The cemetery lay before them, hushed and calm under the moonlight. Leaves whispered overhead, but the crypt's loose tape lay still. The driveway was empty. No police lights lit up the gravestones.

For a moment, he couldn't breathe. "The girl..." he whispered.

"Ah. You mean Verity Hawkes."

Ford nodded. "Where is she?"

"Safe in bed, I assume. And yes, she went inside the church. But not tonight." The shape bent over, engulfing him in shadows. "Why don't you wait for her? She'll be back. Can't leave well enough alone, that one. But next time—"

With a bitter laugh, he released Ford's arms and shoved him against the fence. Ford stumbled and fell to his knees on the stony ground.

"Next time, she'll be *under* one of those gravestones."

Ford lurched to his feet and staggered down the path toward the river.

Twigs snapped as footsteps rustled through the grass behind him.

He picked up his pace.

CHAPTER TWENTY

JEFF WALKED into Leafy Strike Lanes wearing a snug black T-shirt tucked into black jeans. I jumped up from my seat at an empty lane and waved. He grinned and walked over.

"Sorry I couldn't pick you up," he said, turning the ringer on his cell phone up to maximum and placing it on the table. "But I may need to leave in a hurry, and this way you'll have your truck."

"No problem." I eyed his phone. "Have there been developments?"

He scanned the neighboring lanes, ignoring my question, before turning to me with a smile. "Come on, let's get you suited up."

I followed him up the three steps that led from the bowling lanes to the lobby, past the row of stools and the fried-grease aroma of the poutine counter, and up to the front desk.

A middle-aged woman leaned a pudgy arm over the counter to tap Jeff's hand.

"Hey there, welcome back. Missed you last week at the tournament."

"Busy at work. Heard the team did okay without me though."

She grinned. "Not as good as they would have done with you."

Jeff smiled. "You could have stepped in for me and bowled one of those perfect games of yours." He nodded at a glass-walled cabinet that displayed dozens of bowling trophies.

"Flatterer," she said, returning his grin. "But yeah, I could still take you. Anytime." She swiveled to the wall of cubby-holes behind her. Each held a pair of shoes, with names etched on plastic labeling tape. She pulled out a pair from a cubby marked J.KATSURO and plunked them on the counter. "You'll be needing your Ebonite, too." She stepped over to the far side of the counter where larger cubbies held bowling balls, most with names painted on them in script. Skulls or giant spiders were painted on some. Creepy.

Jeff's was plain black, which seemed appropriate.

She handed him the bowling ball and turned to me with a big smile. "So, hon, what can I do for you?"

"Tracy, this is Verity Hawkes," Jeff said.

"Ah, Adeline's niece," she said, smiling. "Welcome to Leafy Strike Lanes."

"Tracy and her husband Carl own Leafy Strike," Jeff said. "I'm going to stake out our lane, and then I'll be back. Tracy, Verity's joining the team. Give her your best shoes."

He strode off, bowling ball in hand and shoes slung over his shoulder by their laces.

Tracy looked at me with new interest. "The team, really? About time they filled that spot. What's your average, hon?"

"Oh, I'm not ready for competition," I said, forcing a smile, uncomfortable with the sudden attention of her laser-sharp gaze. "Jeff's just giving me lessons."

"Uh-huh." She gave me one of those *just-us-girls* smiles and leaned over the counter to whisper, "Jeff's lessons are very popular."

"It's not a date," I protested.

Tracy straightened up. "Of course not." She swiveled back to the cubbies. "Now, you're a size nine, I'm betting," she said, pulling out a pair of green leather bowling shoes. "These should fit." She placed them on the counter. Over her shoulder, I noticed another name on the cubbies. N. YATES. And beside it, I. YATES.

"Those are pretty," I said, pointing to Isabelle's pink-toned shoes. "Can I take a look?"

Tracy pulled the leather shoes from their cubby, blew dust off them, and set them on the counter. I picked up the left one. It looked brand new, but dust had worked its way into the serrated edges of its leather trim. "Thanks," I said, placing the shoe next to its mate. "Looks like they don't get much use."

Tracy replaced Isabelle's shoes in the cubby. "Nick's here all the time, but I haven't seen Isabelle in months." She contemplated the wall of shoes. "Been meaning to call and ask her to pick them up. We could use the space."

I whirled at a touch on my shoulder.

"All set?" Jeff asked. He guided me over to the lane with a hand on the small of my back, nodding at several of the regulars. I was surprised how affable he was, compared to the all-business demeanor I knew so well.

While I laced on the shoes, Jeff delivered a quick rundown on scoring. Strikes, spares, misses, and fouls. It seemed straightforward enough. I watched as he released two balls to demonstrate. Each time, he knocked down every pin with a roar and a clatter. "Now you try it," he said.

I smiled. This looked like an easy game. I'd be on that team in no time.

Flexing my fingers, I picked up a mosaic green ball from the return row, to match my shoes. I took a step forward and started my swing.

"Wait," Jeff said. "You're over the foul line."

I halted and looked down at the painted yellow line at my feet. "Oops." After taking a step back, I swung again and let go of the ball.

It hit the lane with a loud *crack* and bounded several times. On the last bounce, it sprang over the gutter and into the lane next to us. With its momentum slowed by that leap for freedom, it rolled forlornly down the polished wooden floor and into the gutter one lane over.

I darted down the gleaming wooden lane after it. "Sorry," I said to the green-shirted man standing stiffly, bowling ball in hand, at the end of that lane.

"S'okay," he said. "It happens."

I returned with the ball, biting my lip. "Sorry," I said to Jeff.

"Try it again." He smiled. "With a little less force this time."

My next three balls went into the gutter, rumbling aimlessly to the far end of the lane. For my fourth ball, I used less effort, hoping for better aim. That ball wobbled down the middle of the lane, which looked promising, until it petered out and stopped halfway. I stomped on the floor several times, determined to urge it along. Nothing happened.

"Never mind," Jeff said. "Let's go over your swing."

I retrieved the ball and returned.

After checking that my finger hold was correct, he snugged up behind me and put his hand over mine. I was close enough to smell his *Old Spice* aftershave. Without thinking, I leaned back onto his chest and closed my eyes for a second. Then I jerked forward. *Focus, Verity.*

"Now, pull your arm back like this, take three steps, and let go. Follow the arrows on the floor to keep the trajectory straight."

Jeff released my hand and took a step back. Not fast enough though.

I dropped the ball on his toes.

"Oh, gosh! I'm so sorry," I said, clapping a hand to my mouth.

Jeff was hopping on one foot, his lips pressed tightly together.

"Sorry! I thought you were holding onto it," I said. "Honestly, I thought you had it. I'm so sorry."

Out of the corner of my eye, I saw the green-shirted bowler chuckling. When he noticed me looking at him, he

RICKIE BLAIR

adopted a serious expression. "Need any help over there?" he called.

"We're fine," Jeff managed through clenched teeth. "No problem." He limped to the bench and sat down.

"Can I get you anything?" I asked weakly. "Aspirin?"

"I'm okay," he said. "Don't worry about it. But I think I'll watch from here for now."

I released several more balls with Jeff encouraging me from the sidelines. If you could call it that. Prodding might be more accurate. Or even nagging.

"You're drifting."

"Don't rush it."

"Foul!"

"Watch the arrows! Not the pins!"

"You're dropping too early."

Then, when I tried to correct that, "You're lofting."

Finally, I turned to face him with my hands on my hips. "I give up." I marched to the bench and sat down, my back stiff.

Jeff looked bemused. "That's not like you," he said, reaching over to brush a lock of hair off my cheek. "You never give up. It's one of the things I like about you."

"Really?" I leaned in, hoping he might reveal other "things."

Then I heard a cackle to my left. I looked over. The rest of the lanes had filled up while I'd been practicing. Zander and Terry were seated at the lane beside us with their feet up, shouting helpful hints at a group of bowlers in the far lane. Zander was wearing jeans and a plaid flannel shirt, but Terry wore an official-looking polo shirt with his name embroidered on the chest pocket, designer sweatpants, and monogrammed bowling shoes. He waved at me and poked Zander, who swiveled his head and waved, too. Terry said something, and then they picked up their plates and beverages and walked over to our table.

"Mind if we cut in?" Zander asked.

"Please do," I said. "Maybe you can give me some pointers."

Zander placed a greasy platter of fries, with cheese curds and gravy pooled over them, beside me. He sat down, followed by Terry.

"Hi, guys." Jeff stood and pointed a finger at me. "Sirloin burger and a beer?" he asked.

"I'd love that, thanks." I watched as he mounted the steps and strode over to the poutine counter. His limp was barely noticeable.

"Dating the investigator?" Terry whistled. "Nice work, Verity. Now you'll know everything that's going on with the case."

"It's not a date," I said. "And I know nothing."

Terry raised his eyebrows. "Sure." He glanced at Zander's plate, shaking his head. "That stuff will kill you." Terry unwrapped a sandwich I recognized as coming from Emy's vegan takeout, and then took a bite. "Have you thought any more about our request?" he asked between mouthfuls.

"No, because I can't help you. Anyway, neither of you is under suspicion. Why are you so worried?"

They exchanged glances and resumed eating. "No reason," Zander said.

Terry finished the last of his sandwich, crumpled up the

wrapper, and tossed it into the trash. "You know, Verity, you should get your own bowling ball. That way, you can have it drilled to match your fingers. An improperly fitted ball will cause you to drop it at the wrong time." He gestured at the front desk. "Tracy can hook you up."

I glanced over at the poutine counter where Jeff was in a lineup, waiting to be served.

"Maybe I'll ask her about it," I said, getting to my feet. I strolled over to the desk. Tracy was spraying deodorant into a row of rental shoes. She looked up as I approached.

"Hi there, hon. How's the lesson going?"

"Great," I replied, hoping she hadn't been monitoring my progress. "Someone suggested I should get my own ball."

Tracy put down the spray can. "That's always a good idea, if you're serious about the game. I like to watch someone play for a while before I fit them. We can set up an appointment. Pencil in a time on the clipboard over there." She pointed to the end of the counter and then picked up the first two pairs of shoes, twisted to tuck them into cubbies, and swiveled back for more.

I added my name to a list on the clipboard, using the pencil attached with a cord. As I watched Tracy work, I noticed a plastic cubby label that read, X.Roy. I pointed to it. "Does Xavier Roy, the filmmaker, bowl here?"

Tracy followed my finger and then scowled. "When he's not hitting us up for money." I looked surprised, and she winced. "Sorry. Forget I said that. Shouldn't have put it like that."

"It's forgotten." I decided to take a leap. "Are you one of his backers?"

She paused with two pairs of shoes in her hand, looking at me intently. "He told you about that?"

"Well, everybody knows, don't they?" I lied. "About the documentary?"

Tracy put the shoes down, leaned her elbows on the counter with her fingers locked, and heaved a sigh. "It sounded like such a good idea. I mean—Olympic bowling, who wouldn't be interested in that, eh? And we have some terrific players here. So, yeah, Carl and I agreed to back it."

Olympic bowling? I made a face. "I thought Xavier's documentary was on that historian, the one who was writing about the War of 1812."

Tracy's snort was derisive. "It is now. But he originally said he was filming a doc on our best players, the ones headed for the Olympic team. It was a big surprise to us, believe me, when we realized what he was really doing."

I was way out of my depth. "Ah," I stammered. "There's such a thing as Olympic bowling?"

Tracy flicked her hand and returned to the shoes. "Only a matter of time. It was a demonstration sport in '88. More popular than beach volleyball, I heard." She shoved the last pair of shoes into its cubby.

I doubted bowling would attract more viewers than beach volleyball unless it underwent a major wardrobe re-assessment. But, whatever. The important thing here was that Xavier Roy solicited funding under false pretenses.

"Does Xavier still owe his investors?"

"Yes, and some of us are considering a class action to get our money back."

I walked back to our lane, mulling this over. If Xavier Roy

owed thousands of dollars to his backers, he must have been devastated when Nesbitt-Cavanagh cut him from his documentary team. But now that the cranky historian was out of the way, Xavier could do what he liked with his Leafy Hollow footage. Maybe even sell it. And he wouldn't have to share the proceeds with Nesbitt-Cavanagh.

Jeff was tucking into his burger by the time I got back. "I didn't know what you wanted on yours, so I asked them to put everything on the side," he said, pointing at the paper plates laid out beside my burger. "Mustard, ketchup, red onions, French fries, mozzarella, hot peppers, sauerkraut, dill pickles, blue cheese, braised apple, feta, and cucumber slices."

I slathered on everything but the cucumber and replaced the top bun. After a good look at the mounded burger, I reconsidered. Carefully, I removed the onions—because you never knew. "Thanks," I said, and nearly cracked my jaw taking a bite. I chewed carefully and swallowed. "Hey, this isn't bad." I renewed my attack.

"Best burgers in town," Jeff said with a wink.

Zander, still working on his poutine, nodded vigorously. Terry merely sighed and took another swallow of his Gatorade.

We polished off the burgers and sat back, sipping our Molson Canadians—Jeff opted for a cola—listening to the clatter of rolling balls and falling pins, and watching the other bowlers.

"I would have thought you'd prefer hockey to this," I said.

Jeff pondered this a moment. "Because every red-blooded

Canadian male plays hockey?" he asked, raising his can to take a swallow.

"Something like that."

"I used to play hockey—in Ryker Fields' pickup league—but my work schedule's erratic. I get called out at all hours. I missed too many practices."

"Wouldn't that affect bowling, too?"

"Sure, but it's not as... competitive." He smiled. "Besides, you know what I like about this?" He gestured at the lanes with his cola can. "It's possible to play a perfect game. What other sport can you say that about?"

A perfect game? Why was that important? I opened my mouth to ask, but I didn't get the chance. Jeff's cell phone, lying on the table, thrummed loudly. He picked it up, glanced at the display, and rose to his feet. "I have to take this," he said, striding up the steps while holding the phone to his ear.

Zander watched Jeff walk away, his brow furrowed. "What do you think, Tee?" he asked. "Developments in the case?"

Terry nodded. "Oh, I think so, Zee."

Jeff walked back down the steps to our table, sliding his phone into his back pocket. "Sorry, Verity. I have to go."

"I'll walk you out." I gathered up my purse and hoodie and followed him to the entrance, where he pushed open the door. We stepped outside. The slight drizzle that was falling wreathed the parking lot lights and slicked the pavement.

Jeff turned to me with a shrug. "Sorry. That wasn't much of a lesson."

"It was a great lesson," I said. "I'm not much of a student."

He took a step closer. "You'll learn." He reached out to brush that same errant strand of hair from my cheek. "It's raining. You'll get wet out here."

I tentatively rested a hand on his arm. "It's only mist."

Jeff bent closer, smiling. "Are you sure? We wouldn't want you to catch cold."

"I'm fine," I whispered as he bent his head toward me.

Thrummmm. Thrummmm. Thrummmm.

Jeff jerked his head back and slid the phone from his pocket for a quick glance. "Darn," he said. "Sorry, Verity. I gotta go." He trotted to his unmarked car and slid into the front seat. With a brief wave, he headed out onto the highway, pausing at the entrance to the parking lot to flip a cherry light onto his roof. With a blast of the siren, he was gone.

I stood there a moment, watching the rain fall. With a start, I glanced down. My Leafy Strike rental footwear was standing in an inch-deep puddle. I shook my head and reentered the building. Looked like I'd just bought my first pair of bowling shoes.

Wilf looked uncomfortable. "I'm not at liberty to say."

"Did Tracy and Carl from Leafy Strikes ask you to file their class-action suit?"

Wilf grasped the Hummer's padded leather steering wheel with both hands while staring off into the distance. "I'm not at liberty to say."

"They did, didn't they?"

"Verity, I can't talk about that."

I had him on the ropes now. Time to slip in my ringer.

"Can you talk about my aunt's relationship with Nesbitt-Cavanagh? Why did she think he was a *menace*?"

Wilf let out a long breath. "Did she tell you that?"

"She may have mentioned it. Also that she asked for your help."

He slumped back on the seat. "There wasn't anything I could do. You have to understand, Verity—your aunt was a conspiracy nut."

I raised my eyebrows. "Oh?"

"Sorry. I only meant that she was always looking over her shoulder, suspicious of everyone. I thought she was paranoid."

"Until she disappeared."

He made a face. "Yeah." He pointed a finger at me. "But I don't believe that had anything to do with Nesbitt-Cavanagh." He turned the key in the ignition and revved the engine. "Anything else?"

"One thing. Can you recommend a veterinarian?"

Wilf reached into the breast pocket of his jacket and slid out a leather card case. He extracted a card and handed it over.

I took it and stepped away as the Hummer pulled out into Main Street.

———

I was surprised the veterinarian answered her own phone until reflecting that this was Leafy Hollow. Maybe there was only one phone to go around in the vet clinic.

"Hi," I said. "I'm Verity Hawkes—"

"Adeline's niece?" she asked.

I shook my head. If there was anyone in Leafy Hollow who hadn't memorized my entire family tree, I'd yet to meet them. "That's right."

"What can I do for you?"

"It's about a cat."

"It often is."

"Yes." I chuckled. "Well, this cat, I call him General Chang—"

"Star Trek?"

"Yes." I sensed I'd have to talk faster. "It seems he's fathered a litter of kittens and I was wondering—"

"If he has to make support payments?"

I paused. "Okay, now you're making fun."

"Hard not to." She giggled. "Sorry. I'm an old friend of Adeline's. Was, I mean." I heard her sigh even over the phone. "Hard to believe she's gone."

No time to get into the *she's-not-dead* debate. "Yes, it is. But this cat—"

"Right. You want to bring him in for neutering?"

"When could you do it?"

"End of the week looks good. Have him here by eight a.m. on Friday. Nothing to eat or drink after nine the night before."

I started to object, since breakfast was my favorite meal of the day, but then I realized she meant the cat.

"Are you looking after the kittens as well?" she asked.

"No, they're down by the river. With that man who—"

"Ford, yes. I know him well, although I haven't seen him for a few days. I've been meaning to check in with him. I neutered all the long-time residents down there, but I must have missed one."

Again, I took a few seconds to puzzle that out. *She means the* cats, *Verity.*

"Their mother was a recent arrival," I said.

"That would explain it. Tell me, when you were there, did Ford seem... troubled?"

I gawked at the phone before returning it to my ear. Was she serious? "Define *troubled*," I said, narrowing my eyes.

"Usually, he's calm. Never talkative, but calm. But when I saw him a few days ago, he was agitated. Talking over me, interrupting, repeating himself. Seemed odd for Ford."

"I'd never met him before, so I wouldn't know if his behavior was unusual."

"Of course. Forget I asked."

"But, since you mentioned it, he was concerned about something. He was fine when I left though."

"I'll look in on him tomorrow. And check the kittens while I'm there. See you on Friday, Verity. Remember—"

"Eight. We'll be on time."

As I clicked off the call, the General jumped onto my lap

and stretched out for a tummy rub, purring. I complied, feeling guilty.

But it wasn't just the General's upcoming snip-snip that was causing me remorse. I realized I hadn't told Jeff about Ford's ramblings. There was probably nothing to them, but it wasn't up to me to decide what was important. With a start, I realized I also didn't mention it to Daniel McAllister. He and Isabelle knew Ford better than anyone. Maybe they could make sense of his comments.

After giving the General a double helping of *Feline Fritters*, I walked outside to check on Carson's progress. A wet load of composted leaves, spruce needles, and gunk missed my head by inches and went *splat* on the driveway, spattering my running shoes with muck.

"Carson?" I asked, alarmed. "What are you doing?" I craned my neck. The wiry handyman scooped gunk out of the built-in eavestroughs and dropped it onto the ground.

He squinted down at me. "That you, Verity?"

No, I almost replied, *it's the Rose Cottage ghost*. "Yes, and I'm wondering what you're doing up there."

He held up a hand to show surprise at my question. "Clearing out the eavestroughs, a course. I can't repair 'em till they're clean." He scooped up another handful.

"Hang on," I called, stepping smartly out of the way. "Couldn't you put that stuff in a bucket or something?"

He looked puzzled. "Why?"

I glanced over my shoulder. A mounded trail of gunk and wet leaves led around the corner of the house. "No reason," I said with a sigh. I headed to the garage for a shovel.

As I worked, I talked to Carson. "Have you ever heard any local legends about buried treasure?"

"Buried treasure? Like pirates?"

"Sort of, but in Leafy Hollow. The old church—the one that existed before the current structure was built."

Carson, seeing an excuse for a history break, sat on the edge of the roof, flung his legs over the side, and lit a cigarette. He took two puffs before replying. "There was talk about that. That'd be, let's see, 1814."

I admired the way he could slide into another century as if it happened yesterday. "And what did they say?"

"Well, it was Loyalists, a course. Lots of 'em around here then. The story goes that someone hijacked gold meant for them and hid it here."

"Did this story mention the church?"

He took another drag. "Matter a fact, it did. Something about the minister at the time being a Yankee sympathizer. Load a nonsense, a course." He stubbed his cigarette out on the eavestrough and tossed it over the side of the roof, onto the piles of muck. "It was supposed to be buried under the foundation. Lotta people looked for it over the years. With metal detectors and so on. Nothing ever came of it. Why do you want to know?"

"Just curious," I said, bending to my task. An hour later, with the eavestroughs clean and Carson taking a break on the camp stool by his trailer, flask in hand, I went inside for a shower.

My phone rang as I opened the front door.

"You called me?" a male voice said when I answered.

"I don't think so. Who is this?"

"Emil Schmidt. I'm a clerk at the Sleepy Time Motel, on the highway? They told me you had a question."

"Oh, right. Sorry. I didn't realize." I swung the door shut behind me while trying to wiggle out of my muddy running shoes and hold the phone at the same time. "I did. Have a question. It was about—" How could I put it? "A friend of mine was at the motel a few nights ago, and she's convinced that she left something there, but there was no sign of it in the lost and found."

"What did she leave?"

"It was a book, a picture book about... history," I said, improvising wildly.

"I didn't take any book, if that's what you're implying."

"Sorry. I'm not implying anything. I only wondered if you remembered her. Mid-forties, blazing red hair? She would have been with an overweight middle-aged man who smoked a pipe."

"Oh, her." He puffed out a breath. "I could hardly forget her."

"What do you mean?"

"Well, they had a huge battle, didn't they? I actually got complaints from other guests. Normally, our clients are making too much noise to hear anything else if you know what I mean."

I pursed my lips. *Not going there.* "I see. What happened next?"

"She stormed out. That must have been when she forgot her book. But it wasn't in the room, so her date must have picked it up when he left."

"When was that?"

"I don't know exactly. But the room was empty the next morning. So he must have left sometime in the night. And there was no book."

"Thanks. You've been very helpful."

"You're welcome. Hey, what was the name of this book? In case it turns up."

"Ah..." I scanned my stack of self-help volumes for inspiration. "*Top Ten Wars*," I said and hung up.

CHAPTER TWENTY-TWO

I DROVE down the highway to Kirby's, the steak restaurant that served as an alternative watering hole for Leafy Hollow residents. Forget Reverend Daniel's predicament. I had to clear my own name. There was embarrassing film footage out there, and I intended to track it down and destroy it. It was self-serving of me—and hardly important considering there was a murder to solve—but it would take my mind off the larger picture for a while.

While pulling into the lot, I noticed a sleek yellow Corvette parked by the entrance. My date had arrived. As I walked past the sports car on my way into the restaurant, I peeked through the windows, taking care not to breathe on it and set off some hair-trigger car alarm. The Corvette was far from new, but it still seemed an expensive choice for someone who couldn't pay his bills.

The early dinner crowd already jammed the booths, and more people waited in the lobby for the next available tables.

Even the bar, just inside the entrance, had only a single empty stool—right beside the man I'd come here to see, and whose hand was splayed over its leather cover. Xavier Roy looked around and spotted me by the door.

"Verity!" he called. "I saved you a seat."

I worked my way through the lobby, squeezing through the crowd, trying not to feel anxious about the press of strangers. "Excuse me. Sorry."

With a deep sigh of relief, I slid onto the empty stool and beckoned to the bartender, a dark-haired man whose starched white apron stretched across his middle-aged spread. I turned to my companion. The drink in his hand looked as if it had lawn clippings in it.

"Mojito?" Xavier asked, raising his glass. He was still wearing his black baseball cap with *Director of Photography* embroidered in white.

"No, thanks. Molson Canadian, please. Draft," I said to the bartender. He nodded and plunked a paper coaster down in front of me before turning to fill my glass.

I sipped my beer while scanning the booths and tables in the restaurant behind us. I recognized hockey players from the triple rink up the road by their shower-damp hair. And suburban couples on date night, the women's makeup a little overdone, their familial responsibilities tucked up at home with a babysitter.

But no one I knew.

"I was surprised to get your call," Xavier said. "Does this mean you've reconsidered my request for an interview?"

I set my beer on the counter. I wanted to be sober for this discussion. "No, sorry. And honestly, Xavier, I can't add much to your documentary. I'm a stranger in Leafy Hollow. I've been here six weeks. I don't know anything about Prudence Bannon. So there's no way I could comment on that debate."

"Not a problem," he said, puffing out a breath while flicking his hand. "My film has moved beyond the constraints of historical whatever."

I narrowed my eyes. This wasn't good news.

"What do you mean by *beyond*?"

"It's a true-crime doc now, isn't it? Two brutal murders, within days of each other, in a sleepy Canadian village? With a minister as the prime suspect in both? It's gripping." Waggling his eyebrows, he leaned in to whisper, "A major studio has expressed interest."

I sat back in astonishment. Obviously, the first victim in Xavier's "true-crime doc" was the truth. I tried for a casual tone for my next comment, after picking up my glass, taking a sip, and replacing it carefully on its coaster "A major studio? Your backers will be happy to hear that."

Xavier's mojito paused halfway to his lips. "What do you know about my backers?"

"Nothing. I'm only assuming. I mean, it's expensive to make a film, isn't it? Even a documentary? And now that Nesbitt-Cavanagh's no longer in the picture"—okay, bad pun —"you'll need someone else to foot the bill. Of course..." I shrugged, beamed a beatific smile, and picked up my glass again. "I don't know anything about the movie business. Not like you. You're an expert."

"It's highly competitive. You have no idea."

I nodded sympathetically. "I bet it's all about who you know."

"You got it. And until I lucked into this little venture..." His voice trailed off as he contemplated the green mass in the bottom of his empty glass. I nodded at the bartender, who brought over another mojito. Xavier switched glasses without comment and sipped the fresh drink, staring at the bottles on the wall without seeing them. He was miles away. "It's always been my dream to make a feature documentary," he said, still without looking at me. "I was so close with Edgar's film." He shrugged before lifting his new glass. "But this is way better." He took a sip and put the glass down. "That footage at the church is pure gold."

My leg cramped up from the effort it took not to kick him.

"I've been meaning to ask," I said. "How did you know the silent alarm at the church was triggered?"

He chuckled. "What true-crime documentarian doesn't have a police radio at home? I heard about it on the scanner, and I hightailed it out there. In time to film you and your friends." He chuckled again.

"You listen to a police scanner when you're at home? Surely there's not that much happening in Leafy Hollow."

"Not usually. But things in this village have been hopping recently." He winked. "I attribute it to your arrival, Verity. You bring good luck."

Because I attract murder and mayhem? That was one way of looking at it. Ill wind and all that. I cleared my throat.

"Listen, Xavier, thank you for not giving that video to the television station. The one of us leaving the church, I mean. Emy, Lorne, and I were grateful that it wasn't on the news."

His eyes widened. "Why would I? That clip will be the centerpiece of the film's trailer. If I sold it, there might be copyright issues."

My stomach sank. "The trailer?"

"Yeah. Remember that studio I mentioned? They have incredible trailers. They hire a company in L.A. that does nothing but trailers. All the big blockbusters. It's the key to the whole marketing campaign."

Marketing campaign? If my stomach got any lower, it would drag me off my stool. "And this trailer will be available... where?"

He waved a hand. "Everywhere. YouTube, iTunes, network ads, theaters, you name it. It will be great."

"Yeah. Great. So, this studio deal is a sure thing? You've signed it?"

Replacing his glass on the bar, Xavier pursed his lips. "Not exactly. Like I said, they've expressed interest. That's the first move. These big guys"—he shook his head knowingly—"can't just rush into things. They have shareholders, you know. Bean counters and so forth."

My mind raced. Nesbitt-Cavanagh's death brought Xavier's dream a big step closer. Close enough to justify murder?

Xavier was on a roll. "I've already started interviewing potential crew members, and I'm stockpiling props and stuff at my apartment."

"Why do you need props for a documentary?"

"Obviously, we have to recreate some things. Like weapons. I found some great guns online."

"Guns? Nobody's been shot."

"Not yet, but you never know. And it adds realism." He paused, mulling this over, and then raised his glass to his lips. "So, the interview. How about I swing by Rose Cottage tomorrow and we can do it?"

"I don't think so. Sorry."

He shrugged, drained the rest of his glass, and rose to go. "I'm not giving up. Your viewpoint is even more important since you found the second body. I'm sure you'll change your mind." He grinned at me. "I can make you famous, Verity." Then he winked. "Think about it." And he was gone.

Well, that tore it. The last thing I wanted to be was famous. Surrounded by crowds and fans—and cameras. Without knowing it, Xavier had doomed our deal. No way would I step in front of his camera again. Not voluntarily.

I lifted my glass, intending to finish my beer and go home, when I felt a hand on my arm. I looked up—directly into the handsome, tanned face and cool blue eyes of Ryker Fields.

He raised an eyebrow. "Is this seat taken?" Without waiting for a reply, Ryker slid onto Xavier's vacated stool. He nodded at the bartender and said, with a thumb indicating my beer, "Another for the lady, and the same for me, Andy." Ryker leaned back and raised his eyebrows. "Drinking alone?" he asked. "I'm surprised."

"Don't be. My drinking companion only left a moment ago. And I was about to do the same. But thanks for the beer." I smiled at him. Ryker and I got off on the wrong foot when I first arrived in Leafy Hollow, but he had proved to be a good friend since. And I had no complaints about sharing a public drink with a six-foot-two blond Adonis and his impressive pecs. *Take that, Leafy Hollow doubters.*

"How's the biz?" he asked.

"Doing well, thanks to those clients you steered my way. Coming Up Roses may actually deserve its name before long."

He nodded and hunched over his beer with his elbows on the bar, not looking at me. "You know—we haven't had that dinner you promised me." He picked up his beer and took a swig, still not catching my eye.

"I know, and I'm sorry. It's been a busy time." I swiveled my stool to face the restaurant. Ryker had been more than decent, giving my aunt's landscaping business a life-saving infusion of clientele, helping me with lawnmower lessons, and even advising me on equipment rentals. Why was I so reluctant to have dinner with him?

Was I wary of starting over? Or simply not interested in Ryker?

I puffed air through my mouth, but as I turned to swivel back to the bar, something caught my eye. I squinted at the far wall to where a man and woman were having dinner in a booth. The woman was blonde, petite, and pretty. Her tube dress clung to every curve and her earrings sparkled under an overhead spot—fancy dress for Kirby's, but ideal for a date. But the man—my heart thumped. The man was Jeff Katsuro, law enforcement nemesis, bowling guru, and darkly brooding hunk. Out for dinner with a woman who was clearly not his sister. If he even had a sister.

Well, I had my answer—I wasn't interested in Ryker. I'd spotted the handsome landscaper with plenty of female hangers-on, but never experienced a gut-wrenching response like this. Pivoting on the stool, I clapped both palms on the bar and took a deep breath, conscious that my mouth was hanging open. Beside me, Ryker was still talking.

"...and the food's good here. Why not have dinner right now?" With his elbows on the bar, he gave me a slow, sexy grin over his beer glass.

Normally when that happened, I wondered how many women Ryker had tried to stun with his alluring smile over the past twenty-four hours. Was I the first today? Or the fiftieth? But as I sat there slack-jawed, I realized that I was, in fact, hungry, that Kirby's steaks were legendary, and... and—to hell with Jeff Katsuro.

"Good idea," I said.

"Really?" Ryker put down his glass. His smile was genuine this time.

Andy, who was wiping down the counter with a bar towel, looked up. I hadn't noticed he was listening. "A table just opened up on the far side." He gestured to the hostess, who walked our way. She transferred our beers to a tray and led us to a booth near the back.

As we swept through the restaurant, I couldn't help but glance at Jeff, who was oblivious to our presence. He leaned over the table as his date slid a fully loaded dessert spoon topped with whipped cream into his mouth. Jeff chewed, swallowed, and smiled at her.

What was the matter with the men in this village? Couldn't they feed themselves?

I flopped into our booth, surreptitiously unfastening the top two buttons of my silk shirt. What? It was hot in that restaurant. Believe me, with my lack of cleavage, it made little difference. And would make even less difference once that footage of Xavier's hit the web. Whatever shred of mystery I had left would vanish forever. I accepted a menu from the waitress and turned the pages with interest, pretending not to notice as Jeff and his date rose to their feet. They headed for the exit, Jeff's hand guiding her lower back. Probably worried she'd pitch over in those four-inch heels.

Kirby's corn-fed beef was excellent—juicy and grilled to perfection—as were the crispy frites and the arugula-pear salad. I had a strawberry margarita, and Ryker drank two more beers. We talked about our landscaping jobs—I'd been having trouble starting my aunt's heavy gas trimmer, and Ryker advised a lighter model—and our conversation eventually got around to the churchyard murders. I expounded on my list of suspects.

"The thing is, somebody's lying," I said, scooping up a mouthful of my triple-chocolate brownie sundae.

"Why do you care?" he asked, trying to spear my last brownie piece with his fork.

I evaded his attack by getting there first with my spoon. "The question is, why don't you? There's a murderer running around Leafy Hollow. Aren't you worried?"

Ryker retired his fork, admitting defeat. "Sometimes it's best to leave criminal matters to the police. Anyway, isn't Reverend McAllister the current suspect?"

"Daniel's not a killer," I said, trying to look more confident than I felt. "I promised Emy I would help prove it." I set down my spoon and pushed the empty plate to one side. "You know a little about police procedures, don't you?"

Ryker looked startled. "Me?"

I'd forgotten I wasn't supposed to know about Ryker's

juvenile record. According to Emy, his brush with the law as a teenager was not public knowledge. She also claimed Ryker covered for a girlfriend and didn't commit those break-and-enters himself, but that he "doesn't talk about it."

"Sorry," I said. "My mistake."

He sat back in his chair, tapping the side of his beer glass with a wry smile. "Nah, you're right. Figure you'll hear about it, eventually. When I was in high school, I spent time in juvie."

"Which doesn't matter now."

His expression turned serious. "No, but hear me out. I learned a lot at that detention facility, and the most important thing was that people are not always what they seem. There are some dangerous people in this little hamlet, Verity. You'd be surprised." He shoved his glass aside so he could lean over the table and fix me with a solemn stare. "Just be careful, okay? Don't get in over your head."

Before I could react, he leaned back and gestured to the waitress for the bill. When she walked over, Ryker pulled a credit card from his wallet.

"We're splitting it," I said, reaching for my purse.

He waved me away and handed his card to the waitress. "We will." His sexy smile was back. "Next time."

CHAPTER TWENTY-THREE

THE FACES around the harvest table in the manse's kitchen were pinched and shocked. We now knew who was buried under the church floor, and it seemed impossible. I hadn't known him, but the other three people sitting at Reverend Daniel's table remembered him as a vibrant young man, full of promise. Now their last memory of Charlie Inglis was a skeletal hand.

Jeff had driven Isabelle back from the morgue, and he leaned against the doorframe, watching intently.

"Why didn't anybody look for Charlie?" I asked. "I mean, after he disappeared. Didn't his parents wonder where he was?"

"He didn't have parents," Isabelle said. "Charlie was a foster kid and was moved around a lot. His foster parents at the time assumed he'd gone out West, like he said in his note."

I looked up at Jeff.

"We'll talk to them," he said, "as soon as Child Services locates them. They're not in the system anymore."

Emy leaned into the group with a frown. "I don't understand how you can bury a body in the church basement without somebody noticing it."

I knew the answer to that. "Because of the flooding. Reverend Doctor Abbott said it was so damp in the storage room that summer that they kept the paint and equipment in the Bannon family vault. If the ground was that wet, signs of digging would have disappeared fairly quickly. Especially once the killer put the patio stones back and tamped everything down."

"I'll need Minister Abbott's contact information," Jeff said, pulling out his notepad. He made a brief notation and returned it to his pocket.

"Charlie didn't suffer, did he?" Isabelle blurted.

Jeff frowned. "I don't think that's—"

"Is it true he was strangled?"

Jeff pushed away from the wall. "Where did you—"

Emy fingered her throat. "Can they tell that from a skeleton?" she asked.

"There's a bone in the neck that gets broken," I said.

"The hyoid," McAllister muttered. We all turned to look at him.

"Enough speculation," Jeff said. "How about we leave that to the professionals?"

I decided to change the subject. "Isabelle, what did his note say?"

"That he was going out West," she said, "and that we were... finished. I thought..." She looked at the rest of us with a bitter smile. "I had no idea." Isabelle hung her head. For once, she wasn't crying. I assumed her tear ducts had finally run dry.

Emy reached over and rubbed Isabelle's back. "Nobody did, Izzy. Even I knew Charlie walked out on you. That's what everybody thought. You couldn't have known."

"Are they certain it's him?" I asked. "How did they identify the body?"

Jeff cleared his throat, and I jumped. I'd almost forgotten he was there.

"The pathologist sent X-rays of the teeth to Charlie's dentist in Strathcona. And there was also a signet ring that Charlie always wore," he said.

I hadn't noticed jewelry on the skeletal hand we uncovered in the basement. But then again, ours was a hasty inspection.

"I saw the ring at the morgue," Isabelle said. "It was the one I gave him."

"You didn't have to look at his body, did you?" Emy asked.

Isabelle shook her head. "No. His ring and bits of clothing were spread out on a table, and I looked at those."

That was surprising. "Charlie's clothes were intact after ten years in the ground?"

"Parts of his jeans and his hoodie. There were specks of blue paint on them, so that was another clue."

Emy and I exchanged glances.

"Was the paint... fresh?" I asked, trying to sound casual.

"Oh, no. The examiner said it was as old as the rest of the remains," Isabelle said.

I breathed a sigh of relief.

Isabelle continued. "So, of course, I knew..." She glanced at Reverend Daniel.

He nodded, not looking up from his minute examination of the table's polished pine planks.

I looked from one to the other. "Knew what?"

At that, the minister raised his head. "Charlie Inglis was one of the volunteers painting the church basement that summer. I asked him more than once to be careful. He splashed a lot of paint around—"

"He certainly did," Isabelle broke in, smiling. "He was determined to get those walls covered as fast as possible so he could get a reference from Reverend Abbott and find another job." She studied the table with a faraway look on her face. "I thought that meant..." Her smile faded, and she straightened up. "I thought he'd get a job here, not out West. When he told me what he wanted to do, we had a terrible fight over it." Her face crumpled, and Emy squeezed her hand. Isabelle swallowed hard before continuing. "He wanted us to elope. I said that was ridiculous. I said—"

Emy tapped Isabelle's hand. "You can tell us later," she said, glancing at Jeff.

He was watching Isabelle intently, which worried me. Surely he didn't suspect she had something to do with Charlie's death?

"But you didn't have this argument in the storage room," I pointed out. "So, obviously—"

"Oh, no, we did," Isabelle said. "I went down there to find out when he would be finished. We were going to

227

Kirby's, to celebrate the end of the painting. But that's where he told me about... his plan. And that's where we argued."

Emy shot me a warning glance. She placed a hand on Isabelle's arm. "We can talk about this later, Izzy. I don't think now is the time—"

"Anyway, it's not a big deal," I said, trying to lighten the mood. "Teenagers argue all the time. It doesn't mean anything. You probably made up and—"

Isabelle wasn't listening. She rubbed the back of her hand across her mouth. "The last words I said to him—"

"Stop, Izzy." Emy moved closer and murmured, "Let's go home."

Isabelle stared at her, wild-eyed. "I said I wanted to kill him," she whispered. "And then I... threw something."

The air in the kitchen turned to ice. We froze in place, not daring to look at each other.

Jeff's words cut through the chill. "What did you throw, Isabelle?"

"She doesn't have to answer that," Emy blurted. "Don't say anything else, Izzy. I mean it." Emy glared at me. "Stay out of it, Verity."

I slumped back against my chair, shocked. *Stay out of it?* I was only in it because Emy asked for my help. Now I was the villain?

I glanced surreptitiously at Jeff, who was studying Isabelle's face. Did he imagine that she killed Charlie in a rage, possibly by accident? And that Reverend Daniel helped cover up the evidence? Was it possible Isabelle herself was now a murder suspect? From the worried glances Emy cast at the minister, I could tell she'd come to the same troubling conclusion.

I dropped the rest of my Key lime tart on my plate, uneaten.

"I have to get back to the station, but we'll talk again," Jeff said. He swept his gaze over our group before turning to the front hall.

"I'll let you out," I said, and then walked him to the door. It wasn't locked, and he was perfectly able to open it himself, but I wanted a private word.

"Jeff," I said, once we were out of earshot of the group. "You don't suspect Isabelle, do you? I'm certain she wouldn't have harmed Charlie."

He looked at me a long moment before saying, "I can't discuss the case with you, Verity."

I watched him walk back to his cruiser. There was another question I was itching to ask, but "Who's the blonde?" seemed inappropriate, given the circumstances.

When I returned to the kitchen, Emy had a pot of tea steeping on the counter. She opened the white cardboard box she'd brought with her and arranged more goodies on a tray. Isabelle shook her head, as did Daniel. I glumly contemplated my half-eaten pastry. If Emy's fabulous Key lime tarts were going begging, things were even worse than I thought.

I put an elbow on the table, leaned my head on my hand, and pushed the tart around on my plate. Emy stood to pick up the teapot and poured us each a cup. No one drank it.

"All this time, I thought it was me," Isabelle said, breaking the silence. "I thought I wasn't good enough."

I looked up with interest. "What are you talking about?"

"Charlie. You didn't know him, Verity, but he was the most popular boy at school. He was on the football team and the basketball team. At school assemblies and plays, Charlie and his friends would sit in the back, cracking jokes. Whenever a group gathered in the hall, you knew Charlie would be at the center of it."

While you watched from the sidelines? I wondered.

"Isabelle, did you keep that note he sent you?" I asked.

"I don't think we should talk about the case anymore," Emy said in a curt tone. I glanced at her, surprised. If I didn't know better, I'd say she was angry—at me. But what had I done?

Emy poured a cup of tea for herself and sat at the table, opposite me.

Isabelle didn't seem to notice the renewed frost in the air. "I have it with me. I took it to the station this morning in case the police wanted to see it."

I held out my hand. "Can I take a look at it?" Emy kicked me under the table. I hastily added, "Unless you'd rather not, of course."

"It's not a secret." Isabelle shrugged. "Everybody saw it at the time." She pulled her purse closer and undid the clasp. Isabelle pulled out a daytimer, flipped to the back, and slid two folded pages out of a pocket on the inside cover. She slid them across the table.

I picked up the flimsy pages and unfolded them, taking care not to tear them along their well-worn creases, and read:

Dear Izzy,

You must make a decision. You've had enough time.

Here's what I think. I will go out West to Alberta and get a real job. Those oil jobs pay really good. I could get work as a drilling rig floor hand or a pipeline worker or even a cat operator. The time has come to—

I switched to the second page.

—make a clean break. I can't stay in Leafy Hollow any longer.

Remember, I will always love you.

Charlie

I put the pages on the table, with my fingers holding them down, and stared at them. I wasn't sure what I'd been hoping for. A secret message, perhaps? But there was no secret code here. Nothing more than a heartfelt letter from a lovesick teenager. I frowned at the scrawled note and looked up at Isabelle. "Can I have a copy of this?"

"Sure." She held out her hand for the pages. "There's a printer in Daniel's office that makes copies. I'll get one for you." She took the pages down the hall.

Emy looked puzzled. "What are you going to do with those?"

"I'm not sure. But there's something..." I knew what puzzled me about Charlie's letter, but it seemed ridiculous. And I had no way to follow it up, anyway. "It's probably nothing," I said.

Truthfully, with my concerns over Aunt Adeline, Gideon's strange disclosures, and worries about my upcoming test for the shadowy Control, I had conspiracy fever on the brain.

CHAPTER TWENTY-FOUR

GIDEON STARED at the sharp edges of the faces on the monitors in Rose Cottage's basement. "How do you know Adeline's note is not genuine?" he asked.

The cubist faces dissolved, and then reformed into the exact image of Adeline Hawkes as a young woman. Gideon started at the resemblance. How well he remembered that face.

A synthetic version of Adeline's voice said, "You know better than to ask." The images swirled, regaining their sharp edges. Control's mechanical tone resumed. "How do we know anything, if it comes to that?"

"By trusting operatives in the field."

"You haven't been in the field in a long time. An age."

"Some things never change."

"Some things do. You're decrepit." A chuckle echoed against the metal walls.

"Very funny." Gideon heaved a sigh. "So now that you

have a Twitter account and an Instagram page, feet on the ground mean nothing?"

"Social media is the new frontier. That pretty-boy prime minister of ours wouldn't have been elected without it. Although his opponent did have the cat-video crowd on his side."

"Balderdash."

"Perfect example. Who says *balderdash* anymore?"

"I do."

"Look, Gideon, we'd like to help you, but you don't represent the new generation." The faces wavered and re-arranged themselves again. "We don't need you."

Gideon pursed his lips, watching as the faces bopped in time to unseen music. He sat back and crossed his arms before replying in flat tones.

"Cocoa farms. Ivory Coast. Laura Secord." He paused. "Are you detecting a pattern?"

The faces stopped bopping and zeroed in on Gideon's nose. "Tell us what you know."

"Why should I?"

"To safeguard the national interest. You took an oath."

"That was an age ago. As you said."

"Are you refusing to help?"

"You said you didn't need my help. That I'm—how did you put it—*decrepit*."

"What do you want?"

"You know what I want."

"One moment, please." The faces dissolved into concentric swirls. Snippets of Bieber's "Somebody to Love" filled the interval until the cubist faces reappeared.

"Your request is approved. As of today, you are a temporary agent. Tell us what you know."

"I believe the Syndicate funded Nesbitt-Cavanagh's book project to enhance the Prudence Bannon legend and slander the memory of Laura Secord."

The images' expressions turned black. "A true Canadian heroine. Bastards."

"There's more," Gideon said. "The Syndicate is buying up land in Ivory Coast. It wants to corner the cocoa market and form a competing global chocolate conglomerate. Candy production across the country would be affected."

"So the book was a smokescreen, funded by the Syndicate?"

"Until Nesbitt-Cavanagh turned on them. His new version of events would have restored Laura Secord's reputation as the official Canadian female celebrity of the War of 1812."

The face looked thoughtful. "She's big on Wikipedia."

"Chocolate production is a three-billion-dollar industry in this country."

"We're well aware of that. Can you prove any of this, or is it simply conjecture?"

"Adeline has the evidence, I'm positive."

"Adeline is dead. No one misses her more than us—"

"Unlikely."

"—but that doesn't change the fact."

"Her niece doesn't believe she's dead, and neither do I."

"Then you're both delusional." The faces turned as if listening to someone off-screen. They swiveled their glances back to Gideon, head tilted. "Your temporary status has been revoked. Sorry, but this is eyes only." The faces dissolved into multicolored swirls again before fading into black.

"No! That's not our—"

Locks thudded into place, one after the other. Gideon took a hasty step back a second before the metal walls closed in front of him with a *whoosh* and a teeth-rattling clang. The wall wavered and reformed into storage shelves—stocked with two-fours of Molson Canadian and warehouse-sized boxes of toilet paper and maple syrup. Gideon thrust a hand into the hologram and watched as his fingers disappeared.

Nothing happened. With a curse, he pulled out his hand.

Control could revoke his status. But he didn't have to go along with it.

CHAPTER TWENTY-FIVE

DROPS OF RAIN were falling as I left the manse, so I returned to Rose Cottage to pick up a windbreaker before joining Lorne at our first job of the day. I turned the key in the lock before I saw the note pinned to the door.

"*Ave.*"

I recognized that scrawl, and the code word. More clandestine nonsense from my neighbor.

Sighing, I walked out to the driveway and my aunt's ruined Ford Escort. After glancing around to make sure no one was watching, I bent over and ran my hand along the underside of the right front fender—the spot where my aunt and Gideon had exchanged messages over the years, as he told me when I first arrived in Leafy Hollow. My fingers bumped up against a smooth metal object.

I pulled out the key holder and slid it open to remove the note inside. It read:

Message from A. On intercept mission. Don't try to follow. G.

I closed my eyes, shaking my head in frustration. Why couldn't Gideon simply tell me in person instead of leaving this ridiculously cryptic, secret-agent note? A message from my aunt could be the evidence I needed to reopen the police investigation into her disappearance.

I thrust the note and key holder into my pocket and strode up the lane to Gideon's bungalow. My pounding on the front door got no response. I twisted the handle. It turned, and the door swung open. I stepped inside.

The first time I'd been in Gideon's home, I was startled to discover a life-sized replica of the Starship Enterprise's command deck in his living room. The mock-up was old hat by now, but it still made me smile when I saw it, despite my current irritation. Gideon told me that Adeline's critiques were instrumental in his design of the controls. I pictured him and my aunt sitting in the swivel leather chairs, sipping their version of Romulan ale.

Today, the wall screen was blank. Even the beeping LCD panels were quiet and dark. Dust motes shimmered in the light from the open front door as I walked through the rooms, calling Gideon's name.

Eventually, I slumped into the captain's chair, staring at the blank screen while idly fingering the control keys on the chair's arms.

Darn it. Why hadn't Gideon let me come along? I was tired of being the outsider. Given how easily I'd messed up his knee, he must know I could look after myself. *Intercept mission*, my fanny. Adeline was my aunt, not his. And both of them were old enough to retire and join a knitting circle. I was certain my aunt had no idea what to do with a knitting needle—other than to use it as a weapon—but she'd earned the right to kick back. Maybe watch a few *Star Trek* episodes in Gideon's living room. Eat a few donuts. Let herself go.

Instead, I was the one sidelined, cutting lawns and pruning shrubs until the two of them decided to let me in. Meanwhile, as far as Leafy Hollow knew, Adeline Hawkes was dead and gone. My misgivings about her accident had been dismissed as wishful thinking by the public—and by her lawyer, Wilf Mullins. Jeff's higher-ups in the police force had refused to reopen my aunt's case without new evidence. A recent note penned by my supposedly deceased relative was "new evidence." But Gideon was withholding that note.

Vicious circle, indeed.

I got to my feet and shuffled to the door, closing it behind me. I couldn't lock it since I had no key. Maybe that was why Gideon left it unlocked in the first place, so I could get in. Or perhaps he'd been forced to leave in a hurry.

That thought didn't calm my nerves any. What was he protecting me from? And what if he didn't come back?

Still, this was Leafy Hollow. Lots of residents didn't lock their doors. Which made it even weirder that Rose Cottage had so many deadbolts. Especially the two on the front door that seemed to have a mind of their own. One time, they'd both snapped shut when I was certain I hadn't touched them. Although I'd been tired and distracted that day, so perhaps I imagined it.

Speaking of Rose Cottage—I had time before joining

Lorne to check on the hologram. Perhaps with Gideon gone, Control would reappear.

Back in my aunt's kitchen, I wrenched open the sticky basement door and started down the narrow stairs, stepping carefully on their worn wooden treads. At the bottom, I toggled the antique wall switch and a lone bulb flickered overhead. The rough-hewn ceiling beams cast ragged shadows on the unfinished stone walls of the musty room.

I walked over to the shelving units along one side of the space.

"Control," I yelled. "Verity Hawkes here. Show yourself."

No answer.

"Please?"

Still no answer. I tried again. Same response.

I turned to head back up the stairs.

"Verity Hawkes?" a synthetic voice boomed behind me.

I whirled around, heart racing. "I'm here." I stepped closer, thrusting my hand into the nearest case of Molson Canadian. "I'm here. Verity Hawkes."

"One moment," the voice boomed.

I held my breath, waiting for the hologram to dissolve and reveal the control booth and keypad.

The voice spoke again. "You must stand by, Verity."

I stood there so long that my outstretched hand trembled and ached, but I heard nothing else. "Stand by for *what*?" I asked repeatedly. "Are you there?"

No reply. I waited. The air-conditioning unit chugged on and off. The lightbulb overhead flickered and winked out, leaving me in darkness.

Stand by? Was that it? I cursed under my breath.

Lowering my hand, I turned to the stairway, trying to make out the shape of its bottom tread in the nearly black room.

That was when I heard footsteps in the cottage above me.

My heart leaped into my throat and I froze, remembering I didn't lock the front door. *Now* the deadbolts decided to live up to their name?

"Verity?" a woman's voice called. "Where the heck are you?"

I puffed out a breath as my shoulders relaxed. Emy must have found the door open and walked in.

"Here," I yelled as I started up the stairs, abandoning my vigil for now. The basement door opened. Light from the kitchen framed Emy's dark curls.

"What are you doing down there? Talking to that thing again? It's a waste of time."

I gained the top step and closed the basement door. "That's your opinion. What are you doing here, anyway? Who's looking after the bakery?"

"No one. I shut down for the day." Emy crossed her arms and leaned against the kitchen counter, scowling. "You haven't heard, I take it?"

"Heard what? Would you like some lemonade?" I swiveled to open the fridge, and then slid out the pitcher. I'd made a new batch, with fresh lemons, only that morning.

Emy ignored my offer. "Izzy and Daniel have been arrested."

"What?" I released my hold on the pitcher's handle and closed the fridge door, feeling dizzy. "When? And... for what?"

"Today. They've been charged in Charlie's murder. That fancy forensic pathologist from Strathcona concluded he was whacked on the back of the head with a shovel." Emy hadn't moved from her position at the counter, nor unfurled her arms. She pressed her lips together, glaring at me. I'd never seen my normally sunny friend smolder like this.

"It must be a mistake," I said. "They're bound to let Isabelle go, at least."

"The mistake was trusting you to help her. My cousin is in jail, Verity."

The words *it's all your fault* were unspoken, but definitely hanging in the air. I felt a piercing pain in my chest. "Emy, what did I—"

"Why did you have to go on and on about that terrible argument Izzy said she had with Charlie? Couldn't you have changed the subject? She wouldn't have brought it up at all if you hadn't pressed her on it. And now the police..." Unfolding her arms, Emy pushed off from the counter and paced the kitchen floor. "She said she wanted to *kill* him. In front of Jeff. And now the police know how she felt." Halting, she swiveled around and pointed a finger at me. "Because of you."

This was spectacularly unfair, and I tried to say so. "We all say things when we're angry, but everyone knows we don't mean them. Anyway, I'm sure the police—" I intended to point out that anything Isabelle told them couldn't be used against her until she was officially cautioned—which I knew from *Mystery Theater*.

Emy did not give me the chance.

"No more of your theories about the police, please," she

snapped. "You promised to help Izzy. And now look what's happened."

Technically, I'd promised to help Reverend Daniel, but I didn't think this was the time to mention that. "I'm sorry if I did the wrong thing, but I think you're overreacting."

Oops.

Emy glared at me. "Overreacting? Really? Because my cousin is in jail, charged with murder?" Her voice had risen almost to a squeak.

I had never seen her angry like this. I wouldn't have thought it possible.

I took care to keep my voice calm. "If the police really suspect Isabelle of murder—and I find that hard to believe—they must have more evidence than her shaky recollection of a possible argument a decade ago."

Emy's petite body slumped and her face fell. "They do. Someone told them Izzy and Daniel were having an affair."

"Who told them that?"

"I don't know. I'm not even sure it's true, to be honest. Although, she does have a thing for him. Whether it's mutual or not..." She shrugged.

I scrunched up my face. "Wait a minute—how does that make sense? They couldn't have been involved back then. McAllister had only just arrived in Leafy Hollow, and Charlie and Isabelle were still an item."

Besides, I had trouble picturing mousy Isabelle as a likely candidate to spark a love triangle. Maybe she'd been more adventurous as a teenager.

"I guess the theory is that Daniel was drawn to her even then and agreed to help her with Charlie's body," Emy said.

"That's ridiculous. No one could believe that. A teenage girl and a minister ten years her senior? No way."

Emy straightened up. "Yet, the two of them are at the police station this very moment." She walked out of the kitchen, toward the front door.

"Wait," I called after her. "Do the police have a copy of Charlie's note?"

Emy whirled, her eyes wide. "No, and don't you dare give it to them."

"I wasn't going to. But I think that note—"

"Haven't you done enough damage?" Pressing her lips together, Emy pivoted on her heel and walked out the front door, leaving it open.

I stared after her, feeling strangely chilled, until I heard her Fiat rev up and then crunch across Rose Cottage's gravel driveway. Looking out the window, I watched as she drove up the road and out of sight. I walked over to the door and closed it with numb fingers. How was any of this my fault? Why hadn't she waited to hear my theory about Charlie's note? I stood in the tiny foyer, wracked with regret, feeling sick that I may have jeopardized my friendship with Emy.

I should stay out of the murder inquiry. None of the people involved were relatives. Or even close friends if Emy's behavior was genuine. I had no reason to probe a decade-old murder that had nothing to do with me.

And now Gideon was gone as well, leaving me with nothing to investigate. Or anyone to care that I had nothing to investigate. The walls were closing in, the vein in the side of my neck was throbbing, and my chest was tightening.

I retrieved a beer from the fridge—it was still morning but

at least I'd had breakfast—and screwed off the top. Then I scooped up my copy of *Organize Your Way to a Better Life* from the coffee table and retreated to the bedroom. After pushing off my running shoes with the toes of either foot and placing the beer on the side table, I tossed back the coverlet on my aunt's four-poster and tucked myself under it, settling the book on my stomach. I leafed through the pages.

Chapter 1: Setting Your Priorities.

"Mrack."

I peered over the edge of the mattress. General Chang leaped up, purring, and curled up on the pillow next to me. I scratched his head. "Looks like it's just you and me, fella."

The General stretched out to his full length before curling up again, still purring. Cats were solitary creatures, which was smart. They wouldn't need us at all if it weren't for the can opener problem.

With a sigh, I snugged down in the coverlet and started to read.

"Empty your cupboards, keep what's important, toss the rest..."

CHAPTER TWENTY-SIX

I AWOKE with a start and reached for the ringing phone, intending to shut it off, but winced when I saw Lorne's name on the display. I had fallen asleep over the pages of *Organize Your Way* without calling him. He probably wondered where I was. With misgivings, I clicked on the *Answer* button.

"Hi, Lorne. I'm sick today. Can you carry on without me?"

"Sure." He paused. "Is it anything serious?"

"No, a touch of flu, I guess. Thanks." Without waiting for his response, I hung up, set my phone to *Do Not Disturb,* and burrowed back under the coverlet. I considered rising to get another beer from the kitchen, but it seemed too much work. I glanced at the pillow beside me. The General had disappeared, no doubt on a search-and-destroy mission. Or his approximation of one. When the one-eyed tomcat moved in, we agreed that I would supply the *Feline Fritters* as long as he took care of the mice—but so far, the vermin were winning. I sighed, reflecting that the General and Gideon were both outdated warriors past their prime. And that led to thoughts of the darkly handsome Jeff Katsuro, who was definitely *not* past his prime—followed by the recollection of his blonde date. I sighed again. Maybe outdated warriors were the best I could do. And that thought made me feel guilty, since Matthew had been dead barely two years and what kind of person did that make me, to even be *thinking* about dating other men?

I flipped the sheet over my head, vowing never to emerge.

I lay there, my eyes closed against the light that filtered through the cotton fabric, until other thoughts intruded. About the note Charlie left for Isabelle when he disappeared. I'd puzzled over it at the manse, but now I realized the problem. It was the number of pages. Why two? Charlie could easily have written the entire note on one page. Something about the stationery nagged at me, too. It could be an important clue to his killer. And that killer wasn't Isabelle, I was convinced.

So what? asked my annoying inner voice. *You're not involved in the investigation anymore, remember? So far, you've only made things worse. Even Emy thinks you're a screwup.* My breath caught in my chest. The thought that my new friend now hated me was even worse than my guilt over Matthew. Emy was an important part of my new life. Did I screw that up, too?

The note? asked that annoying voice in my head.

"Leave me alone," I muttered.

Get up. It's important.

I decided to check that one little thing, and then return to bed. I rolled over, extricated myself from the rumpled sheet and coverlet, and touched my stocking feet to the floor. After one last swig from the almost-empty beer bottle, I got up, yanked my T-shirt down over my belly button, and shuffled into the living room.

The photocopied pages were on my aunt's desk, where I'd tossed them after returning from our gathering at the manse.

I sat in the chair and lined up the pages side by side on the desktop.

The first page ended, *The time has come to—*

And the second one began—*make a clean break.* Nothing suspicious there. I flipped them over. Thanks to Isabelle's double-sided printing, I saw that the note was written on the back of two flyers for a church bake sale. The date of the sale corresponded with the weekend after Charlie disappeared. He had torn the 9x11 flyers in half, flipped them over, and written his note on the back of the two top halves.

But what happened to the bottom halves of the flyers? Why didn't he use those?

The explanation hit me like a brick.

Charlie's second page was actually his *third*. There must have been another page to his note, written on the bottom half of the first flyer.

But when did that page disappear—after Isabelle received it, which made no sense unless she was lying, or before? Isabelle said the note was found under her parent's front door. Everyone assumed Charlie left it there. But what if he didn't? What if his killer delivered the note after discarding its middle page?

Which only led to more questions: What did that page say? And why did his killer take it?

I slumped in my chair, tapping my fingers on the papers. Even if my theory was right, it had no connection to the murder of Nesbitt-Cavanagh. The historian lied about his position at Oxford University, and where he was living, but there was no evidence to suggest he'd been in Leafy Hollow— or even Canada—twelve years ago.

But he could have stumbled upon Charlie's body during his search for buried treasure in the church basement.

And been killed because of it.

If my hypothesis was correct, the same person murdered both Charlie Inglis and Edgar Nesbitt-Cavanagh. Further, that person must be a resident of Leafy Hollow who knew Charlie well, lived here twelve years ago, and lived here today.

Which brought my investigation full circle, back to Isabelle and Reverend Daniel.

My hand trembled as I pushed the pages away. Emy was right. I should keep my nose out of this.

After getting another beer from the fridge, I went back to bed.

Hammering on the front door woke me several hours later. I considered not answering, but it didn't sound as if my visitor intended to leave. Or stop hammering.

I tossed back the covers, squinting at the mid-afternoon

sunlight that streamed through the window. "Hang on," I called as I shuffled out to the foyer and threw open the door.

Lorne stood before me, frowning slightly. "Verity? Are you okay?"

Yawning, I rubbed a hand over my face, glancing sidelong in the foyer mirror and recoiling at the sight of my bed head. "I'm fine," I said, patting futilely at my cowlick. "You didn't need to check up on me."

"I know, but Emy insisted."

Emy poked her head out from behind Lorne with a sheepish grin. "Sorry, but it's not like you to ignore your phone."

I stared at her. "I thought you were mad at me."

"I was, for a while. But I realized I was being unfair."

"Hmmm," I said, at an uncharacteristic loss for words.

"You were only trying to help," she continued.

"Hmmm," I said again. "So you're not... angry?"

"No, of course not."

"I can leave," Lorne said, "if you two want to... talk."

He looked embarrassed. With a start, I recalled peeling off my yoga pants before getting into bed the second time. Yikes. Tugging on the bottom of my T-shirt with one hand, I crossed my legs and yanked an afghan off the armchair with my other. Lorne looked at the floor while I wrapped the fabric around myself. The feathery crocheted pattern didn't offer much coverage.

"Come on in, both of you. I'll get dressed." I gestured at the living room as I wobbled into the bedroom—trying not to trip over the afghan's trailing edges—to find my pants. And brush my hair. And—I sniffed with my hand over my mouth —my teeth.

When I returned, Emy and Lorne were bent over the photocopies of Charlie's note on my aunt's desk.

Emy looked up. "Why were you so interested in this, Verity? Do you think it's important?"

I reached between them to flip over the two pages. Pointing at the bake sale flyer on the backs, I explained my theory.

"But how could a missing page have any bearing on Charlie's death?" Emy asked.

"It's just a theory. I could be wrong. Maybe Charlie spilled coffee or paint on the other half of the flyer and that's why he didn't use it."

"I guess." Emy shook her head, sighing, as she examined the note. "I'm worried about Izzy. It was bad enough when she was concerned about Daniel, but now she blames herself for Charlie's death. She feels guilty about their argument. The one you went on... about." She bit her lip. "Sorry."

"Forget it. But why should Isabelle blame herself? She didn't kill Charlie, did she?" I attempted a chuckle, but it was lukewarm.

Emy pressed her lips together before replying. "Of course she didn't kill him. What a notion."

"Sorry."

Emy ran a finger across the photocopied note. "Izzy thinks if she hadn't quarreled with Charlie, he wouldn't have left that same night. And if he hadn't done that, he might not have run into his killer."

"I'm not sure that makes sense."

Emy shrugged. "She's not thinking straight, I'm afraid. And neither was I. I'm sorry I was so hard on you."

"Forget it. And frankly, you were right. I haven't been much help, and I may have made things worse."

"That's not true. Izzy appreciates your help, and I do, too." She paused. "I could use a cup of tea. Mind if I make some?"

"Be my guest."

Emy disappeared into the kitchen, and I plunked down on the sofa, next to Lorne. He was checking baseball scores on his phone. "How are the Jays doing?" I asked.

"Their pitching could use some work."

I nodded. "I'm glad to see the two of you back together."

Lorne looked up with a startled expression. "What do you mean?"

"Emy? And you? Together?"

His cheeks flushed red, and he shook his head. "That's ridiculous. We're only friends."

I leaned in to whisper, "You'll never be anything else if you don't get off your butt and tell her how you feel."

His eyes widened until he resembled a cornered deer.

I sighed. "Well, at least she's forgiven you for popping Nick one in the bakery. That's something, I guess."

"What's something?" Emy asked, returning with a tray loaded with a teapot, mugs, and the last of the Oreos I'd been hoarding.

I grimaced. Emy didn't know I sometimes ate store-bought biscuits. "These were my aunt's," I blurted.

She smiled without looking up from pouring the tea. "Milk and sugar?"

"Just milk for me." I plucked an Oreo from the plate and took a bite. "It's amazing these aren't stale."

After the cookies were eaten, and our mugs drained, I straightened up and puffed out a breath. "Gideon's gone."

"Gone? Gone where?"

"I don't know. I think it has something to do with my aunt's disappearance. And Control."

"Verity—" Emy started.

I held up a hand. "I know. You think it's dangerous. I'm not trying to restart that debate. I only want to tell you—both of you—that I'm done investigating. From now on, I'm a landscaper and that's it. No more poking around. I'm sorry about Isabelle, but you were right, Emy. I should stay out of it."

They regarded me silently before exchanging a sidelong glance.

I pretended not to notice, pouring myself another mug before settling back on the sofa. "In fact, if anybody else gets killed in Leafy Hollow, I don't even want to hear about it." I sipped my tea.

"Well, that's too bad," Emy said, "because we've got an idea."

I flashed her a warning look over the rim of my mug. "Didn't you hear me? Not interested."

"This has to do with Zander and Terry," Lorne offered. "Not Isabelle."

I narrowed my eyes, and then put down my tea, intrigued despite my misgivings. "What about them?"

"We think they told Wilf Mullins the legend about buried treasure. And that Wilf told Nesbitt-Cavanagh."

"That's interesting," I agreed, "but hardly evidence of guilt on anybody's part."

"No, but it helps clear Reverend Daniel, don't you think?" Emy asked.

"How?"

"Daniel told the police he discovered Nesbitt-Cavanagh checking the floor in the basement storage room, looking for buried gold. Daniel said he argued with him, took the shovel away, and escorted him out of the church."

"So?"

"Well, the police don't believe him. They think Daniel killed Nesbitt-Cavanagh to keep him from digging up Charlie's body and revealing Isabelle's secret. And that the treasure was a cover story he dreamed up to account for the shovel."

"We were in the basement. Digging. There was no sign of buried gold."

"But don't you see? We don't need the actual gold. If we can prove that Nesbitt-Cavanagh knew about the legend, then Daniel's story makes sense. It also explains why Daniel's fingerprints were on the shovel. It had nothing to do with a buried body. Daniel was only trying to get the historian out of there before he damaged something. He said he left Nesbitt-Cavanagh outside, in the cemetery, by the crypt."

"Yes," I said slowly. "But how would we prove that?"

"Up until now, there's been no reason to believe Nesbitt-Cavanagh knew anything about supposed Loyalist gold buried under the old church. But Wilf can prove that he did."

"Will Wilf back this up?"

Emy beamed. "He will if you ask him."

"Me? Why does he care what I think?"

"Wilf's always blustering on about something, but he wants to do the right thing, I know he does," Emy said.

"And you're a client," Lorne said, "so you have reason to drop by and talk to him. Then you can maneuver the conversation around to the gold."

"So you see—you can't give up investigating just yet," Emy said.

"But I thought you said—"

Emy flapped her hands. "Never mind about that. I was wrong."

I slumped back against the sofa. "No."

"What do you mean, *no*?"

"I mean, I'm not getting involved. I'm serious. Leave it to the police, Emy. Let them ferret out Wilf's story. Or better yet, tell them outright. But leave me out of it."

"But what about Izzy? You promised—"

"Absolutely not. Don't you remember telling me what a screwup I was?"

"I never said—"

"Whatever words you used, you were angry. And I don't blame you. Let's not go there again. Let's leave this to the professionals."

"Verity, I said I was sorry."

"Don't you get it? We're *friends*, Emy." I mumbled my next sentences while staring down at the empty mug in my hand. "I spent the past two years holed up in my apartment, afraid to go out. If it wasn't for you..." I gripped the mug in both hands, willing my heartbeat to slow. "I don't want to risk our friendship with my half-baked theories about a decade-old murder."

The room fell silent. General Chang swiveled his gaze from one to the other of us, his hind end twitching. He strolled off into the kitchen, the rigid set of his upright tail broadcasting feline disdain. *Humans. So dumb.*

Emy reached across the coffee table to place her hand on my arm. "It's not that easy to get rid of me, bestie."

I smiled, conscious that my lower lip was trembling.

Lorne cleared his throat, obviously embarrassed by all the girl talk. I took pity on him.

"Okay," I said, setting the mug down. "What do you want me to do?"

Emy opened her mouth, but I raised my hand to stop her. "But first," I said, "you must do something for me."

"What?"

"Write me cheat notes on *Anna Karenina*? I'll never finish it before your mom's book club meeting next week."

Emy flicked a hand and grinned. "No worries. I've got the DVD in the car. I knew you'd need it." She turned to Lorne. "Can you get it? It's on the backseat."

As soon as Lorne shut the door, Emy turned to me. "Remember telling me about that blonde you saw at Kirby's?"

I drew a quick breath. "You mean Jeff's date?"

She nodded. "I asked Mom to check the usual sources."

"And?"

"You won't like it."

My shoulders slumped. "Go ahead."

"She's a nurse from the hospital in Strathcona. Emergency room. They met when Jeff escorted a prisoner into the ER for treatment."

"Is it serious?"

"Maybe."

I plucked at my T-shirt, removing invisible flecks of lint. "Well, good for him. He deserves to be happy."

"You're not disappointed?" Emy asked.

I glanced at Matthew's photo on the mantel. "I'm not interested in Jeff. Or anyone else," I said.

And I almost believed it.

Emy opened her mouth to say something, but then Lorne walked back in.

"It's a library copy," Emy said, reaching for the DVD in Lorne's hand. "You can drop it off in the overnight returns box when you're done. That way, Mom won't see you." She winked at me, handing over the disc.

I planned to wear a hoodie anyway, in case of cameras. Whatever Gideon was up to, it couldn't be any more covert than misleading the founder of Leafy Hollow's Original Book Club.

CHAPTER TWENTY-SEVEN

GUFFAWS WERE ISSUING FROM WILF MULLINS' inner office when I pushed open the door and entered the carpeted waiting room. Blue carpet, blue walls, blue upholstered chairs. I waved a hand at the elegantly dressed woman with gray hair who rose to greet me. "Don't get up, Harriet," I said, pointing at the door to Wilf's sanctum. "I just need a quick word. Is he in?"

Another roar of laughter floated through the yellow pine door with *Wilfred Mullins* engraved on it in gold leaf. Obviously, the diminutive lawyer was in. I was only trying to be polite.

Harriet—a woman of few words, in marked contrast to her employer—nodded and dropped gracefully back into her seat. I took that as permission to enter.

I opened Wilf's office door and found him perched on his executive chair, talking on the phone. When he saw me, Wilf flicked off the speaker.

"Verity," he said, still shaking with laughter. "Great to see you." He wiped tears from his face and picked up the handset. "*Ciao* for now, Nellie. Let's catch up later."

I dropped into the armchair opposite his desk. The glamorous Nellie Quintero was my real estate agent—or would be, if I ever sold Rose Cottage. She'd been a valuable source of information on the local market. "Tell Nellie 'hi' for me," I said.

Wilf replaced the handset and slapped both hands on his desk. "Too late. I'll tell her next time."

That wouldn't be long, I figured. Wilf and Nellie were BFFs.

"What can I do for you, Verity?"

"I've been researching village history," I lied, "and I read about a legend that says Loyalists buried Yankee gold under the old church—the one that predates the current building."

"Uh-huh," Wilf said, narrowing his eyes, hands flat on the desk before him. "And?"

"Well, I'm trying to confirm it and wondered if you'd ever heard of it. Since you're the village's only lawyer, I figured you'd be up on local lore."

Wilf tapped his fingers on the desk, looking away. "Well, there is a legend that says something like that. But it's probably nonsense." He pressed his lips together, looking uneasy—an unusual pose for the sociable attorney. I sensed there was more.

"Did you ever talk to Zander or Terry about it?"

Wilf looked at me intently. "I may have. But it's nonsense, like I said."

"Humor me, please. I'm reading my aunt's journal, and

I'd like to make a few annotations." I adopted a look of despair. "It brings her closer, somehow." I tried to eke out a tear, but since I was no actress, my expression more likely suggested gastric distress.

"I am sorry about your aunt, Verity. What was I thinking?" Wilf nodded, his face a perfect example of faux-anguish.

Neither of us would win any Oscars—or whatever we had in Canada.

"Yes, there is a legend like that," he said. "Zander and Terry came across it while they were working on the installation for the museum."

"Installation?"

"On Prudence Bannon. It's quite something. You should get them to show it to you. Audio-visual, role play, everything. There's an app, too."

I wrinkled my brow at the mention of role play, but decided not to question it for now. "I'll check it out. So, the legend?"

"According to this tale, Yankee sympathizers stole gold from a Loyalist shipment, intending to smuggle it across the border to the rebels. But something prevented them, and they buried it in the church's dirt floor for safekeeping. I guess they were killed before they could dig it up."

I nodded. "The current church includes part of the original structure."

"That's what I understand. A crawl space or a storage shed or something. I haven't been down there myself," he added hastily.

"Did Nesbitt-Cavanagh know about this story of buried Loyalist gold?"

Wilf's face darkened. "That man—" He spit out the words. "If he wasn't already a murder victim..."

I raised my eyebrows. Wilf smoothed a hand over his face, relaxing his scowl. "Sorry. It's not like me to speak ill of the dead. But that historian was a very trying individual. I did my best to help him, you know."

"In what way?"

"Well, the story you speak of, for one. I told him about it."

"But my aunt said he wasn't trustworthy."

"I never really believed that. I figured your aunt was—"

"Paranoid." I frowned.

"Yes, but there was another reason. I thought if I told Nesbitt-Cavanagh that British gold was buried in the village church, waiting to be discovered, he would postpone the exhumation. Academic kudos are all well and good, but nothing beats cash. So I called him."

"When?"

Wilf flinched. "The night he was killed."

"Do you think that's why he went into the basement?"

Wilf stiffened, giving me a suspicious glance. "It's not my fault."

I tried to smooth over my blunder. "Of course not. How were you to know he would do that?"

He nodded sagely. "Indeed."

"Speaking of the exhumation—is it going ahead?" I asked.

"I've spoken with the authorities and we've reached a consensus." Wilf tented his fingers on the desk, looking solemn. "Since the person who brought the original application is... no longer with us, we can forget the whole thing."

Yet another benefit to the historian's murder, I thought.

"You know, that story about the gold..."

"Yes?"

"It might help clear Reverend Daniel if you told the police the buried treasure tale. It supports his version of events."

Wilf rubbed the back of his neck, wincing. "I've been thinking the same thing."

We resumed our Oscar-caliber expressions of despondency.

"Okay," he said. "I'll call Jeff and tell him. I'm not guaranteeing it will help. Though... there is the bail money to think of." He looked thoughtful, and then brightened. "Yes, it's a good idea all round. Especially now that the waterpark is back on."

"I didn't know it was off."

"Wait till you see this." Wilf switched on his Ferrari-styled electric executive chair. He descended slowly, smiling the entire time, until his chin was on a level with the desk. When the motor stopped, Wilf hopped off and walked over to the far wall. A roll-down chart was attached to the wood paneling, two meters off the floor. He jumped for the dangling cord, missed it, and jumped again. He missed again. I got up to help him, but the third time, he snared the cord's tassel. Puffing, he pulled down the map and turned to face me with a triumphant air.

The map portrayed the area west of the village, judging by a tiny road sign that read, *Leafy Hollow, two kilometers*, with an arrow pointing to the far edge. Wide-eyed occupants of miniature cars waved multicolored flags, headed for The Prudence Bannon Waterpark in the middle of the map.

Something else caught my eye, and I walked over to take a closer look. "Prudence Bannon" was crossed out with black marker, and "Cameron Wurst" penciled above. The sign now read, "The Cameron Wurst Waterpark."

"Wilf?" I asked, my forehead wrinkled. "Isn't Cameron Wurst the name of that sausage factory in Strathcona?"

"Yes, isn't it great?" He gazed proudly at the map. "The waterpark must move with the times. Business can't stand still."

"I guess not." I studied the edges. Someone had drawn sausages with smiling faces and tiny, dancing legs.

"So when the Cameron Wurst people contacted me with a generous proposal to change the name," Wilf said, "I was more than happy to listen." He leaned in with a conspiratorial air. "Let's face it—a good sausage will always be more popular than a history lesson." With a frown, he noticed a flattened fly stuck to a prancing sausage. Wilf pulled a handkerchief from his pocket to scrape it off.

Then he stepped back, admiring his new project. "All in all, I think we've had a lucky escape."

I walked the few doors that separated Wilf's Main Street office from Emy's bakery, to let her know how I'd fared.

"That's good news," Emy said, nodding over her teacup at the small table in the back. "Don't you think so?"

"I'm not sure how much weight the police will place on it. But it can't hurt."

She nodded. "Have you thought any more about Charlie's note?"

"A bit, but my theory's pretty thin. There's no reason to think there was another page."

A bell tinkled over the door of Emy's adjoining vegan-takeout business. "Back in a jiff."

"Should I hide these bacon scones?" I asked with a grin.

She mock-slapped my arm before rising to her feet and walking through the connecting door. "What can I get you?" she asked her customer.

A low hum of conversation followed, but I paid no attention. I was thinking about Isabelle and her note from Charlie. I had made light of it to Emy, but I was convinced there must be another page. Charlie's note was crude and messy—not the work of someone who cared about being tidy. He was a lovesick teenager in a hurry to leave town who'd written his goodbye on the back of a church flyer. So he must have been in the church—maybe even the basement—when he wrote it.

Did his killer surprise him there?

If so, Charlie couldn't have delivered the note. But who did, then?

I was thinking in circles. Either Charlie's killer slipped that note in the Gagnons' letter slot—or Isabelle was lying. Maybe when they quarreled in the church basement, Charlie died—perhaps from hitting his head, which could look like a shovel attack.

Or from being struck by a heavy, thrown object.

Then Reverend Daniel helped Isabelle clean up the

scene, fearful perhaps that he'd be implicated in a murder during his first weeks on the job. Or, if it was an accident, to shield a young, innocent woman from a lengthy inquiry and possible trial.

The bell tinkled again as the door to the vegan takeout closed. When Emy returned, she placed a palm against the side of our cooled teapot, and then took it behind the counter to refill with hot water.

"Emy, do you have a picture of your cousin taken ten or twelve years ago? Back about the time Charlie disappeared?"

She turned on the burner under the kettle, wrinkling her forehead. "I might have one upstairs. Wait here and I'll look." She slipped two pistachio macarons on a plate and deposited it in front of me before darting up the staircase that led to her apartment.

I munched on the cream-filled meringue-and-almond biscuits while I waited. Investigating was hard work.

I'd barely finished the first cookie before Emy clattered back down the stairs.

She handed me an old photograph. "Mom's never trusted digital copies, so she printed this for me. It was taken at Izzy and Charlie's prom. That's them"—she pointed to a young couple dancing in the photo—"in the middle of the floor. This was only days before he disappeared."

"That's Isabelle?" I asked, staring at the pretty girl with the flowing hair, tiny waist, and apple-cheeked face who smiled back at the camera.

"Yep. You can see why Mom wants to do that makeover. Izzy used to be a knockout."

"What happened?"

"I guess she was broken up about Charlie leaving her. She's been depressed ever since, according to Mom."

Depressed—I thought—*or guilty?* I puffed out a breath. Where did *that* thought come from? "Was she sad before that?"

"No. Izzy was quite lively. In fact, she was a bit of a troublemaker. I remember her getting into it with one of the other cheerleaders—a fight over their lockers or something. Izzy ripped up the other girl's uniform right in front of her."

"That sounds mean."

Emy shrugged.

I stared at the radiant young woman in the picture for a long minute before recognizing another face. I pointed to a young man standing next to the dance floor. "Is that Nick?"

Emy took the photo from me to hold it under the light. "Yes. I never noticed him there before. You've got a good eye." She handed back the picture.

I studied it again before placing it on the table and sliding it to Emy's side. It was unsettling, years later, to see the young couple's happiness and know Charlie would be dead within days of that prom.

"Did anybody see who put Charlie's note in the Gagnons' mail slot?"

"No. It was at night, so they were asleep. Isabelle said her mother gave it to her when she came down for breakfast."

"Was it sealed?"

She nodded.

"Charlie used a church flyer for notepaper, but sealed it in an envelope?"

"I guess. Is that important?"

"Probably not. Although it means Isabelle was the first person to read the note."

So there was no way to tell if the killer, or Isabelle herself, hid the third page. Of course, my theory about a mysterious third page was impossible to prove. I was being ridiculous.

"Everyone assumed that Charlie walked out to the highway after dropping off the note, and then hitched a ride into Strathcona," Emy continued. "A lot of truckers go by at night. He could have taken a Greyhound bus from the Strathcona station. Or even hitched the whole way to Alberta, on the Trans-Canada Highway." She sighed. "But everyone was wrong. He was here all along." She picked up the photo and rose to tuck it behind the counter.

The bell tinkled over the front door, and we looked up. Nick Yates stood in the entrance, glaring at us. He walked in, letting the door bang shut behind him.

"Izzy's not here, Nick," Emy said.

"Don't you think I know that?" He scowled, which made his ruddy face even redder. "She's at the police station. I thought you might know when they're letting her come home." He lowered his head, scratching absently at his arm through the sleeve of his cotton shirt, and issued a heavy sigh. "I've been there all day. They won't tell me anything."

I felt a pang of sympathy. Just because Isabelle wanted nothing to do with her husband was no reason for us to be unfriendly. And besides, I had a few questions for Nick. "Why don't you sit down?" I asked. "We're having tea."

He shot Emy a sidelong glance.

She pressed her lips together and then jerked her head at

the empty chair. I noticed she didn't rush behind the counter to get him a cup, though.

Nick pulled out the wooden chair and slumped into it, his generous rear spreading over the edges. He stared at the table, worrying a patch of eczema on his neck.

The kettle boiled and shut off with a *click*. Emy ignored it.

"I'm sorry I started a fight the last time I was here," Nick said. "I shouldn't have." He looked up at Emy with a sheepish expression.

She uncrossed her arms and puffed out a breath. "You were upset. No harm done." She walked behind the counter to refill the teapot.

"I just want to get Isabelle out of jail," Nick said.

Emy replaced the filled teapot on its trivet in the center of the table. "We all do."

I pursed my lips. "There is one person who might know what happened that night. It's a long shot, but..."

Nick shot me a look. "Who?"

Emy nodded, pulling out the third chair and sitting down. "You're thinking of Ford, aren't you? Izzy mentioned that he might know something."

Nick frowned. "Are you talking about that crazy guy who lives in a tent by the river?"

"He's not crazy, Nick," Emy snapped.

He issued a derisive snort. "It's not exactly sane to poop in the woods like a bear."

I cleared my throat, mostly to deter Emy from whacking Nick with the last of the bacon scones. True, he was infuriating, but that was no reason to waste pastries.

"Regardless of where Ford... lives," I said, "he was at the cemetery the night Nesbitt-Cavanagh was killed."

"Then he's the one who killed him," Nick said with a scowl. "A guy like that shouldn't be walking around free. It's not safe for the rest of us."

Emy put both hands on her hips. "What do you suggest we do with him? Lock him up?"

Nick shrugged. "He'd get three squares that way, wouldn't he?"

Emy sighed heavily and turned away.

Sensing that detente had ended, I hurried on to my next question. I pulled Ford's crumpled map from my purse and smoothed it out on the table. "This is where Ford was standing." I pointed to his scrawled X behind the cemetery's back fence. "I checked online—there was a full moon that night. If Ford was there at the right time, he would have seen the killer drag Nesbitt-Cavanagh's body into the crypt."

Nick drew my hand-drawn map toward him, frowning as he studied it. "I'm telling you, the guy's crazy." He pushed the map away. "This is some wild vision of his. It doesn't mean anything."

"Maybe, but I'm going down there to ask him again. Maybe this time, he'll be calmer and able to remember more. If Ford identifies Nesbitt-Cavanagh's attacker, we can clear Daniel."

"You can't go alone, Verity," Emy said. "It's already dark. Why don't you call Jeff? He'll go with you."

I recalled Ford's distress at my mention of the police. "I don't think so. Ford might panic, and then we'd be no further ahead. I'll drive there and talk to him myself. It's on my way home. It's not a big deal."

Emy crossed her arms, blowing air through her lips. "Nick, you have to go with her." He sputtered, and she gave him a level look. "Verity shouldn't go alone, and you're the only one available. I can't close early because I'm packing up a trial dessert order for Fritz's restaurant." She turned to face me. "I'll cancel if I have to. And I will if you're investigating on your own."

"No need. I'm fine."

"You're not fine, Verity. There's a killer on the loose. None of us should be alone." She glanced at the front door.

"What about you, then?"

"Fritz will be here shortly. Besides, I'm in the middle of Leafy Hollow—not alone in the woods."

"Ford's campsite isn't in the woods," I said. "It's in the Pine Hill Conservation Area. People go through there all the time."

Emy looked unconvinced. "Not at night."

"Why don't I text Jeff to meet us here? Nick and I will be back by the time he arrives, and then I can tell him about Ford." I shrugged. "Assuming he says anything useful. Don't hold your breath."

I pulled out my phone and tapped in a message.

Meet me at Emy's. I know who the killer is.

To be honest, I wasn't one hundred percent sure, but I had a pretty good idea. And a visit to Ford would confirm my suspicion. So, I hit send.

"Done." I replaced the cell phone in my pocket.

Emy cocked her head at Nick. "Well?" For such a tiny person, she had a commanding presence.

"Okay," he said, raising both hands. "I'll go with Verity. But don't expect me to talk to that lunatic."

"You don't have to," I said. "You can stay in the truck. Let's go."

CHAPTER TWENTY-EIGHT

AS THE TRUCK crested the hill outside the village, the headlights flashed on the words carved into a wooden sign by the road. *Pine Hill Conservation Area. Closed at sunset. Please vacate park before dark.* Ignoring the instructions, I swerved onto the unpaved road that led to the river.

Nick braced one arm on the dashboard as we bumped over the winding, uneven track.

"That rain last week really brought out the potholes," I said in what I hoped was a friendly tone.

Nick, staring straight ahead, didn't reply.

"This won't take long," I added.

He grunted.

Trees and shrubs crowded the narrow road on either side, and branches met overhead, obscuring the night sky and making our route into a tunnel. I wondered how Ford would react to our nighttime visit. I didn't want to frighten him.

If only there was another way to shake loose the truth.

I glanced at my cell phone, lying on the padded console between the front seats. Still no text from Jeff. Where was he? He must have gotten my message by now.

We hit another pothole, and Nick muttered under his breath, furiously scratching his neck. I shot him an uneasy glance.

"It's good of you to be concerned about Isabelle," I said. "To look after her, I mean. I'm sure she appreciates it."

He gave me a puzzled look. "It's my job to look after her." A rabbit darted out of the trees and across the pavement in front of us. I braked, and it disappeared into the foliage on the other side. I stepped on the accelerator.

"And if anybody tries to harm her," Nick added with a scowl, "I'll look after them, too."

When we reached the end of the road, I pulled into the empty parking lot and turned off the engine. With the headlights out, there was nothing to illuminate our surroundings except the overhead cabin light in the truck. I switched it off.

"Hand me that flashlight in the glove box, please, Nick."

He opened the hinged door, fished out the light, and handed it over.

I flicked it on and climbed down from the cab. "Wait here. I don't want you to spook Ford."

"No worries." He snorted in disgust. "I'm staying here, where I can't step on anything gross."

Seriously? I rolled my eyes, shut the truck door, and walked around to the back to get the plastic bag of cat food I'd stashed there earlier in the day. It was wedged into a box of garden tools, and I climbed into the truck bed to retrieve it. With the bag hanging from my arm, I walked to the opening in the fence that marked the path to the river. I shone the flashlight beam on the trail. Other than a few fallen leaves, the footpath was deserted.

I started down the track. The flashlight kept me from tripping on rocks and tree roots, but it was almost useless for lighting the way ahead, since branches and undergrowth hemmed in the trail on either side.

Sticks snapped behind me. I froze, holding my breath. It was probably one of the feral cats, hunting mice. When nothing happened, I resumed my course along the path to the river.

After a dozen steps, I heard shuffling. And more snapping. I halted again, this time fearing that the Leafy Hollow coyote I'd narrowly escaped during a previous investigation had returned to claim his prize.

That was silly. Everybody knew coyotes rarely attacked humans. Even if they did, a predator on the prowl wouldn't be snapping twigs like gunshots. I imagined furry canine feet trotting down the path behind me. You wouldn't hear a coyote at all, until...

I stopped to listen, my chest tight.

Nothing. I shook off my nerves and started back down the path, picking up my pace as the trail got steeper where it neared the river.

In the moonlight, I could see Ford crouched by his fire pit, poking at the ashes. Judging by the can of lighter fluid perched on a camp cot beside him, he was getting ready to cook dinner. A pair of yellow eyes flashed briefly in the bushes that surrounded his campsite. Now that Diana's kittens were tucked into Ford's tent for the night, the tabby must be doing some solitary hunting. I wondered if she repaid Ford in rodents. General Chang wasn't the best mouser, but at least I didn't have to dispose of half-chewed carcasses.

Ford looked up as I approached. I lifted my plastic bag in the air. "Cat food," I said, placing it on the ground.

"Thanks," he mumbled.

I stepped closer, pointing to the nearest boulder. "Mind if I sit down?"

He grunted again.

We sat, admiring the stars overhead. The river gurgled and churned, headed to Paradise Falls a hundred meters away. A breeze whispered in the trees.

"Why do you camp so close to the water when you can't swim?" I asked.

Ford shrugged. He got up to stack sticks and kindling in the fire pit. After sprinkling lighter fluid over them, he dropped a match in the middle. The kindling flared, and the flames caught the larger pieces of wood piled around the edges. Once the campfire was blazing, he walked past me to retrieve the cat food.

I reached out my palms to the crackling flames. The night was turning chilly, and the heat felt good against my face and hands. "Can you show me how to build a fire like this?" I asked, turning my head to watch Ford pick up the bag.

Without warning, a shape charged out of the bushes and tackled him.

Ford hit the ground in a tangle of arms and legs and rolled over twice. Then he was dragged upright, onto his feet. Firelight glinted off Ford's terrified eyes as a man's arm gripped his chest from behind, pinning his arms to his side.

The fire also lit up the face of his attacker—Nick Yates. I gasped. Nick was holding a knife to Ford's throat.

For a moment, I couldn't breathe. Then, instinctively, I stepped toward them.

"Stop right there or I'll cut him," Nick snapped.

I halted, raising my hands. "I've stopped."

We stood for a long moment, staring at each other. Rushing water gurgled and splashed a few feet away, the sound almost drowned out by the pounding of my heart.

Ford tried to wiggle out of Nick's grasp. "Hold still," Nick growled, tightening his grip.

"Nick," I said, slowly. "What are you doing?"

"You figured out what happened at the church twelve years ago, didn't you?" The hand holding the knife trembled. "Didn't you?" he barked.

"How could I? I wasn't there."

"And this moron was at the cemetery, sneaking around," Nick continued, almost as if he hadn't heard me. He jerked the knife, and Ford gasped.

I said nothing, biting my lip and keeping my hands in the air, waiting for Nick to speak again.

"You don't know anything," he muttered. "You don't know about Charlie Inglis. He was so special, our Charlie." Nick spat on the ground. "Charlie on the basketball team, Charlie on the track team—always showing off. He played the guitar, did Isabelle tell you that?"

I shook my head, not willing to risk speech.

"He carried it all around the school. Played it whenever he felt like it. 'Impromptu serenades,' he called them." Nick snorted. "Noise pollution, more like. Weren't even proper songs. The girls liked it though. They flocked around him in the halls. Even the teachers liked Charlie."

I attempted a sympathetic tone. "I can see how that would be infuriating."

Nick shifted his weight from one foot to the other. "You can't see anything. You can't see what he was like. He and his pals made fun of me, called me pumpkin face and porker and... worse. Charlie would bump into me in the hall to knock books out of my hand, and then laugh when I bent over to pick them up." His expression took a dark turn. "But never when the teachers could see him. They thought he was an angel. Even after I showed them..."

The knife wavered in his hand as he stopped talking.

I tried to slow my breathing as I studied him. A four-finger eye strike would disable Nick if I could do it with enough force and perfect aim. But I'd have to be much closer before I could jab at his eyes. And I'd need to get my arm inside his. If he raised his elbow, he could knock my arm away and kill us both.

"Showed them what, Nick?" I edged a step closer.

"What Charlie wrote in my locker. They said I did it myself to get him in trouble. But I was the one who got blamed. When I came out of the school after detention, it was dark. Charlie and his buddies tackled me in the parking lot. And gave me this."

He stuck a finger in his hair and pulled it back, revealing a jagged scar on his scalp.

"Why didn't you report them?"

"Because," he shouted, eyes flaring. "No one ever believed me." He lowered his head. "Except Isabelle."

I took another stealthy step. "Why was that, Nick?"

"Well, she knew him, didn't she? Knew what he was capable of." His voice dropped. "Didn't try to stop it, though." His hand sagged, lowering the knife.

"Tell me what happened the night Charlie died."

"I was looking for Isabelle, in the church. I knew they'd been painting the basement and figured they were still there. But when I went inside, Charlie was cleaning brushes. I asked him where Isabelle was."

Ford tried to wiggle away. Nick tightened his grip. His hand holding the knife, which had relaxed during our conversation, moved up. A drop of blood appeared on Ford's throat and trickled to his collar.

I raised my hands in the air, using the movement to mask another step forward. "Nobody needs to get hurt, Nick. Please give me the knife."

"No. Not until I tell you what happened."

"I'm listening." I lowered my hands. "What did Charlie say?"

Nick snorted. "He said Isabelle left early so she wouldn't have to tutor me. He said that she thought I was an idiot, and she was tired of me following her around like a lovesick puppy. Charlie said he was sick of it, too."

I shook my head, trying to appear sympathetic. "That was cruel."

Nick tightened his grip on Ford. I calculated the distance. Still not close enough. He could cut Ford's throat before I reached him.

"When I said Isabelle was my friend, Charlie laughed. He said they were eloping, and I'd never see her again. I said he was a liar, that Isabelle loved her parents and she wouldn't elope with anybody, never mind him." Nick stared over my head at an invisible scene. I knew he was back in that dank basement facing his greatest fear—that the girl he loved would be taken away from him.

I took another step.

He shook his head with another snort of disgust. "Charlie laughed. He pulled a note out of his pocket and waved it in my face. He said it was proof that they'd be gone by morning." His voice dropped to a whisper. "I didn't mean to kill him, I swear. I only wanted to see that note. I tried to grab it, and we fought over it, and somehow... I don't know what happened. He hit his head, I guess."

I glimpsed a movement off to my right and shot a sidelong glance at the bushes, hoping Jeff had arrived. But it was Diana, the kittens' mother, emerging from the undergrowth with a mouse clenched in her jaws. She crouched, her eyes on the two men, tail swishing back and forth.

"And then you buried him," I said.

"The floor was soft from the flooding. It was easy. Afterward, I slopped more water over the ground so it would settle. I had to bury him—you can see that, can't you? I couldn't tell anybody what happened because..."

"Because Isabelle might hate you."

He nodded miserably.

"Give me the knife, Nick. It was an accident. You didn't mean it."

His grip tightened and his knuckles turned white. "You don't know what else I've done."

Feigning ignorance seemed the wisest course. "It doesn't matter, Nick. Ford has no idea who attacked Nesbitt-Cavanagh. He didn't see his face."

"How do you know?"

"I asked him, days ago. He doesn't know. Charlie's death was an accident, Nick. Don't make it worse. Lower that blade." I took another step.

Nick complied, but only by a few inches. "Stay where you are. Don't come any closer."

I eyed the knife, recognizing it as one of the garden tools from my truck. Lorne took pride in sharpening all our implements to razor-sharp edges. An attack was too risky. Which meant I had to play for time. Surely by now Jeff was at the bakery and would realize something was wrong.

"Nick," I said slowly. "Who delivered Charlie's note?"

"I did. But I kept one page. I still have it."

"Can I see it?"

He ignored my request. "Throw me the keys to your truck. At my feet." When I hesitated, he barked, "Now."

I pulled the key chain from my pocket and raised my hand as if to toss it. The chain held over a dozen keys, and it was heavy. I thought about hurling it at his face. I drew my arm back, lining up the throw, praying it would startle Nick enough that he would drop the knife.

But I was caught short by a new development.

A blinding white light lit the campsite from behind me.

With a gasp of pain, Nick released his hold on Ford, using that hand to shade his eyes. But he kept his other hand—the one with the blade—trained on Ford's neck. More blood appeared on his throat, crimson in the harsh glare.

Before I could swivel around to find the source of the light, a baseball-capped figure stepped up beside me. I gaped at the pistol in Xavier's hand.

"Put the knife down, Nick," Xavier said, his hand trembling. "I don't want to shoot you."

I let out the breath I'd been holding.

But Nick had no intention of surrendering. He yanked Ford back, squeezing his ribs, walking backward.

"Come any closer and I'll kill him," he barked.

My breathing quickened as I realized he intended to drag Ford into the river, leaving us to pull him out while Nick swam across and escaped up the opposite bank.

Ford's eyes widened as he realized they were headed for the water. "No," he hollered, digging his heels into the ground.

I cast an anguished glance at Xavier, who didn't realize the danger. Ford couldn't swim. If Nick tossed him into the river in his panicked state, he would go under and drown. The campsite was lit up, but the water beyond was in darkness. We wouldn't be able to find him before the river surged over Paradise Falls, taking him with it.

Nick fought to restrain the struggling Ford, dragging him toward the bank, step by step, holding the blade at his throat. The trail of blood grew thicker.

Xavier stepped closer with the pistol and raised his outstretched arm. "Drop the knife, Nick."

Nick continued to move backward until he was steps from the water, dragging Ford with him.

Beside me, Xavier took careful aim. My heart rose into my throat. Xavier couldn't possibly shoot Nick without hitting Ford. We were out of time. I had to take action. If I rushed Nick, he might simply turn and dive into the river, leaving Ford behind.

But we were all outmaneuvered.

A scraggly gray warrior bounded from the bushes, leaped onto a boulder, and hurled himself at Nick's face.

Nick dropped the knife and staggered back—with a hissing, shrieking mound of fur clinging to his head. Nick whirled, lurching and screaming, trying to detach General Chang from his scalp. The General hung on, digging in his nails, hissing and snarling, his back arched and his tail puffed. Blood streamed down Nick's face.

Nick whirled again, right into my well-executed arm chop to his neck. But my foot slipped on a muddy patch of ground and the impact with his throat threw me onto a nearby boulder.

I heard a loud *crack* as Xavier's gun went off, coupled with a stabbing pain in my chest. I slid off the rock and onto the grass. When I tried to rise on all fours, pain exploded in my solar plexus.

I collapsed onto the ground, flopped over, and lay there.

I wasn't certain what happened after that. I think I drifted in and out of consciousness. But I remember a pair of strong arms picking me up and carrying me.

"Hi, Jeff," I mumbled. "About time." My head lolled against his chest.

I couldn't make out his reply. But I remember being lowered onto a stretcher, grabbing someone's arm in a Vulcan-like grip, and saying hoarsely, "Tell the General it should be, 'Let slip the *cats* of war.'" Grinning, I collapsed onto the stretcher. Then I passed out.

CHAPTER TWENTY-NINE

I AWOKE IN A HOSPITAL BED, feeling surprisingly chipper for a gunshot victim. Daylight streamed through the slatted blinds on the window. A water pitcher and glass sat on a wheeled table by my elbow, next to a box of tissue. An electronic *beep-beep-beep* sounded by my head.

Gingerly, I lifted the sheet to check my ribcage, wondering if I'd have a scar. My skin was intact, except for a huge purple bruise. What happened to the bullet? As I let the sheet drop, the room swirled, and I cringed. I had one heck of a headache. Maybe I was delirious, and that was why I couldn't find my gunshot wound. I was daydreaming about my public-service award when I heard a familiar male voice.

"There you are."

With a smile, Ryker dropped into the armchair next to my bed and stretched out his long legs, running a hand through his hair. He looked tired. "Doctor's releasing you tomorrow morning. They're keeping you for twenty-four hours because you have a minor concussion."

I reviewed his statement, one word at a time, until I reached the end. "Concussion?" I asked.

"And a cracked rib. Also minor. You'll be fine in a few weeks. They're sending you home with painkillers and an ice pack."

I struggled to sit up, which was when I discovered that "minor" was medical-speak for "hurts so much you might actually be dead." Gasping in pain, I collapsed back onto my pillow. "Are you sure? I heard Xavier's gun go off. I thought —" My minor concussion made itself felt, wiping all rational thought from my brain. I looked around. No sign of the promised painkillers.

"That you got shot?" Ryker grinned.

I nodded, gesturing at the water glass. He handed it to me, and I sipped the straw.

"It was a prop gun," he said. "From Xavier's movie equipment. Nobody got shot."

"What was that loud crack I heard, then?"

He grinned again. "Probably your head hitting that boulder."

I nodded, but more carefully this time. "So I was unconscious when Jeff carried me up to the road."

I recalled mumbling Jeff's name, but everything after that was blurry. At least I had an excuse for whatever idiocy I might have spouted.

Ryker shot me a curious glance. "Is that all you remember?"

"After the boulder attacked me, you mean?"

He nodded.

"I'm afraid so. Although now that I think about it, I might have rattled on a bit in the ambulance." With a wince, I remembered saying something about cats. I propped myself up on one elbow, ignoring a sudden wave of pain. "Is General Chang all right?"

Ryker looked confused, so I added, "My cat? Gray-tabby tom?"

"Oh, right. Emy took him to Rose Cottage. She'll be along soon, and you can ask her for the details, but I think he's fine."

I settled back on my pillow. "How did Xavier know where I was? And why the stunt with the prop gun? He could have gotten himself killed."

Ryker pressed his lips together and tilted his head, giving me an odd look before replying. "Dunno." He pushed off from the chair and rose to his feet. "Glad you're okay," he said, turning to go.

A buxom student nurse came through the door to my room, carrying extra blankets. Ryker bestowed one of his sexy smiles. She melted under his gaze, tittering. I thought he added a wink, too, although his back was to me, so I couldn't be sure.

"See you around, Verity," he said over his shoulder. "Take care."

Ryker had barely left when Emy and Lorne burst through the door. After noticing I wasn't dead, Lorne slumped into the armchair and picked up a well-thumbed copy of *Sports Illustrated*. He leafed through the pages.

Emy stood by the bed, patting my hand. "Ryker said you've been drifting in and out for hours."

I frowned at her, puzzled. "How would he know?"

"Because he's been here the whole time. I had to stay with Izzy, but he sent us texts. He kept the reporters out, too."

I did a double take. "Why didn't he..." I closed my eyes. *Later.* "Never mind. How's Isabelle?"

"Devastated. I took her back home just now. She wants to be alone for a while."

I nodded. Seemed reasonable.

"Actually, it was lucky that Ryker dropped by the bakery when he did," Emy said. "He's been following you—"

"He's been doing what?" I blurted, sitting up without thinking. I clapped both hands to my forehead. "Ow." When the pain subsided, I added, "What do you mean, he's been following me?"

She made a face. "I shouldn't have told you. Ryker said you wouldn't like—"

"Being stalked?" I finished the sentence for her.

"It wasn't like that. He was worried. None of us knew who killed Nesbitt-Cavanagh, and Ryker thought someone should keep an eye on you."

"He should have been keeping an eye on Xavier. That idiot nearly got us all killed."

"That wasn't Ryker's fault. Xavier got into his truck before he could stop him and refused to get out. Ryker didn't want to haul him out of there, so he let him come along. When they reached the conservation area, Xavier offered to act as cover for him."

"Cover for what?"

"Ryker was circling around through the bushes to get behind Nick and tackle him."

"But the General got there first."

"Exactly."

I picked at the sheets, wondering again why Ryker didn't mention his role. "How is Ford? And the cats?"

Lorne looked up from his magazine. "Ford's been talking a blue streak. More than I've ever heard. The cats are fine— better than fine, since they got extra rations this morning. And somebody started a Facebook page for them. The whole group's online now, with mugshots." He got out his phone, clicked on it, and held out the phone. I saw blurry feline faces, with Greek and Roman names superimposed on each one.

I chuckled. "I'll check it out later." As Lorne put his phone away, an unpleasant thought nagged at me. "Did Xavier... film any of this?"

Emy winced. "I'm afraid so. Ryker said the first thing Xavier did was put his camera on a tripod and turn it on— before he switched on the light. Xavier's excited about the footage. He says your confrontation with Nick will be the best thing in the film. After his own heroics with the prop gun." Emy rolled her eyes. "And then Jeff showed up in his cruiser, siren blaring." She pursed her lips, looking apologetic. "Which tipped off everybody else."

Any parts of my body that weren't already on red alert tensed up. "Was everyone in the village at the scene?"

Emy brightened. "I wasn't. I was at the bakery, waiting for Jeff. When he arrived, I sent him after you and Nick." She paused, considering her next words. "I meant to say—I didn't arrive until much later. Mom picked me up when Jeff left, and, of course, we drove up to the conservation area."

"Of course."

"It was hard finding a place to park, though."

I lowered my head on the pillow to stare at the acoustic tiles in the ceiling, hoping they'd fall down and knock me out for good. I imagined how my rescue would look on film, what with my head lolling around and my nonsensical statements. I puffed out a breath. "Did Xavier film Jeff picking me up and carrying me up the hill?"

Emy looked confused. "Jeff didn't carry you up the hill. That was Ryker."

I held my head off the pillow and stared at her. "Why didn't he tell me?"

"Didn't he?"

A double tap sounded on the open door, and we turned.

Jeff slipped off his police cap, leaned his tall frame against the doorframe, and looked directly at me. He had a smile on his face.

I felt as if that smile was intended only for me, but that was ridiculous.

"How are you feeling?" he asked.

I raised myself up on an elbow. "Good, thanks. Going home tomorrow. Lorne might have to take over my work for a day or two. Bit of a headache, but... good." I pressed my lips shut—if only to stop the pitiful babbling.

Lorne looked up at the mention of his name and nodded briefly before diving back into *Sports Illustrated*. Emy ducked around the other side of my bed to make room for Jeff.

He walked over and lifted my hand from the bed. Jeff caressed the back of my hand with his thumb as his dark eyes probed mine. "That's good news."

All thoughts of concussion fled. I'd never felt better, in fact.

Lorne noisily flipped a few pages while I stared into Jeff's eyes.

With a sudden clatter of wheels, a blue-gowned nurse pushed a gurney past the open door of my room, triggering a flashback of a blonde in four-inch heels. I slid my hand out of Jeff's and tented my fingers on my stomach.

A flicker of something—was it disappointment or was I still delusional?—flashed in his eyes. He took a step back. "Well, that's also good news, because I have a question and I want your full attention."

"Oh?" I asked, attempting a nonchalant tone that fooled no one.

Jeff pulled his cell phone from his pocket, scrolled, and then held the phone up to face me. He flexed his eyebrows. "Explain this text, please."

He turned the phone around and read from the screen:

Meet me at Emy's. I know who the killer is.

Jeff gave me a stern look. "If you knew Nick murdered Nesbitt-Cavanagh, why on earth did you go to the conservation area with him?"

"That's a good question," Emy muttered from the other side of the bed. I shot her a look, and she studied her cuticles for a while.

"You could have been killed," Jeff said.

"It wasn't like that. I knew Ford couldn't identify Nick as the killer, so neither of us was in danger, not really. I wanted to see if Nick would implicate himself. I told him not to follow me to the river, to see if he would come after me and try to question Ford." I winced. "I never dreamed we might be at risk. Anyway"—I pointed a finger at Jeff and attempted a sorrowful look—"you were supposed to read my text and rescue us if things went south."

"Why would I? According to your message, you were safe and sound in Emy's bakery, not roaming around in the woods with a suspected killer."

"Why does everyone keep calling it the woods?" I protested. "It's a public conservation area minutes from the village, not the wilderness."

Jeff shook his head, sliding the phone back into his pocket. "You took an awfully big chance, Verity. I don't think you realize how close you came to being attacked yourself."

Emy—still examining her cuticles—muttered something under her breath.

I'd deal with her later.

Jeff wrinkled his brow. "And you still haven't explained how you knew Nick was the killer."

I flicked my hand. "That was easy. He was scratching."

"Excuse me?"

"*Urtica dioica*," I said.

Lorne looked up from his magazine and nodded thoughtfully. "Of course."

Jeff and Emy looked puzzled, so I spelled it out for them. "Nick dragged Nesbitt-Cavanagh's body through a patch of stinging nettles outside the Bannon family crypt. That's why he was scratching so much. I thought at first he had chronic eczema, aggravated by stress. But he wasn't scratching at the village hall meeting. So it had to be the nettles."

I raised my hand and Emy slapped her palm against mine

in a high five. Jeff merely shook his head before turning away, his lips twitching.

To tell the truth, I was disappointed at his reaction to my startling breakthrough in investigative gardening. Well, Aunt Adeline would be proud of me. If she ever turned up. I picked up my water glass and sipped at the straw before replacing it on the table. "Nick did do it, didn't he?"

Jeff turned back, nodding. "He confessed with his lawyer present. He was eager to tell us the truth, in fact. I think Charlie's death has been weighing on him all these years."

"How did Nick know Nesbitt-Cavanagh was digging in the basement?" I asked. "Or even that he was at the church that night?"

"Because Nick drove him there."

I could feel my eyebrows rise. "How did that happen?"

Jeff pulled over a chair, spun it around, and straddled it with his arms leaning on the back, facing me. Lorne and Emy leaned in to listen.

"After Isabelle moved out, Nick followed her around the village quite a lot. As part of his routine, he used to drive by the Sleepy Time motel on the highway, looking for her car."

"Which is creepy, by the way," I said.

Emy snorted. "No kidding."

"That night, he was driving around as usual and slowed down while passing the motel. And who should he see in the parking lot but Nesbitt-Cavanagh, trying to hail a cab."

"But cabs never stop up there. You have to call one."

"Nesbitt-Cavanagh didn't know that. But Nick did, being a Leafy Hollow resident. So he pulled into the lot and offered the historian a ride back into the village. He figured he would want to go back to the B&B."

"But Nick was furious with Nesbitt-Cavanagh at the village hall meeting. He threw a cupcake at him. Why would he drive him into the village?"

"He said he wanted to apologize."

I mulled this over. It fit with what I had observed of Nick's character. He lost his temper, caused a blowup, and felt guilty the next day. Until the cycle started over. "Go on."

"On their way back into the village, Nesbitt-Cavanagh asked Nick to drop him at the church. When Nick asked why, he told him some garbled tale about buried treasure. He said he was digging up Loyalist gold, but that Reverend McAllister would never agree, so he had to do it at night."

"Why would Nesbitt-Cavanagh tell Nick that?" I asked.

Jeff shrugged. "The motel staff said he was stinking drunk when he left."

"After his big fight with Madeline," I said.

Jeff shot me a look. "You knew about that?"

"Uh... maybe." I rubbed my head, feigning pain.

Jeff looked suspicious, but he continued his tale. "Anyway, Nick claims Nesbitt-Cavanagh staggered across the lawn to the church, and then whacked at the door handle with a rock until it broke."

"But the lock wasn't broken when we entered the church a few days later. And why didn't the silent alarm go off?"

"Because there wasn't one, not then. Reverend McAllister said the board of managers fixed the lock and added that alarm the next day, after the exhumation." He paused, collecting his thoughts. "Anyway, Nick parked his car out of sight and waited behind the Bannon family crypt for Nesbitt-Cavanagh to come back out."

"Nick must have been sitting in the nettles," I said, unable to help myself.

Jeff shrugged. "A light came on in the manse, and McAllister walked out onto the lawn and over to the church. When he saw the damaged handle on the vestry door, he went inside."

"And hauled Nesbitt-Cavanagh out of the basement."

Jeff nodded. "Nick's confession confirmed everything the minister told us. They came back out the vestry door and argued in the cemetery. Nick overheard the minister berating Nesbitt-Cavanagh for digging in the basement. The historian had a shovel with him that he'd found in the storage area. McAllister grabbed it away from him and propped it up against the crypt. He told Nesbitt-Cavanagh that he was going back to the manse to call him a cab and he should leave the minute it arrived."

"What did the taxi driver say?"

"We haven't found him yet, but I imagine he'll say no one was around when he arrived. Nick confronted Nesbitt-Cavanagh right after the minister went back into the manse. It was all over in minutes."

"Confronted how?"

"Picked up the shovel and whacked him on the head from behind. Nesbitt-Cavanagh fell against a corner of the crypt, which made a second wound, but he was already dead, according to the coroner."

I nodded. "And then Nick dragged his body through the nettles and into the crypt. But why didn't he find a better hiding place? He placed the body in the one spot where everyone in the village couldn't fail to see it."

"That was the point, according to Nick. He wanted to implicate McAllister for the murder because he suspected Isabelle and the minister were having an affair."

I nodded thoughtfully—and gingerly. "Is that true? Were they?"

Jeff shrugged. "You'll have to ask them that."

"But you must have—"

He raised his eyebrows in a gesture that said, *none of your business.*

"That explains why Nick left the body in the crypt, but how did he get it open? There was no sign of tampering on the lock, was there?"

"Nick used to drive Isabelle to her job at the library when her car was in the shop. One day, she left her purse behind. He copied all the church keys on her key chain before delivering the forgotten purse to her at work."

"Why?"

"He figured the key to the manse would be among them. I suspect he meant to barge in one day and confront the two of them. So, when he found himself with a body to hide right outside the old Bannon vault, he realized the big key—the antique skeleton key—must open the crypt."

"And then he dragged the body inside," I said. "So Ford really did witness a murder. Will he have to testify?"

Jeff shook his head. "It's up to the prosecutor, but I doubt it. Nick intends to plead guilty, according to his lawyer." Jeff got to his feet and placed his chair by the wall. "I've told you this because you're involved in the case. But I'd rather you keep it to yourselves for now." He glanced at all of us in turn.

"Naturally," we said in unison.

After Jeff left, Emy whipped out her phone. Both Lorne and I stared at her.

"What? I have to tell Mom *something* or she'll kill me," she said.

Having experienced Thérèse Dionne's wrath in the past, we merely nodded.

CHAPTER THIRTY

EMY, Isabelle, and I stared at the full-color postcard that lay before us on 5X Bakery's tiny table.

MADELINE STUART
"SECRETS OF LEAFY HOLLOW"
EXHIBITION OF RECENT WORKS ON CANVAS
OPENING RECEPTION 7-9 P.M.

Madeline's portrait of Prudence Bannon—minus the cherry custard—covered two-thirds of the card.

"We're all invited to the opening?" I asked.

"Looks like it," Emy replied.

"Are we expected to buy something?" Given the state of my bank account, that might be tough.

"I doubt it. Wilf said Madeline's showing is oversubscribed. Everything's already sold. The exhibition is for publicity. And maybe to garner some new commissions."

"Good for Madeline." I tapped the card with my finger. "At least something worthwhile came from all this."

"And it's not the only thing. Xavier's true-crime doc is a go. He's signed with a big studio, according to Zander and Terry."

I sighed. "I know. I agreed to do his interview. Xavier is coming to Rose Cottage next week with a film crew."

"How did he talk you into it?"

"Remember that video he took of us outside the church?"

Emy groaned. "How could I forget? Mom will kill me if that makes it onto YouTube."

"Well, your worries are over. I struck a deal. I do the interview, and Xavier takes that footage out of his documentary." I leaned back in my chair and tilted my head to stare at the ceiling. The last thing I wanted was to be front and center in anybody's film, but I couldn't see a way out of it. And maybe my aunt or Gideon would see the publicity stills—or the "incredible" trailer—and call home.

I glanced at Isabelle, sitting silently in her chair. My troubles were nothing compared to her ordeal. "Jeff will be here any minute," I said. "Then it will be over."

She raised her reddened eyes to mine. "It will never be over. I've been a fool."

Emy patted her hand. "You didn't know."

Isabelle tugged her hand away, shaking her head. "I knew what Charlie was like. I didn't care. Being the girlfriend of the most popular boy in school was all that mattered. Reverend Daniel tried to tell me what Charlie was doing to Nick. He was the new minister. He'd only been here a few weeks, and I told him he was wrong." Lowering her head, she ran a finger along the edge of the table. "But I knew," she whispered.

The bells over the front door tinkled, and Jeff walked in. He had a gusseted file folder in his hand.

"Have you got it?" I asked.

Jeff nodded and walked up to the table, unfastening the string on the file. He reached inside and pulled out a single sheet. "It's a photocopy," he said. "The original has to be retained in evidence." He laid the page on the table, between the two that were already there.

"Nick kept it all these years?" I asked.

"In his wallet, believe it or not."

Isabelle touched the photocopy with the tip of her finger and shivered.

"You might want to read it alone," Jeff said.

She stared at the sheets for a long moment before pushing them into the center of the table with trembling fingers. "You read it, Verity. Please. I can't." She clutched Emy's hand and hung on.

Jeff took a step back.

I picked up the original worn, creased pages—and the new photocopied page—and read them out loud.

Dear Izzy,

You must make a decision. You've had enough time.

Here's what I think. I will go out West to Alberta and get a real job. Those oil jobs pay really good. I could get work as a drilling rig floor hand or a pipeline worker or even a cat opera-tor. The time has come to—

I switched to the new second page.

—get married.

Emy gasped. Isabelle's face was white. I stared at the words on the page a moment before clearing my throat and continuing.

I know your parents don't approve, but once the deed is done, what can they say? My foster parents can't tell me what to do. They're not my family, not really. By the time we come back, we'll both be over twenty-one. Maybe with a family of our own.

You feel the same, I know you do. If we hang in here, nothing will ever happen. Let's elope, like we planned. Let's—

I switched to the original second page.

—make a clean break. I can't stay in Leafy Hollow any longer.

Remember, I will always love you.

Charlie

I folded the papers together, with the missing page tucked between the others, and placed them in front of Isabelle. For a long moment, nobody spoke. She gathered up the papers and clutched them to her chest.

"I'll drive you home," Jeff said.

Isabelle nodded, and he helped her up with a hand on her elbow. The bells over the door tinkled as they walked out.

I bit my lip against sudden tears. I knew how fleeting love could be. Isabelle missed her first two chances. Would her third—the budding relationship with Daniel McAllister—survive this latest revelation? I hoped it would.

Enough of that. I slapped my hand on the table and rose to go. "I think this calls for a drink. Care to join me?"

"Can't. I'm meeting someone," Emy said with a sudden blush.

"Ah. I see." I grinned. "Talk to you later, then." I left the bakery and walked along Main Street until I reached The Tipsy Jay, a small bar a block away.

As I turned to enter, the door of the florist's shop across the street opened. Lorne stepped out with a bouquet of gardenias and roses in his hand. I smiled, recognizing Emy's favorite flowers. I lifted my hand to give him a brief wave, but he didn't see me. He strode resolutely in the direction of the 5X Bakery, obviously on a mission.

I smiled again. Had my shy gardening assistant finally taken the hint? From behind a parked truck, I watched his progress. The bakery door opened and Emy walked out.

She wasn't alone.

Fritz Cameron stepped out after her. They were facing away from Lorne, toward Fritz's new restaurant, Anonymous, up the street.

I swore under my breath. I should have seen that coming. Here I'd been egging Lorne on, when all the time, he had a rival. He didn't even suspect.

Or did he?

Lorne halted, watching them.

Emy twisted her key in the lock. Then she turned to Fritz with a huge grin and tucked her hand under his arm. They strode off, Emy talking and gesticulating.

The bouquet trailed from Lorne's hand. Even from across the street, I could see his shoulders slump. He glanced up at the Tipsy Jay sign behind me and started across the street.

I ducked behind the truck, hoping he hadn't seen me. Then I darted inside and slid to a seat at the far end of the bar. "Molson Canadian, please," I said, a little breathless. By the time the bartender placed a filled glass on the paper coaster in front of me, Lorne was slumping onto the next stool.

Lorne looked surprised to see me. He nodded grimly while dropping the bouquet on the bar beside him. "Verity."

I nodded back. "Lorne. How are you?"

"Never better." He ordered a shot of whisky and a beer. Lorne tossed back the whisky, choked, then slammed the glass on the counter and picked up the beer. He took a long swallow and then motioned to the bartender. "Same again."

"Take it easy, Lorne," I said with a chuckle. "You're not used to hard liquor."

"How do you know?" he asked, not looking at me.

The bartender complied, and Lorne tossed back another. He choked several times before slamming the shot glass down on the counter.

I slapped him on the back.

Then I sliced a finger across my throat at the bartender, who nodded and winked. Hopefully, he'd water Lorne's next shot. Or at least delay it.

And maybe by then, I'd have learned not to interfere in other people's lives.

The door opened and closed, letting in a whoosh of night air.

Emy stood in the doorway. When she saw us at the bar, she walked over and gave Lorne a playful punch on the arm.

"Didn't you hear me calling?" she asked, sliding onto the stool beside him.

He glanced at her before raising his beer. "I thought you

were busy with what's-his-name." He took a sip before using both hands to center his glass on its paper coaster.

"Who, Fritz? He wanted to show me his new menus with my desserts on them. They're gorgeous, with little pen-and-ink drawings on the margins." Emy chattered on about Anonymous and all its trendy features—and its trendy owner —seemingly unaware of Lorne's black mood.

Well, this was awkward. I glanced under the counter to see if there was room to crawl under it and disappear, but no luck. I picked up my beer and swiveled on my chair to check out the rest of the bar. Since The Tipsy Jay only had three tables, there wasn't much to see. I swiveled back.

"—so we decided on the maple-bacon and the lavender-lemon, since they're my best sellers, but Fritz suggested a few twists to make them exclusive to Anonymous."

"Spending a lot of time with him, aren't you," Lorne said, raising his glass. It wasn't a question.

Emy looked puzzled. It must have been a shock, Lorne not hanging on to her every word. She chuckled weakly. "Hah. If I didn't know better, I'd say you were—" Her eyes widened. "Lorne," she said, dragging out his name. "Why do you care who I spend time with?"

He slammed his beer on the counter and turned to face her.

"Because I'm crazy about you," he blurted.

She stared at him, her eyes wide.

I held my breath and froze, hoping to be mistaken for furniture.

Emy's face broke out in a grin. I'd always said her smile could light up a room. But today, it was focused only on

Lorne. She clasped her hands around his arm, snugged up close, and leaned her head on his shoulder. Emy whispered something I couldn't hear.

But I saw the look on Lorne's face when she said it. He closed his eyes and leaned his head on hers.

I dropped a ten-dollar bill on the bar to cover my drink, nodded at the bartender, and slipped past Emy and Lorne to the entrance.

Outside, I looked up. Leafy Hollow's quaint streetlights did their best, but they couldn't dim the constellations that shimmered in the velvet sky. I took a deep gulp of cedar-scented night air and walked down the street to my truck. Vancouver was thousands of miles away, and that was where it would stay. I couldn't imagine leaving here.

EPILOGUE

ON THE MORNING after The Big Operation, General Chang was walking gingerly. "It's for the best," I said as he haughtily passed me in the kitchen, pausing only long enough to chew the handful of liver treats I tossed at him. I winced. The General was not happy.

When I propped open the basement door for a laundry run, he peeked around the corner, saw his chance, and trotted down the stairs. Perhaps he smelled a mouse. Or, more likely, he wanted to make me feel even worse about my treachery by banishing himself to the dankest, darkest part of Rose Cottage. The betrayed warrior, licking his wounds. Literally.

I flicked on the light switch in the stairwell and followed him down. "Come on, boy," I said at the bottom of the stairs. "I have a tin of salmon for you," I wheedled, ducking under the low-lying wooden beams. I glanced at the dusty pipes that crisscrossed above my head, and at the ancient washer and dryer on the opposite side of the room.

Something flashed on my left. I whirled in time to see a gray tail disappear into a holographic case of Molson Canadian.

Shaking my head, I followed the tail. "There's nothing to see here. The salmon's upstairs." I reached out a hand until my fingers disappeared. I'd tried many times to reactivate Control and obtain details about my promised "test" without success. I expected today would be no different.

I was wrong.

"Verity Hawkes," a synthetic voice thundered.

I jerked my hand back.

Locks thudded off, the hologram wavered and disappeared, and the riveted metal wall opened. The two sides drew back with a creak and a groan and settled into place with a clang.

I stared at the multiple faces on the monitors. "Look, when are you going to tell me—"

"Sit down," the voice barked.

I dropped onto the swivel chair that faced the electronic console and pressed my lips together.

"Congratulations, Verity Hawkes," the voice continued. "You are a successful candidate."

I swiveled my gaze across the smug faces, trying to take this in. "I passed your test?"

"Correct."

"But I didn't take any..." I stopped talking, conscious of their curious stares. I cleared my throat. "Thank you," I said.

"No. Thank *you*, Verity, for preserving the fame of a true Canadian heroine. And fending off an attack by the Syndicate."

"Yeah. About that—"

My words were drowned out by the opening chords of "O Canada." I scrambled to my feet and snapped to attention. Since our national anthem is rather leisurely, I had time to mull over this latest development. *How could I pass a test without knowing it?* I beamed. I must be a natural.

The last notes faded away.

The faces on the screen adopted a solemn expression. "Verity, we need your help."

I winced. "You know... can I get a raincheck on that? I've been helping a lot of people lately, and it rarely turns out well." I had a flashback to Emy and Lorne's blue-painted faces. "I only want to find my aunt."

The faces looked incredulous. "It wasn't a request."

"You can't make—"

"Silence," the voice roared.

"That's it." I waved my hands emphatically and turned to the door. "And don't bother threatening to blow up Rose Cottage. I'm not falling for that again."

"We know where Adeline is."

I halted and slowly turned. "Are you going to tell me?"

The faces regarded me sadly. "Well, we don't know *exactly* where she is."

With a snort, I swiveled to face the door.

"But we can tell you where to look for her."

I pivoted. "Is Gideon Picard involved?"

"He's gone rogue."

"Rogue?" I crossed my arms and glared at the screen. "I don't believe it. If you want my help, you need to explain a few things. Like what Control really is."

The voice muttered something I couldn't make out.

"I can't hear you."

Control made a throat-clearing sound and then spoke so rapidly the words ran together. "A loosely aligned group of highly skilled experts who maintain the global reputation of our great nation."

I stared at the monitors, bile rising in my throat. I'd had enough of this pretense. "You're kidding, right?"

"No." The faces looked surprised.

"You're flacks?"

"We prefer the term *public relations specialists*."

"Yeah. Flacks. As if."

"We have no time to debate labels. Your aunt is in danger."

I drew a deep breath and released it before uncrossing my arms. "Tell me what to do."

"Find Gideon Picard. He'll lead you to Adeline." The faces dissolved into an extreme close-up of Niagara's magnificent Horseshoe Falls. "Start here—at our head-quarters."

I peered at the thundering wall of water. "What you mean, *here*? In the water?"

No answer. With a *click*, the screens went black.

"Control?" I called.

The metal walls rumbled on either side of me. I stepped back, watching as the panels closed and the locks thudded shut. The hologram flickered back on, although, this time, the cases of beer were upside down. I studied them for a long moment, remembering the gushing torrent I'd seen on the monitors, wondering what it meant.

The air conditioning unit in the corner rumbled on, thought better of it, and switched off.

I slapped a hand across my forehead. *Of course.* I knew the location of Control's HQ. It was obvious.

"Mrack." General Chang wound himself around my legs. I bent to pat him. Then I straightened up and headed for the door.

Time to gather the team.

ALSO BY RICKIE BLAIR

ABOUT THE AUTHOR

When not hunched over her computer talking to people who exist only in her head, Rickie spends her time taming an unruly half-acre garden and an irrepressible Jack Chi. She also shares her southern Ontario home with two rescued cats and an overactive Netflix account.

Made in the USA
Middletown, DE
27 November 2020